WOLF HEALER

Library of Congress Control Number:
2021919226

Printed in the United States of America: First Printing, 2021.
ISBN 978-1-7378376-0-2 (eBook)
ISBN 978-1-7378376-1-9 (paperback)

www.huckleberryrahrauthor.wordpress.com

Editor: Wes Imrisek
Copy Editor: Angela Grimes
Cover Art: Crimson Phoenix Creations
Formatting: R. L. Davennor

CHAPTER 1

"Jade, are you ready for today?"

With a thunk, I dropped my bag onto the lab bench and started unpacking my materials for class. Two notebooks, one for notes, and a smaller one for notes.

Bevin, my lab partner, watched me, eyes sparkling. Standing, he was just over six feet tall with mousy brown hair. He always wore plaid button downs that looked like he stole them from his dad's closet. You might mistake him for trying to blend in if it weren't for his mischievous personality and stunning sapphire blue eyes.

Sliding into my lab seat until our shoulders bumped,

I nearly fell to the floor. He caught me and I bit back a laugh. "What do you think?"

In a teasing tone he said, "Obviously not." He smiled widely.

My nose wrinkled in mock annoyance, and I poked him in the shoulder with a pencil. He laughed loud enough to catch the attention of the few students around us. Class would start soon so we had to stop goofing off. I dropped my head into my folded arms to hide my smile, took a breath, and straightened back up.

Bevin eyed me and we both lost it again.

We had been brought up together, our families connected. Always thrown together since he was only a year older than me. Then there was the fact that Bevin, like me, was probably going to grow up to be a pack healer, so we'd better learn to love science classes, especially biology. Though we both knew we were destined for medicine, his path into healing hadn't been as abrupt as mine.

"Why do you have black hair, or red hair, or even blond hair? Is your hair straight? Curly? Is there baldness in your family?" My pencil flew across my larger notebook as Ms. White began her lecture. The chapter I'd read last night had covered this, so this material wasn't new.

On the smaller pad I scratched out, `Movie, board game, or social tonight?` and passed it to Bevin.

He read it and passed it back. `Movie for the kiddos, my dad got that new movie they` all want to see. Social for us. If we start playing a game, my sisters will want to play. I haven't had much time to talk to José this week, it'd be nice.

Huffing a laugh, I shrugged. With Owen there, it isn't like you two will have time to talk, but sounds...

"Jade?" Bevin's urgent whisper pulled me back to class.

Looking up, I saw the teacher's gaze boring into me.

My heart raced in my chest as I gazed at her. I tried to keep my expression blank. "I'm sorry, Ms. White, I missed the question."

We had been discussing Punnett squares, small two-by-two grids that let us compare parent traits to predict offspring traits. It was interesting to learn about our own characteristics and to see how they played out in our families. My mom had auburn hair, but you couldn't see any of that with my black locks. My color was recessive to my dad's black hair. My eyes were what gave me my name; they were the exact shade of the green stone.

Genetics were a bit more of a spectrum than these boxes told us, but they were a fun place to start.

Both my parents had brown eyes, but I had my grandparents' green eyes. My brother's blond hair was a recessive trait that no one had expected, but his brown eyes were a mirror image of our dad's. Outside of his hair, he could almost be our dad's twin.

Ms. White continued to stare at me, a smug smile on her face. "It is always easier to be prepared for a quiz when you pay attention in class, Jade."

She loved to catch me daydreaming.

"Sorry, Ms. White," I mumbled, feeling the heat rush to my face. The battle of hiding my emotions was lost. Being caught not paying attention by my teacher irked me more than just about anything in school.

A half hour later, biology class was over, and it was time for lunch with Sarah and the rest of the group. Sarah had been my best friend since kindergarten. We had hit it off when we realized neither of us played with dolls or loved the color pink. We weren't normal little girls. We camped in her backyard, played in the mud getting dirty, and rode around on our bikes all summer. Though she could be girly now, dresses, makeup, and magazines were never our focus. As we grew up, we realized we enjoyed the same books, music, TV shows, and movies.

We were alike in all ways except looks. Where I was of average height and looks, Sarah was tall and stunning. She was several inches taller than me, with dark terra-cotta skin and deep brown eyes. Modelesque yet athletic. Her dominating presence and charisma commanded any room she entered. She played sports, and though she normally slummed with us, on game days she socialized with the athletes.

Our group was eating inside today for lunch. February

was the worst month of the year in Wisconsin, cold and miserable. All we had to look forward to was more snow, and maybe icy wind. Once the cold broke, in March or, say, July, and the warmth came, it would be beautiful for a day or two, and then the heat and humidity would hit. It could be quite lovely in the summer, or miserably sticky. However, staying indoors all the time was driving us crazy.

Sarah sat down at our spot. "Hey, Jade, how were classes?" She dropped her tray with a healthy array of pizza and fries.

My face heated up all over again. "I was goofing with Bev last period and got caught. How does Ms. White always know? I swear. I pay attention, take notes, and do my best, and she ignores me. One note written to Bev, and bam! she immediately calls on me. Every. Single. Time. It's like she has radar."

Sarah laughed at me. "You know Ms. White loves you. When does she ever ignore you? She practically volun-told you to join the senior biology class at the end of freshman year. She knows you want to go into medicine. I'm sure she just wants the best for you…and she probably likes to mess with little Miss Perfect Student."

Groaning, I rolled my eyes. "I am, by no means, a perfect student. I just know my family expects a lot from me."

"Could have fooled me."

Bevin slipped onto one of the table's benches as I shot Sarah a chagrined stare. He started to unpack his lunch, joining in on the conversation. "Not to mention, *you* expect a lot from you. I will admit that Ms. White is exceptional at catching you when you're distracted. It's awesome." He chuckled.

Sarah amusement permeated the table. Instead of fighting them, I took some of her fries, deciding eating was better than getting mad.

The lunchroom was loud as students took their assigned seats. Okay, they weren't assigned, but no one ever veered from the areas they occupied the day before. There may have been a bit of shifting once in a while, but it was rare.

Bevin took a quick bite of his sandwich and swallowed. Apparently, we weren't done with my humiliation during biology. "But your mishap wasn't that bad." He turned to Sarah. "Jade likes to exaggerate. She was in the middle of one of our notebook convos, missed a question, politely requested it repeated, and then wowed the class with her brilliance once she knew what was going on." His tone on the word politely was a bit mocking, as if he wouldn't have been just as polite.

He shook his head in disgust, though his eyes were dancing, and faced me again. "Ms. White can't lose you for long, Jade. She just catches you like a dog chasing a cat up into a tree."

I threw a fry at him. He deserved it. "Jerk." I laughed. Bevin always knew how to get me to laugh.

Sarah turned to Bevin. "Plans for spring break?"

Bevin blushed. "I know I have a year plus before I turn eighteen, but spring break I'm meeting up with some people from a local organization. I found them through Instagram. They're a group of people at different stages of gender confirming surgeries."

Sarah and I both paused. A huge smile broke out over my face. I threw my arms around him. "That's awesome! I know your binder sucks. The end is in sight."

Bevin had known he was different at a young age. We all started calling him Bevin in middle school, though he'd always bought clothes from the boys' department. His family had started the official change on paper, and he began hormone treatment with his transition to high school.

He nodded. "How about you?" His focus shifted between both of us.

Sorting my mental list, Sarah interrupted me before I could share what I'd decided was just me and Sarah, and what the three of us could do together. She made a noise, like a squeak in the back of her throat.

She turned to me. "So, my family wants to take a trip this spring break…" She paused staring back and forth between Bevin and me, then screeched, "To *Florida*!"

Bevin flinched at her pitch.

"Really?" I tried to sound excited, my cheeks pulling my mouth into a smile, of sorts. But my heart dropped to my belly as disappointment flowed through my body. We were supposed to spend this spring break together. It had been a particularly hard winter, we'd all been fighting cabin fever for weeks. I was anticipating doing something fun together, even if it had to be indoors.

The squeeze Bevin gave me on my knee under the table let me know my act hadn't worked. At least I knew he'd be around to keep me company.

Eyes shut, I tried to transform my smile into something sincere. When I stared at Sarah, it was through a bit of misty vision. "That's great. You're going to have so much fun. Are you going to the beaches? Orlando? The Keys? What's the plan? Is your whole family going?"

Even to me, my voice sounded flat.

Sarah stared at me deadpan, and then snorted. "You are trying so hard to be happy for me, yet you look like a drowned cat. You didn't let me finish, silly. Yes, we're going to Florida. Yes, we are going to the beaches. Yes, my whole family is going, all *three* of us. You didn't let me finish, idiot." She paused, staring at me dramatically. "We want you to come with us."

Everything in the world around me stopped. My jaw dropped along with whatever I was holding. My eyes began to sting, and I had to force myself to blink.

Sarah rapped on the table to get my attention. "My mom is going down to the University of Florida for a conference that coincides with our spring break. You won't even miss any classes. We can go on a tour of the University. We'll spend most of our time in Gainesville, not that interesting, but Dad said he would take us to Orlando for at least one day, maybe out to Kennedy Space Center, too. We can see if there are any launches happening."

Bevin knocked into me to snap me out of my shock. Finally, I replied, as my heart raced, and my breathing got ragged. "Really? You aren't kidding me? Me, too? To Florida? With your family? Really?" My words stumbled out of me. "You aren't kidding? This is real? And you really thought I would worry about missing school, dork?"

We were both laughing at this point.

"Yes, it's real, but you need to talk to your parents to make sure they're okay with it. If you can't come, it will be horrible." Her hand flew up to her forehead for emphasis.

Like a bucket of ice-cold water being dumped over my head, my mood deflated. My parents. A chill ran down my spine. My dad. "Yeah, that makes sense." *Focus on the good: Florida.* "Oh, my gods, this is so awesome, I hope they say yes. How many more classes until I can go home and talk with them? This is so cool. Florida!"

It was my turn to squeal.

José, a senior who recently started hanging out with us, and the last of our group, finally arrived. "What's so cool?"

His dad was Mexican, and his mom was from Florida, so his family spoke both English and Spanish at home. His accent always had a way of centering me.

Gazing at him, like a lifeline who held my future, I spoke fast enough my words practically blurred together.

"Sarah's family is going to Florida over spring break, and she just invited me to go." My smile was starting to hurt my cheeks.

"Do you really think your parents will let you go?" His words hit me like a punch to the gut.

Deflated, I slumped and ate some pizza.

José's family was part of the pack, unlike Sarah's, who didn't even know werewolves existed. He used to hang out with my older brother, Owen, another senior, but José got fed up with that crowd. He tended to be more academic than the lot of them. He had been on the basketball team for a few years and was good, but he never seemed liked it. Overall, he would rather hang out with us than a group of dumb jocks. At least that was my theory.

He said he'd started hanging out with us this year, when, as he put it, I became less annoying. He had been offered several engineering scholarships all over the country. Though, he planned on staying local, or at least that is what we all hoped. Having our friend close was important. The local university, the University of Wisconsin-Madison, was a great college.

"Mom? Yes. Maybe. I don't know. Yes! Don't ruin this for me." I felt defensive and defeated at the same time. My heart started racing. Gesturing wildly, I almost took Bevin out. My face heating up in the combination of embarrassment at how important this was to me and frustration that he was probably right.

Bevin carefully grabbed my wrist as José continued to speak.

His warm eyes took me in, calming me. "Jade, I'm not trying to ruin anything, chica, but your dad is not known for being the most easygoing father I've ever met. I mean your mom is awesome, but your dad is as controlling as they come." José had had a few run-ins with my dad over the years, so I guessed I should cut him a little slack.

Focused on José's words, I took a deep breath, ordered my thoughts, and slipped my wrist from Bevin's grip. "That's why I'm going to ask my mom first. She can convince my dad about how educational and amazing this will be for me. To get to my dad, I'll go through my mom."

There, a plan of attack.

Huffing out a laugh, José shook his head and gave me a half-smile. "Fair, but delusional, chica."

Sarah watched us like a tennis match, her eyes bouncing back and forth. "Wow, José, you seem to know Jade's parents almost as well as she does."

Though José had been hanging out with us for a few months now, my parents had not been a subject of discussion. Sarah didn't really understand the neighborhood and how close we all were. Everyone in the pack lived in the neighborhood, and all the kids of pack members grew up together. We spent every full moon night together while our parents were out running, honoring Mondara, the werewolf moon god.

Sarah and I had been best friends forever, but to Sarah, werewolves were just the stuff of legends and books, so she didn't know about that part of my life. I didn't think she even realized how close I was to Bevin. She probably thought José hung out with us because he used to hang out with Owen and knew me through him.

"It's hard to not know River and Hazel Stone if you live in the neighborhood. I've been mowing lawns and shoveling walks since I was in seventh grade. I *know* them."

We all laughed at the chagrin in José's tone.

Bevin tilted his head towards me. "I don't know, it's only Florida. It's not that far away. What? A thousand miles? Her dad might like to get rid of Jade for a bit."

I threw another fry at him.

It wasn't that my dad was awful, it was just that he was very particular about, well, everything, and the people in the neighborhood knew this. My family hired the neighborhood kids to mow the lawn and shovel the walk. It was one of the ways for them to earn money. But if the job wasn't completed up to River Stone standards, you would be doing it again.

Despite that, the kids in the neighborhood loved my parents. They arranged a lot of community events and outings, which was another reason José and I knew each other so well despite the two-year difference in our ages.

The bell rang. Sarah grabbed her bag and stood. "Okay, after school, you will convince your parents."

Bevin leaned down, gave me a hug, and whispered, "Good luck with that," then sauntered off to class.

José's eyes softened and he shook his head as he left.

Sighing, I grabbed my bag. Images of beaches and crystalline blue waters floated through my head. Then I thought about the possibility of seeing a rocket taking off. Shaking off my daydream, I gathered my stuff and went to return my tray.

Florida!

CHAPTER 2

"God, she is such a freak." The words were forced out around the smacking of gum.

There were several students around me all placing trays in the return window. Closing my eyes for a second, an elbow jammed into my rib cage. Wincing, I took a calming breath and headed for the exit, shooting a quick glance towards the voice I'd recognized.

A little behind me and to my left were two of the pretty people. Seniors. Popular. A guy a bit taller than me, blond with wavy hair, arms wrapped around the waist of a petite cheerleader with her hair up in a ponytail. It was game day, so he was wearing his school jersey and she was in her form-hugging tiny uniform.

Go Stolzburg Pumas. Yeah…escape was the best plan.

His voice reached me as surely as hers had. He wanted to soften her sharp evaluation of me, a mere sophomore. "Don't be mean, Brooke."

Her voice slithered out like a snake. "Why do you defend her? I thought you didn't like anyone in your family?"

"She's my sister. No reason to call her out. No one here is as perfect as you."

Gag. Shaking my head, I made a beeline for the door. Their voices still reached me, even as I quickened my pace.

Why did the words hurt? Owen, my brother, loved me. Brooke on the other hand was broken. His decision to try to date her was beyond anyone's comprehension. Everyone knew they were a bad couple. Something was wrong in her family, and it made her hate all families. She had a group of friends and outside of them, she was nasty.

The crowd to get out of the cafeteria thickened. Squeezing through with a desperation to escape, I tried not to knock too many people over. Lunch had been so good, and now this. Suddenly, gym didn't loom as horrible. My attempts to flee were thwarted by the throngs of students.

"Brooke!" Owen's voice came over the crowd.

Her brown ponytail flipped its way through the pack of students. No one was willing to stand in her way.

What had he said to set her off? Did I want to know?

Nope, not really.

The hallway to the gym had no other classrooms so it was free of most students, I could finally breathe. Rolling my shoulders to release the tension that was Brooke, a hand fell on me, stopping my progress to class.

My brother stood there, contrite. "What?" I snapped.

"Sorry."

Releasing a breath of air, I glared up at him. "Whatever."

"No, really. I don't know what it is about her. I really like her, she just isn't about family. I guess hers is pretty awful."

"But Owen, you *are* and yours isn't."

"I know. I just…I dunno…I'm sorry…" He checked his watch. "I gotta run, class." And he was off.

"Whatever," I mumbled again to myself as I resumed my trek to class.

Relationships were dumb. Cheerleaders were dumb.

In the locker room I changed and finally dragged myself to gym class.

There was a foot of snow on the ground outside, so class was indoors. Basketball.

Mr. Nelson, the gym teacher, loved his job. He was a huge bear of a man, well over six feet tall with thick muscular limbs. He wore gym shorts and a t-shirt regardless of temperature and was hairy enough that he looked like he was wearing pants.

I giggled at my own joke.

He eyed me suspiciously before starting class. "Listen

up. Warm up, three laps. Then we will get into our teams from last week."

Three laps…around the room…doable. No problem. I was fit. My family worked out regularly. We had to, it was part of our lives.

"Go!"

The mass of sophomores went.

Jogging. Working out for me meant martial arts training or weights, not running. Though exercise was important in the pack, what we choose varied. *Stay in the middle, Jade. Is that Piper ahead of me?*

Focus on running. The back of the pack is okay, right?

One lap done. *Keep your breathing steady.*

"Pick it up, Ms. Stone!"

The snap of his voice shook me from my thoughts. I'd fallen behind everyone else. Crap.

Why did he always point out that I was falling behind? Couldn't he tell I tried? Couldn't he focus on someone else?

Okay, faster, running faster, that was possible, wasn't it?

Pushing down deep, my legs moved faster and suddenly there were the other trailing students. One, then two. *Ouch!* A knife spiked into my side as my heavy breathing led to a stitch. I had to slow down, but that wasn't an option.

Two laps done.

Why do Sarah and Owen enjoy doing this? Could this be enjoyable?

Pumping my arms harder, trying to get my legs to

comply, the stitch in my side got sharper.

A quarter of a lap to the end. Most of the other students were just standing there watching those of us who were too slow to have finished already. Gods, that chapped my…

The room rolled around me as I tripped on nothing, falling. I continued the motion out of the way of the other runners…both of them. There were more balls stuck in the ceiling rafters than the last time I'd ended up like this. Four this time.

Groaning, my face burned with embarrassment. Lying on my back, panting, my side hurt, my legs hurt, my soul hurt. Was this why Brooke called me a freak?

"Ms. Stone, on your feet." Mr. Nelson called out, his voice a mixture of exasperation and disappointment.

A small hand waved in front of my face. I shifted my focus from the balls stuck behind lights to two lovely blue eyes. Piper. My heart pounded in my chest as a small smile grew on my face and I let her pull me up.

"Thanks," I said shyly.

"No problem," she replied, before running off.

Mr. Nelson surveyed the class. "Ok, now that the excitement of the run is over, get your jerseys so we can play ball."

My arms dropped and my shoulders slumped. The scratchy green jersey, the last available in the bag, was an extra extra-large and fit like a potato sack dress. I knew since I'd gotten it in the past.

As Mr. Nelson handed me the jersey, he looked me up and down and sniffed. "How is your brother the captain of every sport, including basketball, and you end up falling on your face nearly every class?"

The burn of humiliation started at my toes and spread to my ears. Smirking, he left me to join the other students stuck with the burden of me on their team.

He turned to the class. "Start off with drills. Everyone find a group with a matching jersey color. Start with passing, then shooting. There are six nets and thirty of you, do the math. Again, your group should all share the same color jersey."

After classes I found Bevin at his locker. Sarah was at basketball practice. "I fell in gym class…again."

He chortled.

My face dropped into a flat stare. "You know, that isn't very supportive."

His laugh turned into a huge smile and his eyes danced. "Jade, you're so good at everything." He swung his arm around me. "It's nice to know you're still human."

I elbowed him in the side and slipped away. At my locker, there were many layers to put on before facing the outdoors and walking home.

Bevin's head cocked to the side. "Forgetting something?"

Pausing, my mind went blank. Full moon night,

couches, pizza, home. "What?"

"We need to finish our extra credit lab. Ms. White said if we didn't finish it today it would be too late. If it's not done now, then there's no point in finishing it and no points in the grade book."

Dropping my shoulders, all my gear got stacked in my arms instead of put on. It would be nice to be able to leave directly from class. "It's so cold out there. I wish Owen weren't being such a jerk right now. I would ask for a ride. We'll get done about the time his practice ends."

"What did he do this time?"

Slamming my locker to release some frustration before we headed back to biology class, I grumbled, "As I was leaving lunch, I had a run-in with him and Brooke. I just don't know what he sees in her. Apparently, she hates family, hers, his, everyone's. He's trying to charm her. That means, when around her, he's acting weirder than normal, almost like he hates family, too."

Bevin looked thoughtful. "Can he pull off hating his family? I mean, you two fight, but you've always had each other's backs. He's never hated you or your parents."

A huge sigh knocked me into him, and he wrapped an arm around me. "I'm not sure, but I'm not going to be his punching bag." We walked down the hall for a few minutes in silence. "In the long run, I don't think so. Pack is too strong. He's wanted to go wolfie for too long. Waiting to go furry may be hell, though. He's eighteen, so, what? At most, two years?"

"Let's hope it doesn't take him two years."

I rubbed my eyes, stressed. "I know he would love the transition to happen today but knowing my luck it will take longer and this thing with Brooke will last."

"Are they actually dating?"

"They weren't before, but he had all afternoon to convince her."

"You said she walked out on him at lunch, so there's still hope," Bevin said, ever the optimist.

We reached the classroom. It was time to focus on biology and our challenge lab. Most students weren't given these labs, but most students weren't me and Bevin.

CHAPTER 3

Bevin and I opened the school doors to the parking lot into a starry, cold night. The moon was out, and it was freezing. It was only five, but during winter in Wisconsin, night came early.

The wind cut through my scarf as we headed towards the parking lot. I reached up to pull my hat snugger over my ears. "When does the temperature hit double digits again?"

Bevin slid his eyes to me. "Should we call for a ride? I already can't feel my toes."

Staring at him, I didn't notice Piper as I ran into her. She was a few inches shorter than me with sassy auburn hair that matched her freckles. "'Scuse me." My teeth started to chatter.

She was standing there, shoulders curled in, practically a ball. Her hat matched her auburn hair. Her blue eyes shot up to look at me. "What are you two still doing here?"

"Finishing a lab. You?"

"Man, school's rough. I didn't think you would need to stay after school to work on a late assignment. Don't really know why, you just seem so put together when I see you around." She shrugged. "Maybe not so much in gym, though…I had to finish a math test. I suck at math."

Bevin moved forward. "We weren't…"

Glaring at him to say, 'shut up', I said, "We had a bio lab. Had to finish it now or not get credit."

Bevin raised an eyebrow in question.

Piper's brow furrowed as she looked back and forth between us, but she finally nodded. "Yeah, same, getting whatever credit I can scrape up. Well, it's too cold to think. I'm waiting on my dad. See you tomorrow in gym." She gave a small nod in lieu of a wave.

Giving a small nod back, a slight warmth bubbled inside me. Looking up at Bevin, he gave me a strange, penetrating stare. My eyes went wide; it was too cold to get into this with him right then. I grabbed his hand. We started to move away and ran smack into another person. Gazing up, my eyes met those of my brother.

"Owen!" His face was pale, and he was hunched over.

Immediately, I grabbed his arm, Bevin grabbed the other. Pulling him down, I kissed his forehead since every other part of me was bundled up. Warm, even in the freezing cold air. Fever-warm. "You okay?"

He shook his head. When he looked up, his eyes were wild. "It hurts." It came out low and gravely.

His focus was off, eyes glazed, and he was shaking. "What hurts?"

He just shook his head unable to elaborate.

Bevin and I stared at each other and started to move around to the side of the building where there weren't several dozen students. We needed privacy to figure this out and make a call.

"Is he okay?"

I turned to see Piper following us. "Yeah, he gets this way after practice. Muscle cramps. We're just helping him walk it off. Water. You know the drill."

"You sure? The door is that way." She pointed to the left and a bit behind us.

"His locker is by the door over there. This is faster. He has some energy drinks. We're fine. See you tomorrow."

She stuck on our heels. For some reason, she wouldn't get the hint.

"Are you sure?" She kept following, concern deep in her eyes. "My dad gets cramps. I may be able help."

"Yeah, I'm sure," I snapped. We needed her to leave.

Shrugging, eyes wide, she finally stopped and, looking

hurt, headed back to the parking lot.

Bevin watched her for a minute before staring at me. "What's up with you and her?"

"I don't know what you're talking about."

We headed around the corner out of sight of the parking lot as he said, "It's just you two…"

Before he could continue, Owen moaned, "What's wrong with me?"

We navigated into the school's courtyard where there was a small garden. It wasn't an area students went to often because it could be seen from a classroom's windows during the day, but right now that room was dark and empty. During winter, the garden was too covered in snow to be interesting.

We leaned Owen against the wall. We were blocked from the wind, and it felt almost warm. Stripping off my mittens, I felt his head again. "Owen, you're burning up." Fully in triage mode, his wrist was next. "Your pulse is high. What happened during practice? Are you feeling sick? We should call home."

Bevin started to pull out his phone.

Owen bent over and groaned in pain. "Oh, gods, Jade, what's happening to me? It hurts."

I gently put my hands on Owen's arms to calm him. I felt his muscles contracting. This wasn't sick. Waving my hands to signal Bevin to take a few steps back, my heart sank at what was about to happen. "Owen, I need you to take off your shirt and pants."

I was trying to project as much calm as I could. If he knew how scared we were, things could go horribly wrong for him. Peeking over my shoulder at Bevin, he was holding it in—good. Eyes wide but taking deep breaths to keep his peace.

Sounding frazzled, Owen said, "What? No. We're at school, it's the middle of winter, you're kids, and I'm not stripping naked."

He was shaking with fear, cold, everything. Taking his hands in mine, I squeezed hard, and his eyes shot to mine. Knowing his full attention was on me was important. "First of all, we are currently your medical help. Secondly, you'll have underwear on. I didn't say naked." He nodded. He was scared, confused, and didn't know what he was doing. We had a silent conversation, it was almost like we could hear each other, though we couldn't.

Do I have *to do this?* His eyes widened.

Yes. You do. My hands rotated in a hurry up motion.

I don't want to. He dropped his shoulders.

Too bad. My hands flew out to the side as I shrugged.

Fine. He slouched in defeat.

He finally stripped down, panting. When he was done, the whites of his eyes shone around the brown. He was still scared. "What's wrong with me, Jade?" Practically naked, he was shaking, but not shivering, fearful but not cold.

"Not completely sure, Owen. If I were to guess, you're

about to become a werewolf and howl at the moon, run with your pack, and become a bigger pain. If I'm wrong, you're going to freeze out here with me and Bevin to stand as witnesses."

He gaped. Apparently not knowing how to react. We had both seen our parents change, as well as our pack, but this was new for him.

"Remember what we've been told: the important thing is to relax, and to not fight the change. Let it happen. I mean, you will be ridiculous as a wolf with skivvies on, but it is what it is." I gave him a wicked grin.

His breathing roughened.

Bevin spoke up, controlling the situation. "Remember, do not bite us if and when you change. That would mean you'd be out of the pack. This isn't a joke, Owen; you must take this part seriously. If you are about to change, the one thing you must remember is: we are family, we are friends, and you do not bite people."

Owen looked at us with huge brown eyes. He nodded with each word. These were the ideas and concepts that had been drilled into us. The problem was, there should have been an adult werewolf here to help him. Someone who, if Owen did bite them, it wouldn't matter.

His first change shouldn't be here, at school, with us. There hadn't been a change this young in recent pack history. Changes had always happened to older children of werewolves. An accidental bite would mean more than one new werewolf. What if he bit someone who didn't know about werewolves? That would be even worse. It would mean our secret could get out.

"Owen, if you change, you have to stay here and wait for Mom or Dad. No running. No one can see you. There are too many people here who would see your wolf," I reminded him. Standing a bit back from him, I put my mittens back on.

He continued to nod, then his body tensed as if in pain and rippled. He fell to his hands and knees. Fur began to flow out of his body and his face began to elongate. His body was changing, and he whimpered. It sounded like it hurt. We knew it could hurt, and it would take a few minutes for everything to change, but in the end he would be fine.

Transfixed with all the changes, the cold and worry of being on school grounds left me. Everything was all happening in slow motion. The bones rearranging, the fingers getting shorter, the claws coming out, digging into the snow.

His eyes grew. He seemed like he wanted to yell with the pain, but we were at school, and we were near a bunch of norms, people who knew nothing about werewolves. His whole body shook. His eyes said he wanted to curl into a ball with all his hurt, but his body wasn't under his control.

Owen became a grey wolf. His fur was darker near his back, growing lighter as it got closer to his head. It had the same ombré effect on his ears. His wolf was bigger than those in the wild; he weighed about a hundred and eighty pounds, and that was what he would weigh as a werewolf. His wolf was beautiful.

When he was almost done, I told Bevin to back up more. If Owen was going to go crazy, no reason for both of us to get hurt. When Owen finally finished, he got to his feet, shook himself out and gazed up at me. He seemed oddly calm.

"Okay, Owen, turn around if you want help with your undies. Bevin will call home and get a ride so that you can get home safely. You'll run with the pack tonight."

Bevin's voice was full of awe from behind me. "I already called. Someone is on their way."

Deep brown eyes turned up at me, for a moment serious and dangerous. Then his tongue lolled out. He turned so I could see him in all his glory, a huge wolf with tighty-whities on.

A chuckle escaped me, releasing the tension of the last few minutes. He backed up and shook his tail. I helped him with his skivvies—ew.

Just as he stepped out of them, he turned and ran.

Heart dropping, I gave chase. It took mere seconds for Bevin to pass me. He had gathered Owen's clothing at some point and was carrying the pile under one arm. He darted into the parking lot. Screams from the dozen or so students still milling around flowed around me as I made my way to the parking lot, heading to their cars. Following as quickly as I could, focusing on the two in front of me, and not on the ground below me, the icy ground had my foot sliding out from under me. As happened in gym class, the world spun around me and suddenly my face was in the snow.

The cold seeped into my stomach and the icy snow made me want to cry. What made me suddenly think I could run? Owen had turned furry at school. Students exclaiming about what they saw overlapped in a cacophony of sound. Pouting wasn't helping. There was damage control and finding Owen to be done. Oh, gods. My body was frozen to the ground. I sent a thought to both Sonnara, the sun god, and Mondara, the moon god. One of them had to help me out of this. Probably Sonnara, she helped with the human side, though we were in it up to our furry noses on the werewolf side. Or maybe I'd just freeze right here in the snow.

Werewolves believed in set of twin gods: Mondara and Sonnara. Mondara was the moon god. They watched over the animals of the forest, protecting the run and the hunt. They protected the werewolves from being detected. Mondara was the reason werewolves spent at least one night a month as a wolf singing to her in love and acceptance of their animal side.

Mondara's twin was Sonnara, god of the sun. Sonnara protected our humanity and kept us human despite the animalistic urges. They kept the wolf from eating humans and going rogue. They watched over us and guided us when our path was murky. Sonnara sang of love and acceptance.

The two of them became the guiding image of the werewolf's dual nature: person and animal. They represented day and night. They showed that every person had both good and bad in them, and we shouldn't be ashamed of ourselves. Neither one of them individually represent good or evil, but together they represent that everyone has aspects of both. They taught that we needed to learn and understand who we are to grow.

Was this hypothermia? *Get up Jade!*

Groaning, pushing down with one mittened hand, I managed to get to my back. My face felt like it had turned to stone. My eyes were still closed from all the snow stuck in my lashes. The cake of snow on my gloves scraped my forehead when I went to wipe my eyes. Defeated, my arms flopped to the ground with a thump.

"Are you okay?"

Using my sleeve to knock some ice off my eyes, one of my eyes finally opened. A bit of blurry redness wavered in through the snow remaining in my eye, floating above me.

"Piper?"

"Can I help you up?"

I lifted my hands. She grabbed them, hauling me to my

feet. Once up, I took off my mittens and wiped down my face. "I thought you had gone home."

"My dad isn't here yet. You fell. You looked dead…or hurt. Are you okay?" She reached out and touched my face. "You have a small cut. Good thing you iced it." She had a bit of a wicked smile as she said that last bit.

Suppressing a snicker, I was amazed anyone could make me feel anything but frustrated. Still frozen from the temperatures and my fall, it was nice to laugh.

Bevin stomped up to us. "I'm going to kill…" He suddenly took notice of Piper and his scowl turned into a smile. "Piper, you're still around."

"Bevin? Right?"

He nodded. "Yeah, hi, nice to meet you."

"Was that your dog that went running past me? Where did he come from?"

Sending a prayer to Mondara, my eyes on the moon, I took a deep breath. "No, not Bevin's dog. He's…"

Just then a horn honked. Piper whipped around. "That's my dad, I have to go." She gave me a small smile. "See you tomorrow." And she ran off.

Freezing, I moved close to Bevin. "Did you get ahold of my parents?"

"Yeah, they're on their way. But Owen's long gone."

"Thank the gods, I'm turning into ice. What do the other students think?"

"Most thought he was a dog, like Piper. He was running

fast. A couple thought it was a wolf." His eyes narrowed. "So, what aren't you telling me about Piper?"

I had been watching the movements in the parking lot, but at that I shot my gaze up to him. "Nothing…yet."

CHAPTER 4

The cold was seeping into every pore of my body. Shivering, I bumped my shoulder against Bevin's. "Did you actually call anyone?"

"Yeah. I called your mom. She said someone would be here."

"No one in the parking lot seems too freaked out."

Bevin surveyed everyone left by the cars. "Most people are convinced it was a dog. I can't believe that happened."

My hands started to shake. "I've never seen someone change for the first time. It was crazy. I thought he'd be…I donno, less calm, maybe."

"I'm talking about you and Piper. I can't believe I've never seen it before."

Everything in me froze, well, it was freezing outside, but…slowly my searching gaze shifted from the students milling around the parking lot up to his piercing blue eyes. "What?"

"Were you ever going to tell me?" His voice came out so softly. It almost broke my heart.

I reached out and grabbed at his hand. He fisted it and pulled it away. "Bevin."

"What, Jade?"

"Don't do this. I didn't…I'm…I…I don't know. I didn't try to keep it from you. I'm sorry. Please don't be mad."

He huffed out his breath. "Fine. So, you like her. You like girls? Not boys?"

My head dropped and I focused on my feet and nodded. Before either of us said anything more, T.J. pulled up. We leapt into the car, desperate for heat.

T.J. watched us shivering and jacked up the heat as high as it would go. "What happened?"

My teeth started chattering, but I turned to him. "Owen went furry. Didn't wait. Ran through parking lot. Kids screaming. I fell in the snow."

T.J. chuckled at me as I glared back. A few minutes later we arrived at my house, and I jumped out and ran inside. It was a full moon night, so Bevin and T.J. followed me in. Freezing and wet, all my thoughts swirled around warm clothes in my room. Halfway there, a call from the kitchen had me swinging around.

Dad's commanding voice filled the room. "Jade, Bevin, kitchen."

We both turned and made our way to him. When we got there, the noise from the kiddos in the basement told me most of the pack was here. Since my cousin Dillan and José were sitting at the kitchen table there didn't seem to be any older kids down there watching the younger ones. The smell of pizza wafted up, causing my stomach to growl. Mom was sitting at the counter eating a salad. Seeing how cold we looked, she got up and started making herbal tea.

Dad came over, looking frantic. "Tell me what happened. Where is Owen?"

Bevin and I filled my parents in on the situation. As we finished up the story, T.J. came in from the backyard.

"Owen's in the back. He ran home. He looks fine." He headed into the basement to grab some pizza.

Dad went into the backyard to check on Owen, but Mom stayed with us, handing us our tea. We must have looked as awful as we felt.

"Mom, who's staying with us tonight?" I asked as I held the mug, letting it heat me up.

"I'm not sure, everyone is busy. It's hard when the full moon has the audacity to happen mid-week." She looked distracted.

She kept glancing back towards where Dad was with Owen, obviously worried about my brother. She also wanted to get out and run; the pull of the moon must be getting strong. There was usually an adult who stayed with us kiddos to make sure everyone stayed safe. It was practical, since the change could happen at any time — although most of us were still too young. It didn't tend to happen before age nineteen. Owen just turned furry; the likelihood of another wolf tonight was small, hopefully.

"No extra adults tonight." Dad walked in from the backyard. He turned off his phone. "Everyone in the pack is running. Everyone else is busy. There are all sorts of SNAFUs going on tonight, so you and the boys will have to be the adults. Well, you and Bevin, at least."

SNAFU: situation normal, all fouled up, or other fun f-words. It was the main description for a day in IT, or so I'd been told. It was also one of my dad's favorite ways to describe a situation.

"Hey," exclaimed Dillan, as José said, "I think we've been disrespected, bro."

Giggling, I weaved through the kitchen to refill my drink.

Mom stared at Dad. "How is he?"

Dad nodded. "Good. Really good." He turned to me. "You said he was calm after his shift?"

Bevin answered, "It wasn't anything like we expected. He recognized both of us right away. He didn't attack or anything."

Mom shook her head. She looked worried. "We'll have to figure this out…" She tilted her head, looking very wolfie, gazing at me.

Dad took out plates and cups from the cupboard. "There should be enough pizza in the basement for everyone, so enjoy," he said, getting back on topic. He passed them to José, who was closest to him. "Movies, games, not too much sugar, and bedtime by ten for the majority of the kiddos. You all, don't stay up too late. We should be back before morning."

Mom wrote a list of numbers down, mumbling to herself, "I hate it when full moon nights are on a school night."

She turned to us and handed me the numbers. "Everyone should have everything they need for school with them. Breakfast is cereal and bagels."

Three of the younger kids ran up the stairs. A low growl came from Mom, and she shot them a look. An alpha teacher-look. Wow. They all quickly lowered their eyes in submission and walked slowly back down the stairs.

T.J. came up eating a slice of pizza as the small kids flowed around him. He watched them escape. He came up to me and wrapped his arm around me. I rested my head against his shoulder. It was automatic.

Eight years ago, we had all been in the basement, all of us kiddos at least, when Dad came down and called me, Owen, T.J., and Candice up. He drew us into the formal living room, far enough away for others not to overhear, unless they were trying.

My dad paced as we sat on the couch.

T.J. was shaking, so I grabbed his hand and pulled him closer to me. We had always been friends, though he was older. All the color had drained from his face. Candice and Owen were sitting on the other side of T.J.

T.J. was still shaking so I put my hand on his knee and he wrapped his arm around my shoulder. My head felt right resting against his chest. Though T.J. was a teenager and older than me, somehow I knew I was the one who had to give him the comfort just then.

Dad spent a minute gazing at the four of us. I don't know what he saw; kids all of us, all under the age of twenty. "Candice, T.J., your parents' dominance fight didn't go well."

That was all he got out.

Candice wailed, "No!"

A tear just trailed down T.J.'s face. It didn't look like he had reacted, but he was trembling. He wanted to be strong. He was the younger sibling, but he was holding back his emotions for Candice. Something in me knew it. He wanted to be strong for her.

He took a deep breath. "What will happen to us now, River?"

My dad just stared at him, then at all of us. "We will adopt you. Candice, you're old enough to decide what you want, but we will happily take you in as well."

Candice took in a shuttering breath. "Let me think about it, it's a lot."

T.J.'s arm around me turned into a hug.

After that, they both moved in. T.J. became like a second older brother. Candice became more of an aunt.

José brought me out of my memory. "Yo, this isn't our first rodeo," he told my dad. "We do this, like, every month. It isn't like we don't know what's going on. Even when an adult is here, we're the ones running the show in the basement."

Smirking, I followed up with, "Go, you two look ready to bite someone, and since you've said you don't *want* to do that, you should probably leave before it happens."

Mom watched José and Dillan head downstairs. "Are you sure you'll be okay?"

Tapping the list of emergency agency phone numbers on the counter, I smiled. "Go, we're fine. Bevin and I have had lots of training, José is great with the kids, and Dillan is a great backup."

If there was trouble and we really needed help, I'd call Sarah's parents. They should be home. Despite not being in the know, if there was an emergency, I would call them.

"I also know the number to 9-1-1."

"Wait, we should write that down," Bevin grabbed the paper and made a show of looking for a pen.

Mom glared. This close to the full moon her wolf was starting to peek out. "Okay, fine, we'll leave. See you in the morning."

Dad eyes were starting to glow. "You're playing with fire, boy."

Though Dad was teasing, his look was fierce.

Bevin snickered.

Mom and Dad gave me and Bevin hugs. They each went over to pay homage to our image of Mondara, the moon god, in guidance for a good hunt and a safe run. Then they ran out the back door with T.J. close behind them. There was a crowd of pack members out back. Some had shifted, some were getting ready to shift and run. Our house backed up to a wooded area, and the backyard was secluded and safe. We had privacy for them to strip down and change before running out to harass the local wildlife.

The smell of pizza and the promise of friends pulled me down to the basement. José and Dillan were sitting on some couches away from the TV near a table filled with food and drink. The kiddos were watching the latest action hero movie. They were riveted. At nine-thirty, the movie ended, and I got the youngest kiddos' teeth brushed, changed into pajamas, and into bed. There were a few bedrooms with bunkbeds in the basement. By ten o'clock there were only four of us up: Bevin, José, Dillan, and me.

Bevin searched José's face questioningly. "How can you not want to be a werewolf?"

Kids of werewolves had the potential of becoming a werewolf naturally. If they didn't change by twenty, they could choose to be bitten or stay a norm.

This debate had been going on all night. It might have been going on longer than that. The two of them had started hanging out Bevin's freshman year of high school when Sarah and I were still in middle school. Over the years, they had gotten closer. It may have been the real reason José started hanging out with our group.

"I just don't. I mean, if it happens, it happens, and I will cope, but I like the idea of just having a life and not having to deal with all the overhead."

Dillan squinted, brow furrowed. "What overhead?"

His dad, my uncle, was middle of the pack and somehow kept Dillan free from seeing how the pack ran. "You're so oblivious."

José shifted his gaze between Dillan and me. "You don't see it." He nodded at me. "Your parents are pack alphas." Then nodded at Dillan. "And your dad was almost alpha. The rest of the pack has to follow. I don't want to be the alpha, but I don't want to follow. I don't want to fight for my rank and position."

He took a bite of pizza and got a far-off look. "I just want to go to college, get a job, meet the man of my dreams, get married, have two point five kids, a couple of cats, and be happy."

Dillan just stared at José like he had grown a second nose. He cocked his head. He looked confused.

"Which part got to you, cuz, the college part? The job part? Or the being happy with kids part?" Dillan was working on a two-year associates degree. His plan was to work as an auto-technician. We were all excited for having this skill set in the family.

"José. Kids. Cats…. Cats?" Dillan sobered a bit. "Really? Cats? Dude, we're, like, werewolves, we eat cats. You want cats?"

"I've always liked cats." José shifted uncomfortably in his seat, embarrassed. "I have a friend who has a cat, and the cat's nice. They cuddle on your lap and purr. I think I would like having a cat."

It was too much. Raiding the fridge for a soda, I plopped down next to Bevin with my drink.

"Cats aren't bad." Bevin nodded. "My cousins who are out of the loop have two cats. We visited last summer. They were cool. They didn't even mind my parents. One of the cats slept in my bed during the trip. Except for trying to sleep on my head, which apparently means he liked me, it was great. Why is a cat's affection shown through trying to kill the ones they love?" He shrugged. "I could see having a cat."

"Dude, you're totally going to be an old cat-lady someday," Dillan teased.

Slapping my hands over my mouth, I bit back a laugh. José glared. He turned to me. "Do not wake any of the young ones."

That got me laughing harder. Squeaking sounds came out from under my hands. Getting myself under control, I asked, "Do you think Owen is eating a rabbit right now?"

That got us all talking about Owen's first meal as a wolf. Shortly thereafter, everyone started to nod off to sleep.

A few hours later, I got up and headed upstairs. It was too cold to go outside, so I sat in a recliner in the living room hoping it would be enough. The minutes passed and my skin crawled with my inability to sleep. Too restless to sleep, and there were too many people in the house for me to walk around. This happened to me sometimes. When it did, I slipped out the back door and wandered in the backyard and the woods behind the house. My parents knew I was restless and some nights I needed to roam. The backyard area was big, safe, and lit.

This need to roam started when I was young. When I was three, my dad found me at four in the morning on the swing set, swinging. When he asked me why I was out there, my only response was my need to move. He didn't yell. He didn't get mad at me. He just nodded and sat next to me swinging. We watched the sun rise together that morning. That was the first of many restless nights.

Too agitated to sit and worried my tapping would wake the kiddos, I took the stairs to the underground hallway that lead to the pack gym. There was an indoor track that allowed me to move and not disturb the others. I clenched my fists and shook out my hands while walking a few laps, and eventually I relaxed. Finally, the itching under my skin released and I headed back to the basement and collapsed into a fitful sleep.

CHAPTER 5

"Oh, my gods, that was so cool. So cool. Like you can't even begin to understand how cool it was. Cool," Owen blathered on and on the next morning.

We were trying to get all the kiddos off to school. Their parents were helping. Owen was not.

"But was it cool?" Dillan was also not helping.

"Oh, my gods, so cool. I could smell, and see, and hear, and taste, and feel, and oh, my gods."

He wouldn't stop.

I yawned and my jaw cracked, My brain struggled to focus, having been up half the night and worrying about him, yet he kept going on and on without actually saying anything. More coffee.

My parents came in from getting showered and ready for work. "I was too distracted to tell you this yesterday, but you did a really good job…"

"I know," Owen cut in, grabbing a box of cereal from the table. "I was with the pack and like just there."

"…Jade and Bevin," Mom finished a little louder than necessary. I looked over at her, realizing she had been complimenting us, not Owen. "It isn't easy keeping a new wolf calm on their first change, but you two got Owen away from the public eye and to a safe place, you got him changed, and no one got hurt. It looks as if nothing was destroyed, and no one was traumatized. Considering it was nothing we prepped you to do alone and in public, that's pretty amazing."

"Thanks, Mom. Bevin and I are the wonder twins."

Bevin gave me a bright, but tired, smile over his own mug of coffee.

Mom shook her head. "I'm surprised Owen wasn't showing the normal pre-shifting signs. But maybe he was. He's been presenting the signs since he was a toddler. Who knew this time they were real?"

Smiling at Bevin as Owen zoomed around the kitchen, I turned back to Mom. "It was probably easier since this is something that Owen has been dreaming about for years. It didn't seem that bad. We just half carried him around the school to the school's garden and Bevin reminded him of the rules. He seemed terrified at first, but it all went smoothly. The only issue was, once he changed, he ran off."

"I was pretty scared," Owen admitted. "I don't know why, but I was suddenly out of my mind with fear. Jade was like a cool breeze on a summer day. I don't know how to describe it. She's normally a pain in the butt. But then I needed to get home fast. And I had to stretch my muscles." He was pacing with pent-up energy.

"Language," Dad sighed, not for the first time.

I looked over at the younger kids and knew that Dad didn't want them going into their elementary classes saying, "Butt."

"But last night she made me feel, I don't know… right? And Bevin knew all the right words to say. They are a powerful team. I'm actually really glad they were there to help, but I'll never admit it again." He added that last with a grin as he ran out of the room to get ready for school.

"You two had a long night, do you want a ride this morning?" Mom asked me and Bevin as I yawned again.

"I'm good." One more stretch, then I started gathering my stuff for school. "I want to go and meet up with Sarah. Having something normal before school will make for an easier transition."

"I'm with Jade." Bevin put his breakfast dishes in the sink.

"Me, too." José walked in from the back hall, grabbing a banana as he walked by.

"Coolio." It was time to suit up for the cold weather.

"You are all bizarre teens." My dad shook his head in disbelief. "You do know it is freezing outside, right?"

"It's good for us, Mr. Stone." José began to peal his banana. "It will grow hair on our chests."

We all laughed.

As we walked to school, we couldn't stop talking about what had happened to Owen.

"How will they determine where he falls in the pack's pecking order?" Bevin was rubbing his hands together to stay warm.

There were a few types of werewolves. The dominant wolves tended to fight for rank. The alphas were the top of the hierarchy. They also had this power. My parents weren't necessarily the strongest, but they had the combination of brawn, brains, and compassion to keep the pack safe and whole, and that put them at the top. Though they shared the position of the alpha pair, Mom was the more vocal and often called *the alpha*.

They were the parents of the pack. Our pack was a family.

The next type of wolf was the submissive. They didn't fight for dominance. They *could* fight, they just didn't want to. They were awesome people, some of my favorite in the pack. If I became a wolf, I hoped I'd be submissive. I didn't want to spend the rest of my days worrying about where I fell in the hierarchy of dominance, always worrying if someone was gunning for me and if I was going to have to fight.

Submissive wolves were the ones the dominant wolves protected. They gave the dominants someone to care for. They were the heart of the pack. Whenever there was high emotions, they seemed to show up and help.

"Do you know how pack ranking is determined?" José asked from my other side. They were acting as wind breaks.

"Why would I know?"

José raised an eyebrow telling me I was slow. "Well, your parents are the alphas, and your mom knows everything. You talk with your parents about everything. Moreover, *you* seem to know everything."

"Dude. You've known me all my life, but most of it through the filter of Owen. How could you stand that, anyway? I've always wondered. You were always so, I dunno, sane, normal, lucid, and then there was Owen. Anyway, I fixed him up when I was young, the pack labeled me next wolf healer, and he put me in the adult category. But I'm not an adult; I mess up, ask Bevin."

"It's true, she's a wreck. I've had to cover for her for years. I'm glad you're here to take over."

I punched him in the arm.

"Do you really not know why I stuck around your brother when I was younger?" José's cheeks colored a bit, and I didn't think it was from the wind.

"Well, I had my suspicions, but beyond those, no."

"Puppy love." He sighed. "I didn't even realize it at first. I mean, I know he's your brother, Jade, but Owen's hot."

"Eeeeew. That's just gross." My nose wrinkled in disgust.

"It's true," Bevin confirmed. "I've always known it, too, but valued our friendship enough not to say anything."

"Okay, this conversation has turned dark." I shivered. Also, not from the cold.

Sarah approached from the opposite direction. "Ooooh, what were you talking about? I like dark things."

Damn, she'd arrived too soon; now our discussion about Owen the werewolf was over. No more figuring things out and getting our thoughts clear about him. Not having gotten much sleep last night, I wasn't sure if I could keep all our secrets straight. Today was going to be rough.

"José used to think—Ouch." José punched me in the shoulder before I could finish.

Sarah's eye's widened, loving a good bit of gossip. "Think what?"

"We were discussing how hot Owen is," Bevin said quickly, as I rubbed my injured arm.

Sarah fell into step behind us as we all continued to school. Sarah scrunched her face up in thought. "Oh, yeah, he *is* dreamy, but don't tell Jade that. She doesn't like guys in general, and really has a blind spot for him."

My mind went blank as I froze in place, eyes wide in shock. Both boys turned, José gaped at me. Heart beating fast, my hands started to shake, and my breathing became shallow. I gazed up into José's dark brown eyes that stared back at me, hurt, confused, and a bit angry. It wasn't like I kept secrets, but I usually just kept my life private. Sarah was an exception.

"What did you just say?" José voice had dropped dangerously low. He spoke to Sarah, but his gaze was locked with mine.

"What? What did I say?" Sarah sounded genuinely confused.

José grabbed my shoulders, pulling me in a bit closer to him. "Jade, please tell me that this isn't a secret that you've been keeping from me. Come on. You've known about me forever. You're like my little sister. Why wouldn't you tell me?"

His eyes were moist. I had hurt him.

"José, I didn't not tell you. I just don't usually talk about myself… like that. You know. Bevin has been one of my best friends all my life, a brother, and he just figured it out himself. It isn't that I was keeping secrets."

My heart beat loudly enough I was sure it was all any of them could hear. My hands lifted part way up but froze. I didn't want José to be hurt. Swallowing hard, I forced words out. "Sarah only knows because she's with me all the time. She sees who I'm interested in. She knows me well. She may talk a lot, but she's observant and knows how to keep a secret. She confronted me halfway through freshmen year."

My eyes dropped to my shoes, then flicked up to his somber brown eyes, filled with hurt. "I promise you, I wasn't trying to keep anything from anyone, I just didn't think it was that big of a deal. Also, I didn't know when or how to tell anyone. I'm sorry," I whispered. "Okay, here goes. José, I'm gay, like you."

I took a deep breath and quirked a small smile. In a shaky voice, I said, "I don't know that I've actually ever said those words out loud before. I mean, Sarah knows, but she just figured it out, asked, and I nodded. Same with Bevin. So, there you go, you are the first person I've ever actually told."

José gave me a half-smile. His shoulder grab turned into a hug. "I'm proud of you, sis. It's hard to admit those words out loud, especially for the first time, even to a friend in a safe place. I'm honored that you said them to me first."

Darting a look at Sarah, she looked half miserable. I gave her a small smile and a nod. She hadn't meant to out me. Bevin and José were our friends, our safe place. They knew so much about me, how could they not know this? A big part of me felt like a weight had been lifted now that these people, my people, my pack, knew.

José smiled playfully at Sarah and Bevin. "So, who is the lucky lady you have your eye on?"

I blushed.

CHAPTER 6

Owen wasn't at school.

We didn't have any classes together, but I usually saw him in the halls and at lunch. He was a force, and that force was missing.

At lunch Sarah asked me about it. I told her Owen had been sick and because of that I hadn't gotten to bring up Florida. My real guess was that he was tired. I mean, he hadn't slept at all. There may have been some issues with the transition as well, but I couldn't tell her that.

Sarah had almost finished her lunch when she leaned in close. "Okay, no news on Florida, but did you hear about that hiker who was killed last night?"

Apple halfway to my mouth, I paused. "Huh?"

Her smile quirked up on one side. "It was in the woods that backs up to your family's property, but pretty far away, maybe five or six miles."

A sick feeling went through me as I look at Bevin and José. That wasn't that far for a werewolf run. Transfixed, I turned back for the rest of the story.

Sarah's smile widened. "I guess the authorities found the guy, like at three or four in the morning. Eaten or mauled by some wild animal. They think it happened last night. Then, did you hear about the dog or wolf that ran through the school's parking lot last night? I bet it was the same animal."

The bite of apple went down wrong, and I coughed. José patted my back as I tried to relearn how to breathe.

Bevin shot me a glance before asking, "Was he just mauled or…I donno…were bits missing?"

Sarah shivered. "Gross, Bev." Then her smile blossomed. "Love it!" She pulled out her phone and opened it up. "Let me check, I have the story up." Her fingers flew over the screen as her eyes scanned the story. "It says that he was mauled, no other details yet."

Trying to hide the shaking of my hands, I took out my phone. Sarah told me which sites had the best news. Nodding, I opened a text to my dad and told him to check out the local news.

He replied: `Yes honey, we knew about that this morning, it is our property. Focus on classes.`

Frustrated, I wanted to reply, but I knew he wouldn't tell me more. My mind wouldn't stop swirling and my hands shook. Bevin, sitting next to me, scooted in. José, sitting on my other side, wrapped an arm around my waist. Between the two of them I started to relax.

Soon after that, the bell rang. The rest of the day floated by in a daze; when I got home, Owen sat on the couch in the living room watching TV.

"Did you grab my homework?" he asked as I walked through the door.

An eyebrow reached my hairline in disbelief. "Was I supposed to?"

"Don't you always do that? I figured you would."

Dropping down on the couch next to him, my shoulder bumped his. "I wasn't even positive you weren't at school until lunch. You could've texted me if you wanted your homework, which you didn't do."

"I have to do my homework." Owen slumped.

I stifled a laugh. He rarely seemed that forlorn. "You also could have asked Brooke." Even saying her name made my whole body tense.

He jumped up to turn off the TV. He started pacing and shaking out his hands. "Don't go there...please."

He paced the room, moving from couch to chair,

agitated. He seemed to be vibrating. "Whatever, bro."

"I mean it, Jade…" He stopped and sniffed the air as if trying to determine what was being cooked.

Distracted, I followed suit. Was mom making dinner?

He gave me a quizzical look. "Did you just go from frustrated to curious?"

Huh? That caught me off guard. "Oh! Are you smelling my emotions?" My shoulders dropped. I was flabbergasted.

He just nodded and plopped down beside me. "I know the Brooke situation doesn't make sense to you, just…I don't know, just drop it for now. I have too much I'm trying to sort through. Can you do that calming thing you do?"

"That what now?"

He took a deep breath. "I don't know, can you feel calm?"

"Can I feel calm? Well, maybe…" Closing my eyes, I imagined I was walking outside, maybe with my friends, and then I took a few breaths.

Owen scooted closer to me so that we were touching. My Aunt Allison had told me about using my breath to relax. I thought about breathing in tranquility and breathing out all the stress of the day. Slowly, the tension drained from my body.

"Wow," Owen mutter. "That's what they all mean."

Opening my eyes I asked, "What are you talking about?"

"You smell like a Christmas tree by a stream."

"A Christmas tree?"

"You know what I mean."

"A pine tree?"

"Whatever. But it's more than that. It's like you radiate peace. I get it now."

"Oh-kay," I said with some level of dubiousness. "Now, tell me what happened this morning." He obviously wanted to tell his story.

"After you left, I went to take a shower and collapsed in bed. Then I slept, or passed out, or something. I dunno. The next thing I knew it was the afternoon and I was ravenously hungry. Luckily, there was a ton of leftover pizza in the basement."

He turned to me and froze. "Jade, I'm not very dominant. Like, I thought I would just be, I dunno, Dad's right-hand man, but, no, that position is taken."

He shook out his hands then made fists in his frustration.

"When I was out there with all the other wolves, it was weird, I could feel it. Mom says not to worry, that not all new wolves get a feel for their dominance right away, but I could tell."

He continued to move with all his pent-up emotion. "You're zeta, right? Until your official rank is figured out?"

"Yeah, I don't think I'm a submissive, but I didn't want to fight, I just wanted to run and play. When I first changed and you said all that about taking off my undies, it was hilarious. You know, you weren't in any danger. Bevin could have stood closer. I mean, it's good that he didn't. But I had no desire to bite either of you."

He deflated back into himself, our arms touching. He seemed to need the physical contact. Werewolves craved contact, and that's what he was now. The pack was always touching. Much more than regular norms.

In all the stories we'd been told, when a wolf first changed, they were violent. They couldn't control themselves. For the first few minutes, they were like rabid animals. First their body shifted, and they got their paws under them. Often, they immediately attacked because they felt vulnerable. Then their brain caught up and got everything under control. The fact that Owen changed and was at peace was weird. None of the stories went like that.

"What else did Mom say?"

Owen dropped his head on my shoulder. "We're going to go out again tonight, just the two of us."

Suddenly he perked up. "I mean, once I was running with everyone else last night, I got caught up in the chase. I caught a rabbit. It was wicked cool. I started feeling more wolfish. I don't know."

"How did your first rabbit taste?" I asked, trying not to laugh at him.

His wide-eyed innocent look was lost on me. "It was weird. I'll admit it. And I had to give it up the line to the dominants. I really don't want to be submissive."

Wrapping an arm around him, I felt him relax. "Don't put the wagon before the horse and all that jazz. Just wait until you change with Mom tonight. Is Dad going? The three of you together? That would be nice. I could have a night to myself, read a book, watch a movie. Some quiet after last night's drama."

"Are you calling me drama?"

"Well, if the paw fits."

The dead body Sarah told me about came to mind, but Owen seemed too preoccupied by everything else. My mind still churned about it, and I didn't have enough facts to share anyway. Giving Owen one more squeeze, I got up to join Mom in the kitchen. Here was my chance to talk to Mom about the trip to Florida. I could hear the oven door close and her setting the oven timer—we had some time before dinner. "Mom, I have to talk to you about something in private. Can we go into your room to talk?"

"Can it wait? If it's important, maybe we should wait until your father comes home. He should be here in about twenty-five minutes."

My heart sped up. When did it get to be so late? This was bad, I had to get her on my side before he got home. "No, I would rather talk with you alone, if that's okay."

She paused before resuming tidying up the kitchen. "Sure. Owen, can you get the dining room set up and finish up dinner?"

His eyes snapped up and he whined. "Why me?"

Mom's mouth turned up in a half smile. "Well, you don't think you need an education, so I assume you wanted to start to cook or be the cook's assistant. I think becoming the family chef is a truly excellent idea. But since I've already gotten the food into the oven, you can finish up the sides. A salad and garlic toast would be nice." She arched a brow in challenge.

Owen learning to prepare food was a pretty great idea in my opinion.

From the look on Owen's face, college was seeming better and better. Though he didn't like the idea, he ambled into the kitchen to get to work. Mom and I left him to it.

"So, what is so important that you want to get me on your side before Dad gets home?"

My eyes widened. Sometimes Mom was too smart for her own good. I mean, I thought I had been way cleverer than that, but apparently not. Had Owen had seen through my actions as well?

Sitting on the edge of her bed, my hands trembled. I sat on them to hide my nerves. "Well, it's like this. Sarah's mom is going to Florida for a conference over spring break, and the whole family is going. Sarah invited me to go with them. We would leave on Saturday and get back the following Saturday."

Mom's eyebrow started to raise then her eyes started to narrow. My fingers went numb and the rushing sound of blood in my ears was distracting. Mouth dry, I had to figure out how to get her hooked on this idea…quick.

I talked faster, and my hands flew out from under my legs to punctuate my words. "I would be back two days before school started up again. We would be staying near a University in Gainesville, and though I plan on having fun, we will be touring the University while there. We may even get to see the Kennedy Space Center and see a rocket launch."

Everything in me stopped and I dropped my hands to my lap. I gazed into my mom's eyes, trying to read her mind. My heart was beating so hard I was pretty sure she could hear it. By the end I had been speaking so fast, my voice had risen almost a full octave, and I was breathing as if I'd just come from gym class.

There was so much more to say, but she was smart, and I didn't want to overdo it. My arguments should be enough at this point to convince her. I tried to give her my most hopeful puppy-dog eyes, anything that might help my cause.

She sighed and her eyes softened. She stood and walked around the room, changing from her work clothes into something less restrictive. When she got back over to me, she rubbed my shoulders to help me relax.

"Oh, honey, you know this is a big discussion. It's not something I can decide without bringing in your dad. I appreciate that you thought I could, but this is definitely a family discussion. If it helps, I think this is a great opportunity and I think your dad will come around."

Her words brought a mixture of hope and despair. I knew then that José had been right, and my plan was short-sighted.

After dinner, Owen said he was heading to his room. He wanted to call classmates to figure out homework. Wow, he *was* serious. This was perfect for me. As I heard the door close, my gaze shot to Mom expectantly.

She stared back at me. "Jade? Do you have something to say to Dad?"

Suddenly there was something blocking my airways, making it hard to breathe. My voice came out as a whisper. Steeling myself, I told my dad about Florida and why I thought he should let me go.

"No." That's all he said, one word. Stricken, I wanted to cry. Heart in my eyes, I just gaped at him, disbelieving. One simple word and all my hopes crumbled.

"Why?" My voice was still barely audible. Trying to be mature, I tried to keep in all the emotions, everything. Today, in this situation, I was a mountain, not a volcano. To get to Florida there would be no screaming or crying. Like him, there would be just one word.

He turned to me. "It's too dangerous. You're asking to travel halfway across the country. No one from the pack is going with you to keep you safe. There's a pack down there, did you know that?"

I frowned in confusion about Dad's assertion that the Floridian pack was a negative to my traveling there.

His voice took on an edge. "What happens if they don't like the daughter of the Wisconsin pack alpha invading their territory?"

Invade their territory? They were mom's best friends. The lone wolf that had attacked Dad all those years ago had also attacked one of the Floridian alphas, as well as my Aunt Allison, Janet, Bevin's mom, and Clare, José's mom. Eventually, my mom and Tilly, the other Floridian alpha had taken him out.

There were only five werewolf packs in the US. They were not known to the general public. I didn't know much about the other three packs, but the pack in Florida and their alphas weren't strangers to us.

General opinion was paranormal creatures didn't exist. Beyond werewolves, I didn't know if there were other paranormals. However, if there were werewolves, there probably were others.

What about other wereanimals? That would be weird. Would they be like the wolves? The wolves in our pack were bigger than their regular wolf counterparts. Though a werebear would make old-time traveling circuses make way more sense. How else did they get them in those tutus? Imagining Mr. Nelson in a tutu would make gym more palatable. He was about the size of a bear.

Focus Jade! Florida. Alphas. Invading their territory.

As I thought about it, my confusion grew. What was he talking about? Why did he claim that I was invading instead of visiting? Going into a friendly pack's territory should be in the positive column, not negative. My face contorted because of my confusion, and I had to straighten it out. I tried to unfurrow my brow, but his words were just too weird.

Breathe.

Dad shoved his chair back and turned it to face me. "How safe is it for you to go with just a friend and her parents? How safe can they keep you? You're our daughter, a pack daughter, and your safety is of the utmost importance to us. You do know you could be seen as a lone wolf, a danger that needs to be eliminated. You're not a wolf but living in this house, you smell like pack. It wouldn't be safe. My answer is no."

And that was that.

My jaw hit the table. Eyes wide, I couldn't believe my ears. My chair scraped on the floor as I rose and moved from the dining room to the living room. Collapsing in one of the many living room couches, I sat in shock. The house was open plan so I could still listen in, but I was separate and away.

My body had gone numb. Maybe this should have been expected, but somehow I thought I would bring good news to Sarah.

Feeling would return to me later, but right then I just didn't know what to feel, what to do. It was too much. I wanted to cry, but I couldn't even do that.

Mom took a quieting breath. "River, I don't think this choice is yours alone. I resent that you would say, 'no,' without discussing it with me first." I don't think the quieting breath worked because Mom sounded pissed.

The tone Mom used was low and scary. If I were him, I would have run and hid.

"You obviously discussed it with Jade without me," he countered.

"As a matter of fact, no, I didn't. She brought it up to me and I said I needed to have you as part of the discussion. *Discussion.* Not a unilateral decision. I'm glad you feel that you are the only parent whose opinion matters here, but I disagree."

I heard Mom stand up and move around the kitchen and dining room area. "You do understand that we're friends with the alphas down in Florida? I went to college with them. They are some of our best friends. We can talk with them and let them know about Jade's trip. They live closer to Orlando, which isn't that close to Gainesville, but maybe they can check in on her while she's there."

There was a pause as I heard her stop moving, then she snapped, "The Floridian pack is more of a benefit, not a hindrance, and you know it."

"She is only fifteen. Of course you approve of her traveling. You traveled your whole childhood, ending up in Papua New Guinea when you were only twenty-two. You have a weird idea of what's safe. It isn't safe, Hazel. She would be flying across half the country with unknown people to Florida. It wouldn't be safe." Dad was almost yelling.

Both of them had scary angry voices. I wasn't sure who was scarier.

"No, life isn't safe. She could get hit by a bus crossing the street here. Life is about experiences, and this would be both educational and remarkable. Her best friend is going with her parents. They're only unknown because you refuse to interact with them. It's as safe as it can be without us being with her. She's smart. We need to learn to trust her," Mom snarled.

Plates were gathered and then she said, "If you want to know Sarah and her parents, we should get to know them. They've been friends long enough. We really should get to know them; don't you think?"

His voice knife-sharp, Dad asked, "Do you really think that this is the best plan? Sending our fifteen-year-old daughter to Florida?"

Secure in her resolve, Mom said, "Yes, I do. I think it will be something that will change her life."

"I don't, Hazel. I have a really bad feeling about her being so far away. However—"

That word woke me from a haze and the world seemed to come into color as I jumped and began to feel again. Until then, I had been sitting in the grey living room barely feeling. Who knew Mom had the power to change that absolute no from before, but then my dad said that word – however – that wonderful magical word, and the numbness began to melt.

I loved that word.

I loved the word "however".

CHAPTER 7

"So, do you get to go? You didn't call me last night…. Jade. Talk to me!" Sarah nearly attacked me as we met on our morning walk to school.

It was too cold to talk, the warmth of the school was a mere two blocks away. I shivered and rubbed my hands together. My mittens were not doing enough.

White clouds plumed from my mouth as I spoke. "I don't know, Sarah." My lungs froze in the frosty air. "That's why I didn't text." Placing my mittened hands over my face to warm up the air a bit didn't even help. "Can I explain all this when there's actual heat to breathe?"

Sarah likewise had her gloved hands up to her face. She nodded and we rushed the last few blocks to school. When Owen passed us in his car, he made sure to honk and wave. Jerk. I could've bummed a ride with him, but he was late more often than not, and in a lot of ways it just wasn't worth it.

As we rushed through the parking lot, Bevin caught up with us. We got into the school, and the heat, before hurrying to our lockers. I finally started to get feeling in my fingers and nose.

Sarah grabbed my shoulders and turned me to face her. "So? Talk." She was bouncing. From excitement or to generate heat?

"Okay, here it is, my dad doesn't want me to go, my mom does, just as predicted. My dad said no. My mom got pissed that he didn't even think to discuss it with her, just flat out said no. I was crushed, devastated."

Sarah deflated, but she hung on my every word, bookbag half-way off her back.

Rummaging through my bag at my locker, I started getting ready for class. Now that there was heat, my layers were stifling. "After my mom told my dad she thought there were benefits to the trip, my dad said he would think about it. He doesn't think me traveling without him is safe."

Now Sarah was offended. She crashed through her locker.

Bevin, who had been listening, cut in. "Sarah, don't get offended. You would have to understand Jade's parents.

Saying her parents are controlling is putting it lightly. I know you've known us forever, but you've never really met her family."

This distracted her from her ire. She stopped banging around and I looked over at her. Her brows furrowed as she thought about it. "It's really weird, I mean, you've been spending nights at my house for years, since elementary school, and your dad never thought it wasn't safe, what gives? Come to think of it, why haven't I ever spent the night at your place?"

We formed a line at the lockers, and I ignored her question about sleeping at my place, hoping she wouldn't notice. "It's the traveling out of state that weirds him out. I think that Mom and I have convinced him it's safe. Also, some of Mom's college friends live in Orlando."

Bevin stopped rummaging through his bag and shot me a look. "Who?"

Sarah kicked his bag and raised an eyebrow. "Why would you know any of Jade's mom's friends?"

I pulled Sarah away before she did more to Bevin's bag. "Tilly and Rory."

Bevin's eyes popped and then he smiled. "Duh, should have thought of that."

"What?" demanded Sarah. "What am I missing?"

Bevin ducked in embarrassment as I shot him a warning glance. "Nothing, Bevin is just goofing, right?"

"Yep, that's it." He shook his head and zipped up his

bag. "Your trip just got more interesting. You two *are* going to be keeping an online blog we can follow, right? I really want to keep track of all of the happenings." Bevin had a slightly evil flicker in his eyes.

"Anyway, Mom thinks she can focus on the educational side of us going down there. That's helping to make Dad less nervous. You know Dad, he's all about the education angle." Sighing, I leaned my head on Bevin's shoulder.

Bevin snorted at that. "Of course he is. I wonder if he can find a hospital down there you can work at for a day or two."

I scrunched up my face at him.

Bevin gave me a half-grin. "I mean, when you went on vacation in California, didn't you get to visit a hospital there?"

Sitting up, I shook my head. "That was because Owen is an idiot and ended up in the ER. That had nothing to do with an education. I don't think either Sarah or I are going to be reckless enough, or stupid enough, to end up needing stitches."

"How did Owen end up in the ER? Or should I ask which time?" asked José, joining us. He sat down on Bevin's other side.

"It was when we were north of San Francisco running the trails of Mount Tamalpais."

"Running?" interrupted Sarah. "Don't you mean walking carefully? Hiking, maybe, but not running, that's crazy."

"Nope, there's a race people run called the Dipsea that starts in a town and ends in the sea, and we were running it. We decided to take a side-shoot to explore. We ended up on a trail that was so steep there was a ladder built in to get down. Owen, in all his infinite wisdom, decided all he had to do was jump down."

José smirked and Sarah snickered. Bevin covered his mouth with his hand, knowing where this story was heading. They all knew Owen and his impulsiveness well enough to know how his adventures often ended.

I shook my head at the memory as I continued. "I thought he had twisted an ankle. Then I thought he lost his leg by the way he was screaming. Anyway, when I got to him, his legs were fine, but he was holding his arm. I felt around, but the bruising was bad."

Searching the faces of my friends, I realized my story was getting more detailed than normal. The boys knew all of this, but Sarah was going to learn a bit more. If I went to Florida, she'd learn at least this much. "I've learned to always have a medical kit with me, especially when my brother is around. I got his arm splinted so we could safely get him moved. I couldn't tell if the bone was broken. We needed a specialist. We got back to the car, and then we got him to the hospital."

This part of the story always annoyed me, and I stifled a growl, trying to keep my voice normal. "The staff at the hospital were impressed with what my parents had done to take care of Owen and had some follow up questions. My mom had to explain they had nothing to do with it and couldn't answer their questions, but I could. The doctors gave me a weird look. After all, I was only ten at the time."

I shook my hands trying to release my frustration.

"Anyhow, Owen's arm had a minor fracture, but they thought without having been tended and splinted immediately, it could have been a lot worse. Traveling with Owen is always an adventure," I ended with an ironic half-smile and shrugged.

Sarah squinted at me, dumfounded. "Damn, Jade, I had no idea we would be bringing a doctor with us. I don't think you ever told me that story. We were friends then, but you never said anything about *that* part of the trip. Wow."

"You have no idea," grumbled Bevin, who knew most of the stuff I had endured. At times, he'd had to help.

"There's more?" Sarah gaped. "Why don't I know any of these stories? I've known you a long time. What gives?"

"Honestly, my family doesn't talk about it. Having a ten-year-old fix up her brother is a bit weird." Embarrassed, I stood and went back to my locker to make sure I had everything I needed for my morning classes.

Sarah put her hand on my shoulder stopping me. "So, there are other stories like this? How old *were* you when you started fixing up your brother?"

I turned and stared at her, my mind racing. I didn't know what to say. There were secrets she couldn't know about. Alpha law stated that no outsider could know about werewolves, and Sarah may have been my friend my whole life, but all my healing centered around pack life, and I couldn't tell her any of it.

I didn't know where to start. My mind was blank.

"Um…" I offered helpfully.

José, who had stood and walked over, bumped shoulders with me. I thought he was trying to help, until I heard his answer. "It was when you were six, right? When you were out with Annie and Dillan. Owen messed up his leg out in the woods. You had to splint it, or it would have been an out-and-out break?"

That day had been bad. Owen's leg had been bloody and twisted. Staring down at it, I had remembered a plant my Aunt Allison had described to my mom, yarrow. The only reason I had remembered it was because it sounded like the cry of a cat. The plant could help stop the bleeding of a wound.

Between the plant and the splint, my aunt had declared I had the healing gift. From that day forward I went on some healing runs, I helped keep the health records for the pack, and my destiny as a healer had been set.

Sarah just gaped at me. "Six?"

My chin hit my chest as I sheepishly looking at my shoes. "Yeah, I guess that was it. We were out there all alone playing some game, and no one else was doing anything for that idiot brother of mine."

I wasn't sure what else to say, but the bell rang.

Never had I been happier to get to class. Up until I heard Sarah say, "We are not done with this discussion!"

CHAPTER 8

Sarah ran after me as we headed for the same first period class. Alyssa, a girl on her basketball team, intercepted us on the way, saving me from continuing our conversation.

"Oh, my God, Sarah, our game this weekend is going to be *epic*!" She elbowed me out of the way, almost knocking me down.

Sarah stopped and grabbed my arm to steady me. "Sorry, Jade, this will only take a minute. Do you want to wait?"

Normally I would, but I really didn't want to continue our talk about my history of healing.

Then Sarah's face transformed to something more

robotic and plastic. "I know, right? It will be amazing."

My pace slowed as I watched the show Sarah put on for her teammate. This act made my skin crawl. Watching her play basketball—any sport really—she glowed, she loved them all, but this other self she felt she needed to become made me sad. I really didn't like it or want to see it. Anything you needed to put on this much of a performance for didn't seem worth it to me.

As she and Alyssa went on about which refs were assigned to their game, I decided to speed up, slip around them, and make my way to English class.

A few students were milling outside the door. I was about to squeeze past when a hand shot out and grabbed my arm…Brooke. Better and better.

"Hi, Owen's sister," she oozed out.

Shutting my eyes for a second, I tried to emulate Sarah's face. "Hi, Brooke." I hoped I didn't sound too flippant. Tugging, she held fast as I tried to pull away.

She pressed her other hand into my chest to stop my motion. "Don't get in my way, Sophomore. Owen has some weird beliefs about family…for now. If you keep getting into his head, I'll ruin you."

My eyebrow shot up before I knew I had reacted to her words. "It's Jade. And Owen can make up his own mind about family. Why are you so insecure?"

She looked me up and down and obviously didn't like what she saw. Personally, I liked my shirt today, it had a glass on it half-full of liquid. There was an arrow pointing to the top half labeled fifty percent air. An arrow pointing to the bottom labeled fifty percent water. The bottom read, "Technically, the glass is completely full." She shook her head in disgust, pushed my chest slightly so I stumbled, then walked away.

"I hope your day is a pleasant as you are!" The words were out as a student behind me stopped me from falling on my butt. They were loud enough to be heard over the din of the other people in the hall.

She paused, turned, and gave me a smile that made me shiver, then spun on her heel and disappeared in the crowd of students.

Rubbing my eyes, my head began to pound. I couldn't believe this was the person Owen was dating. My lip curled in disgust, and I was about to enter class when an arm wrapped around me.

I relaxed when I saw Sarah's nail polish. "What did the princess want?"

"She wants to scare me off from being Owen's sister…apparently."

Sarah's face scrunched in disbelief. Then she chuckled. "Really? Is she that limited?"

As we headed into class, I rested my head on her shoulder and slipped my arm around her waist. "Let's just go to class."

The rest of the day passed without spectacle. After last

bell, I met Bevin and José at the lockers. We planned on facing the icy wind together. Sarah was at practice again.

One more scarf and a pair of gloves and I could face the outdoors. As I was securing the scarf, I heard Owen's voice coming down the hallway.

"José, need a ride? It's cold enough to freeze your—"

He was interrupted by a shrill voice. "Owen, I thought you were driving me home today."

"Brooke, honey, there is room in the car for more than just the two of us. José is one of us. You know him."

She harrumphed. "He used to be cool, but now he hangs out with *her, them.*"

The vitriol dripped from her voice. Finishing up at my locker, I turned towards the action. Brooke stood with a scowl on her face, arms crossed, and her prim little foot tapping. The gum she smacked only added to the overall effect. Owen was looking helplessly between her and José.

Bevin came over to me and whispered, "Drama."

José tilted his head at us then pinned Owen with a hard stare. "Bro, you need to get your priorities worked out."

Brooke's scowl melted into a half-smile of devious success. She wrapped her arms around Owen's neck and kissed his cheek. "Whatever *you* think is best is fine. It's your car after all."

I turned towards Bevin to hide my reaction but couldn't stop myself from shaking my head in disgust. Bevin was trying not to smile at the ugly manipulation. After a minute, I faced them again.

Owen's shoulders drooped a bit, but he wrapped his arm around her. He shot José a guilty look and shrugged the shoulder supporting Brooke. "I guess it's just us. You are my heart." Though he said the words, they sounded flat.

They walked off.

Sticking a finger in my mouth, I made gaging sounds.

The three of us were cold but enjoyed ourselves. We didn't linger and I got home fast.

Once at my desk in my room, I got lost in English and history. A couple hours later, my mom got home and then my dad.

"Jade, we need to talk with you," Mom called from the main area of the house.

Owen still hadn't gotten home from driving Brooke to her house. Surely the two of them were studying together.

I headed to the kitchen, but found my parents sitting at the dining room table. Dad sat at the head. He looked like a CEO ready to evaluate a board of directors. Mom sat on one side of the table with a stack of papers ready to be graded.

The room was tense and quiet, but I sat across from Mom and watched as she slowly evaluated each paper and moved it over to a second pile, methodically making her way through her stack of work. She had a way of getting through her grading while concentrating on the conversation around her.

Dad took a deep breath. "First of all, I haven't decided

if I'm okay with you going to Florida. But, if you go, I *will* have some conditions."

My eyes widened and I nodded quickly, my body vibrating with excitement.

Mom's mouth twitched, as she continued to grade papers.

"First of all, I want you to write a letter to Tilly and Rory requesting safe passage into their territory."

My heart began to beat faster. "Okay."

Not knowing why I had been summoned, I wasn't prepared. Searching for something to write on, I was about to get up when Mom slid me a pad of paper and a pen. Instantly I signed, "Thank you," in sign language, to not disturb Dad and to acknowledgement her help.

Dad's eyes narrowed. His eyebrows lifted and he pointed at my list. "You also need to get a list from each of your teachers of any homework that will be due after spring break so that you can get it done early."

That one was easy. I had been planning on doing that anyway, but I gave Dad a grave nod, writing it down on my list.

"I want you to talk with Mom about house chores as well. You'll be gone during a full moon, so I want the house to be set. You'll need to coordinate with the boys as well. With you gone, that will leave fewer teens to wrangle the kiddos."

That gave me pause; it was a concern. With Owen's transformation, that just left the three older teens.

Dad pointed at my paper. *Full moon night* went on my list.

His squinted at me and tapped his pen on his stack

of papers, starting to get frustrated. I thought he wanted me to get upset at all his rules, but so far, they seemed reasonable. His eyes shifted to Mom and back to me. Slowly, a triumphant look came across his face. "You'll have to give the pack gym a full cleaning when you return."

Slumping, my whole body went slack with shock, and I dropped my pen. With effort, I managed to close my mouth and gulp in some air. The pack gym was huge. Moving my gaze from the center of the table to him, I managed to pick up my pen and force my hand to move. Shakily, I said, "Okay. Sure."

Mom chuckled as she continued to work on her papers.

Dad's voice came out in a huff. "If you go, you will text me every night with an update."

"An update. Check." My voice was a bit steadier as the new item was added to the list.

Dad gave me a piercing stare. "Are these things on your list?"

Checking it over, I gave a curt nod.

Dad let out a gusty sigh. "You're just going to agree to anything I say, aren't you?"

Nodding sheepishly, I said, "Yes?"

CHAPTER 9

That night at dinner, my aunt and uncle joined us, along with Dillan. My cousin Annie had moved out west for college.

Uncle Jackson had come early and made pork chops, corn on the cob, and mashed potatoes. We were all sitting around the table serving ourselves and discussing the dead hiker found in the woods.

Owen gazed at his plate of food. "I didn't do it. I'm not a rogue wolf. I didn't kill and partially eat that man. I swear to you. I swear to the Twins. It wasn't me."

Mom put down her fork and heaved a gusty sigh. "In

my heart of hearts, I know that, love. You're too calm. Wolves, once they get the taste of man and turn rogue, can't control the need to get more. They're dangerous. But love, it was a kill, there was no evidence of eating. We don't think it was a rogue."

Uncle Jackson's brow furrowed in thought. "Could it just be a wild animal? Could we be thinking about this too hard?"

Dad nodded. "That's what I'm hoping."

A low growl emitted from Mom. "We really need to find a connection at the hospital. Not just a doctor, but someone who works in or near the emergency rooms. Someone who could sneak us in or do the investigations themselves."

Aunt Allison blushed. "I'm sorry I only work with animals. I know that you wanted a person doctor, not someone who worked at the zoo. But I do have more information." She gave an apologetic smile to Uncle Jackson. "I've visited the site with Clare. We could smell Violet. She had to be the one who did the kill. We went to her apartment and found L-theanine on her kitchen counter."

My heart rate doubled. "Really? For the love of Mondara! Why don't the wolves in the pack consult me before starting anything new? I have the database. I am keeping track of their health. We've discussed this in pack meetings. Some herbs work differently with our genetics and that is one of them. It may relax us for a hot minute, but then it short circuits our brain. Causes a kind of insanity. A werewolf may act lucid, but they will snap. What the hay?!"

By the end I was practically yelling.

Aunt Allison gave me a small smile before reaching over to squeeze my hand. "Jade, love. I know you mean well, but in the end, you're only fifteen. The pack isn't ready to share everything with you. Moreover, when we spoke with her, she thought it was a simple relaxant. She must have forgotten the warning."

Hands in fist and ready to punch someone, I snarled, "Well, she knows now. Did you dump it all? No wonder she went crazy. Had she eaten the dead guy or just killed him? The only thing I can say is that the herb won't stay in her system too long with her werewolf metabolism."

"It's all dumped. She knows. She didn't eat the man, just scratched him. When he fell his neck snapped. The death brought her out of her killing haze. Clare and I believe she hasn't gone rogue."

Shaking out my hands, I finally took a calming breath. Thank the gods!

Uncle Jackson returned to the topic of the dead man. "Do you know anyone who could get you in to see the body? I still think we need to see the damage."

Mom thought for a few minutes. "No. We knew a nurse a few years back, but she moved out of state. There is a doctor, but she isn't affiliated there. We're out of connections at the main hospital."

Dad finished off his plate and pushed it away. "Well, until we know for certain, we'll have to assume that Violet is clean and clear. Clare and Tanner will set up a watch."

Owen looked over at me with a half-smile. "Now, if only Jade could get people to listen to her."

CHAPTER 10

Late Saturday morning I was lost in the world of biology and math when Dad put his hand on my shoulder. Started, I jerked then gazed up at him.

"Jade, can we go for a walk?"

It had been a while since the two of us had gone off together. "Absolutely. Let me get suited up. It's what, like, thirty-three degrees out there? Practically a heat wave. Are we going out back or on the sidewalks?"

This was an important question: snow pants and boots for the snow, or just regular shoes. Dad and I didn't take walks as much anymore. We used to take them all the time and discuss the ways of the world. But now he was busy, and I was busy. This was a real treat.

"We'll take the sidewalks, no need to get bundled up. We can enjoy the warm weather."

The funny part was, for him, it was warm. My guess was that he wouldn't even put on a coat. Maybe a scarf, but not much more. Werewolves ran warm and being above freezing meant it was time to break out the warmer weather clothing.

Personally, I still wore a winter coat, scarf, and gloves. It was nice being able to wear regular shoes.

"What's up, Dad, everything okay?"

Dad paused for a moment, seeming to try to order his thoughts. "Mom and I took Owen out again the other night to run. The change was much harder for him this time. After his change, he tried to attack us both."

Dumbfounded, I just gaped at him. Despite my concern, Dad seemed pleased.

"Don't worry, pumpkin, this was much more expected than what happened Wednesday night. A newly turned wolf, submissive or not, should act the wolf and attack. You have always had a strange calming scent. Mom and I believe you naturally calmed him down. It's part of what makes you so good at healing."

We walked in silence as he let me process what he'd told me. "How will he fit into the pack?"

"We know that he will be dominant. He may not be as

dominant as he wants, but still dominant. I doubt he will ever be an alpha, but that's probably for the best. He won't be ranked at the bottom either. He needs to learn his place in the pack, as a wolf and as a person."

We continued walking. Dad scanned the neighborhood. "We discussed some life choices with him. He needs to finish school, graduate, and maybe go to a tech school. I don't see him at a university, but maybe a trade."

Dad stopped talking for a moment and shook his head. "I really don't know why I'm telling you all of this, but again, it's in your nature to encourage confidence."

Mirth bubbled out of me, I couldn't help it, and I laughed. It was true, people confided in me all the time. "I'm glad I know all of this. It's also good to know that his first transition was weird because of me, not him. Bev and I were really confused trying to compare the stories we had heard with what we were seeing. Owen doesn't seem the type to be submissive or peaceful."

Dad nodded and flung his arm around me.

"So, now for you. Spring break is in a couple of weeks. Mom and I talked with Sarah's parents. We know you're excited about this trip." He gave a little squeeze. "We want you to be safe. I was serious when I told you that I want you to text me every night with a summary of what you did. That may sound overprotective, but I'm alpha, and your dad, and that's the way it's going to be."

Pausing, my eyes stung as they refused to blink and ruin

the moment. Did he just confirm what I thought he said? Rotating to face him, I held my breath, my brain convinced if I breathed it could all go away.

Dad's eyes started to shrink in frustration, but he just gently stroked my cheek. "Did you hear what I said?"

Gulping in some air, I stuttered out, "Sounds perfect, Dad." Finally, my body forced steady breathing. "I'm excited." My face broke into a huge smile, and I started to bounce. I squealed, "Thank you, thank you, thank you," as I jumped into his arms and gave him a huge hug.

CHAPTER 11

"Where is your list?" We were sitting in the kitchen the morning of the trip. Mom had helped me pack for Florida the night before.

"It's packed." Not wanting to forget to pack anything for the trip, I had made a list of everything I needed — clothes, money, books, and, well, everything. The list was packed so I would have it for the trip back home. We could pack one carry-on bag and one checked bag. I had a big carry-on with my purse inside, very organized.

It was five-thirty in the morning. Sarah and her parents were due to pick me up any minute. We were leaving from

Chicago O'Hare International Airport, a three-hour drive from home. The plane was scheduled to take off at eleven, but we wanted to be there two hours early.

It would be a long day.

Munching on the last of my breakfast, I finished my coffee and was ready to go. My dad and brother were night owls, so I had said goodbye to them last night. Though, my dad surprised me when he walked out zombie-like, gave me a hug and a kiss, wished me well, reminded me that I had to text him every night, and stumbled back to bed.

There was a knock at the door, and I ran to answer, almost falling over my bag blocking it.

The door opened and T.J. walked in carrying a white paper bag, and a steaming travel cup from a local coffee shop, smiling.

I threw my arms around his neck and kissed his cheek. "What are you doing here?"

He let out a gusty breath. "Work training starts early. I knew you were leaving for Florida this morning, so I thought I'd bring you sustenance." He shook the bag under my nose and handed me the coffee. The scent of chocolate come from the bag.

Snatching the bag of goodies and the coffee, I led him into the house. Putting down the coffee, I dug in the bag and found an assortment of pastries.

T.J. leaned over my shoulder. "They're for you, Sarah, and her family, not just you. The coffee is all yours." He quickly kissed my cheek and headed to the door. "I'll be done with training when you get back, so I probably won't see you much before the next full moon. Since there's one while you're in Florida, it'll be a while. Stay safe." And he was off.

As he walked out, I saw Sarah's parents' car pulling in. My adventure was about to start.

Packing the car was quick, and everyone was happy to have the pastries.

It took about an hour for Sarah and me to really wake up and start talking but after that there was no stopping us.

Tom, Sarah's dad, was driving. Apparently, he had sensitive ears. "I know they're happy sounds, but goodness, they're loud." He wasn't wrong. We were so excited. We were about to fly to Florida, away from the cold.

Cindy, Sarah's mom, chuckled. "They're teenage girls. What did you expect?"

There wasn't much snow left, and the weather was getting warmer, but we were excited to get away.

Sarah's parents had met at a party for tall people, or so I assumed. They were both over six feet tall. Tom was heavyset but solid. Most of Sarah's features came straight from him, from the shape of her eyes to her strong, straight nose. Her generous mouth came from her mom.

Navigating O'Hare was a lot smoother than I'd expected considering its size and the number of people.

Sarah searched for seating with an outlet. "When does

the plane leave?"

I double-checked the ticket. "Eleven."

She scoped out the gates and shops. "Mom, Dad, Jade and I are going shopping, need anything?"

Tom gave her a skeptical look. "No, and neither do the two of you, but you'll be stuck in a plane so moving around now isn't a bad idea."

We walked the vast corridors and checked out the stores, but the mark-ups were crazy. We did end up buying some ice cream cones before heading back to the seats.

After waiting at the gate for almost two hours, we finally got to board the plane. As I sat, I was disappointed to see I had the middle seat.

"I'm a bit nervous. You take the window." Sarah stood in the aisle, waiting for me to move into the seat. "Mom gave me a pill for my nerves anyway."

"What did she give you?"

"Something mild and over the counter." She turned. "Mom, what did you give me?"

"L-theanine, it's an herb to relax you. Would you like some, Jade?"

Pausing, I shivered at the name of that herb again. "No, thanks. I think I'll be fine." Though the herb would probably be fine, if I was going to be a werewolf one day, I didn't want to take any chances.

Sitting at the window was thrilling; I'd always wanted to fly. Watching the farmland go by was a bit monotonous after a while, but the mountains were beautiful, and the adventure of flying, even if it were in a plane, was thrilling. I spent my time on the plane reading and watching the land go by.

Once we landed at Gainesville Regional Airport, Cindy went to get a car rental while the rest of us waited for the luggage. The airport was air-conditioned, a circumstance I was ill-prepared for, coming from the chill of a Wisconsin spring, and indoor heating.

One of Cindy's work colleagues had a place where we could stay. It was a friend's home about ten minutes from the university, and about a half hour from the airport.

As we exited into the sunshine, we hit a wall of air. It was so humid I couldn't believe it. Was this air even breathable? Did people really live like this? The air was sticky and thick. Okay, I had to stop focusing on the negative…I was in Florida! I was here to get away from the cold, I was going to embrace the Floridian weather, heat and all.

Sarah's dropped her bag. "Holy hell, it's freaking hot."

Sarah's mom pointed at the bag and gave a mom stare. "Sarah, language. I know you're tired, but please, there are other people around, including children."

"Sorry, Mom, but, wow, I had no idea. I feel like I need a hatchet to slice through this air. I need to get out of these clothes."

"Let's get to the house first," I suggested, smiling at her mischievously. "I mean, think of the children."

Sarah snorted.

Once we piled into the car, Sarah's mom turned on the air conditioning and I started to feel human. It was partially the heat, but mostly the humidity.

As we were driving to the house it started to rain, but only on one side of the car; the other side was dry.

"What the hay?" Head whipping back and forth, I watched in amusement. Sarah, who had been playing on her phone, snapped her head up at me. Pointing, she glanced out each window. Eyes going wide, she laughed.

"Dude, the weather here is confused." Then a rainbow came out. "Wow," Sarah pointed at it. "It's pretty." Then, suddenly, it was sunny again. There was no sign of rain anywhere.

Florida's weather was crazy.

The house was small, but serviceable. There was a combination living room, dining room, kitchen area. Off to one side was the master bedroom with an attached bathroom. On the other side was a second bedroom with two beds. There was a second door on that side with a guest bathroom that Sarah and I would be using.

We went exploring out back and found a pool: score! The house was newly renovated and beautiful. A person could get used to living here, even though it was small. Then again, living in the pack den, the house may not have been that small. Just smaller than I was used to.

Tom picked up a note and started reading. "This says we can have the run of the house while the owners are out of town. They're friends with the neighbors, who will also be attending the conference. We should go over and introduce ourselves. They have a list of expectations for when we leave." He looked up at us expectantly.

"Well, I want to shower." Sarah grabbed her stuff, ignoring him.

As she went off to the bathroom, there was a knock on the door. Cindy went to answer it. The family from the house next door had come over to introduce themselves. They were here from London, in Gainesville on work visas. They had two kids: Georgie, who was three, and Margot, who was thirteen. They had seen us drive up and unpack the rental and were wondering if we wanted to join them for dinner. They knew how rough traveling could be.

Since we didn't have any other plans, Cindy accepted for us. She said we'd be over after everyone had a chance to freshen up.

Dinner that night was a local favorite…local for London, that was. Fish and chips, chips being french fries. The English had weird names for things…or maybe we did?

As dinner was being prepared, Sarah and I hung out with Margot and Georgie. Well, we hung out with Margot. She was younger, but mature for her age, and fit in well with us. She hadn't hit her growth spurt and was several inches shorter than me, with long, straight blond hair and gray eyes.

Georgie was a cutie with chunky cheeks, brown hair,

and the same gray eyes as Margot. He sat and played with his toys. His favorite toy was a panther he named Kitty.

"Look, Kitty." Georgie held up his slightly mangled and obviously loved stuffy.

"We can't have pets," Margot spoke with a bit of a British accent. She had lived in Florida long enough that she was starting to sound native.

As she spoke, she took stock of her room filled with stuffed animals and animal prints. "Mom is allergic. Georgie has always wanted a cat. He calls his stuffed panther his kitty. We got the panther because of all the panther crossing signs."

Amused, I had to chuckle at the memory of those signs. "Smart. I saw those. Are there really that many around here?"

Margot shrugged. "I haven't seen any, but the signs are fun to see."

Sarah started telling a story about a lost panther. Georgie was immediately entranced with her story, swaying as he hugged his kitty.

Shortly after, we were called for dinner.

"How long have you been here?" Cindy passed drinks around to everyone at the table.

"Just over a year," Avery, Margot's dad, answered. "I came here to teach science. I thought it would be good for my family to live in a different country and experience a different culture. My wife works at a local nursery tending plants. We'll stay here a couple more years and then head back to London."

Avery was tall and lean with short-cropped brown hair and blue eyes. Poppy was shorter and rounder, with auburn hair and the same gray eyes as Margot and George.

Sitting there, I could listen to their accents all day.

"That is so cool." Sarah served herself some extra fries. Being vegetarian, she had a grilled cheese on her plate to go with her fries. "I never knew people did that, I mean, to third world countries, yeah, but here, to America? No idea."

"My mom was in the Peace Corps." I grabbed some fries before she took them all. "She was stationed in Papua New Guinea for two years, teaching, like you. I don't think she got to choose what she taught. I do know she loved it, though."

Sarah's jaw dropped, while everyone else seemed interested.

"Your mom was in the Peace Corps? She was in Papua New Guinea? How did I not know this?" Sarah gaped. "How was it even a question of you coming with us? She obviously approves of traveling and experiencing life. I mean, she lived in another country. For two years. This is like, one week."

Sarah glanced around the table trying to get agreement. Then she seemed to think of something and pinned me with a sharp look. "Wait, has she ever gone back? Have you ever been there? Why are there so many stories you haven't told me? I thought you were my best friend."

I wanted to shrink from her questions but concentrated

on answering the ones about the Peace Corps.

"No. I think she wants to go back, but it isn't really on the beaten path, so to speak."

Tom finished a sip of wine and put his glass down. "Do you think you'll want to do anything like that after college?"

Travel. Would I want to travel? Would I want to go off and see the world and experience how other cultures lived? Gods above, that would be wonderful. It would be amazing. It would be…impossible.

My brain started to cycle out of control, and I tried to stop it with a quick drink of ice water. "I think I need to graduate high school first. Get into college and then figure out how to graduate college. Traveling around, joining the Peace Corps, or even AmeriCorps is a ways off."

I turned to Sarah and smiled. "Can you imagine it, Sarah? Going off to another country, immersing yourself in their way of life, becoming one with them? Think of it, it would be like studying with your whole body."

"Leave it to you to bring everything back to studying, Jade. I bet you brought schoolbooks." Sarah grumbled, "Just when you were getting me excited for our next adventure, too."

Everyone laughed at her chagrin, even Margot. Georgie was still oblivious to everything going on around him except his fries, which he stuffed in his mouth.

Trying to get the attention off me, I turned to Margot. "What do you and Georgie do during the day? What is school like?"

While she answered, I enjoyed the fried fish.

"We mostly hang out around here when our parents are working. We have a tutor that comes in to help, especially with Georgie. I do my schooling online. I enjoy most of my classes, but sometimes they get tricky. I'm good at most of the subjects, but it helps to have someone to bounce ideas off of. It also helps to have someone read over my English papers; grammar isn't as easy as it seems."

Everyone laughed at that.

Sarah gave her a sympathetic nod. "Jade and I work together on English a lot. It's hard when you have to go it alone."

I tilted my head and considered her. "Online school sounds interesting. Though, having just your younger brother and a tutor seems a bit lonely."

"I don't know, my classes have a video part, so I end up debating with kids from all over the world. There are some kids in the neighborhood I sometimes see, too. Hanging out with you and Sarah has been pretty cool."

"Yeah, Jade and I are amazing, we can't help it." Sarah raised her glass for a toast with me.

Clinking glasses, I smiled in agreement.

Margot took in everyone's interested faces. "It's weird you know. Most of the time the students have their cameras off, so the class is mostly boxes with initials. Rarely do I see a friendly face. I sometimes wonder how many of the other students are paying attention or doing other things. When my camera is off, it's harder to focus."

Grabbing my soda, I considered that versus sitting in a traditional class. "Do you often have your camera off?"

She nodded. "Yeah. If I don't want to make myself pretty or show my bedroom. Sometimes I just don't want to share my space with other people, ya know. But when my camera is off…" She trailed off.

Sarah put down her fork. "Is there ever a time you have to have the camera on? Do you know the others in your class?"

"Not really. Some students are really shy and aren't comfortable on camera. Some are always ready for their close-up. I'm about fifty-fifty."

Margot's mom appeared concerned. "Margot, has this been hard on you?"

"No, not really. I mean, I do miss my mates back home, and having my brother, my *little* brother, as my main companion isn't ideal, but I love learning about America and what Americans are really like. What you see on the telly isn't really what it's like here. I love seeing the different areas where we've traveled."

She looked around at everyone at the table, then focused on her mom. "I really wouldn't trade in the experience. Someday I'll travel and have people I can visit all over the world. It's hard, but it's a good hard. I do like the fact that I get to see some other kids closer to my age this week. That's a nice change of pace."

After dinner, we moved outside. That late, the heat

wasn't as bad. The bugs, on the other hand, were huge. "It's so different here. I mean, we're in the same country, only an hour outside our time zone, but I feel like I'm in another world. Everything about this place looks and feels so different from where we come from…not to mention the smells. It's so weird."

"It smells weird? You're weird." Sarah punched me in the arm. "Though you're right about the rest of it. I feel like I'm on some alien planet, everything is strange; especially the bugs, they're huge. Do you ever worry they will abscond with Georgie? Where are the alligators?"

"You get used to it," Margot explained. "I was homesick for a few weeks, but then everything inside just clicked, and I started loving it here. When I go home it will be colder and wetter. As for the bugs, you do know I used to have a second brother."

Her face was so innocent and Sarah's shock so obvious that I almost hit the ground laughing.

Margot's parents busted out laughing as well.

CHAPTER 12

The next few days flew by. We toured the University of Florida. It was an official tour where they gave us University swag and everything. Despite enjoying the campus, I couldn't imagine living there.

Sarah's eye's slid over to me as we walked between buildings. "The thermal shock of switching to air conditioning from this humidity would kill me."

I tried to nod, but even that seemed like too much work.

When we entered the next building, we both shivered. It felt like they set the temperature at sub-zero. For about five seconds I couldn't even breathe. Hunched over, hands on my knees, I just let my body adjust and eventually I could stand and smile. "This campus is lovely, but I would miss experiencing all four seasons. Passing between classes would be intense."

The tour guide smiled at me. "I know what you mean. I'm from Minnesota. It took me a few semesters to really get the hang of living in this climate."

Tom seemed interested. "Did it take you long to acclimate to living with air conditioning year-round and all this heat? People here set their temperatures so low indoors! Do you miss the snow?"

"You'd be surprised. A few trips to the beach and suddenly it all seems worth it."

After the first day I texted my dad: Toured the campus, too humid to even consider. Didn't you go here? How did you even survive this torture? Luv ya!

He quickly replied: It was different in the dark ages.

The next day we visited Kennedy Space station. There weren't any planned rocket launches, but it was still awesome.

My text to Dad was just a GIF of a rocket ship.

Dad replied with a GIF of a frowny face. A minute later I got: That isn't a report. Do better.

Amusement rather than disappointment bubbled up as I flashed my phone to Sarah.

My next text was: `Having fun. See you soon.` I added a heart-eyed face. There was no reply. His dissatisfaction flowed all the way from Wisconsin.

Between our tours, we swam. A lot. Both in the pool and at the beach.

On Tuesday, Tom took me, Sarah, and Margot, to Orlando, Universal Studios! The lines were long because of all the spring break vacationers. It was hot and sticky. But it was amazing. We went on rides all day and ate too much sugar. We crashed on the car ride home.

When I finally woke up, I sent Dad a long text telling him about each ride we went on, all the food we ate and how interesting the drive was. He replied with one word. "Better."

Sarah and I rolled our eyes at his enthusiasm.

On Wednesday, Sarah's parents decided to take us camping at Stardust's Campground.

We rented an RV, some bikes, and two large tents. The RV was more for the indoor plumbing than for sleeping. It had a single bed and a bathroom. There was no way the lot of us could all fit. I was happy that Margot's family was invited to join us. We arrived at the camp site early in the afternoon.

Sarah, Margot, and I, were off and biking before anyone could mention setting up the tents. This was Sarah's idea and she thought she was very clever. How did I know this? She told us when we cleared camp.

Sarah was at the lead. "That's the second bug I've eaten, and I'm vegetarian."

Margot yelled from between us, "You may have to turn in your card, mate!"

Trying to keep my mouth shut, I sniggered. The trail through the trees was shaded from the worst of the sun and smelled of eucalyptus. There were tons of trees.

"Margot, do you know what types of trees these are? Are they eucalyptus?"

"No, they are mostly oak trees, a few different species." She was panting.

There was a lake to the left and a field I could barely make out through the foliage to the right.

After about twenty minutes we decided to turn around.

When we got back, the tents still needed to be set up. Breathing hard from the ride, I grabbed a bottle of water and dumped half in my mouth, half over my head.

Sarah was pouring water over her head when I heard her mumble, "So much for getting out of set-up."

Her mom chuckled as she set up the fire and food area.

There were two tent bags, and I grabbed one, dumping out the pieces. Sarah grabbed the instructions and her eyes actually crossed.

Snatching them from her before her brain broke, I saw they were a series of pictures and words. Nothing *that* bad. Each tent could hold four people. They had two rooms, with a dividing wall; it was pretty sweet. The tents went up quickly and easily.

Once the tents were up, we flopped down, exhausted.

While we had been getting our tent ready, Margot's family had gotten theirs set up on the other side of the campground. Margot and Tom set up the mosquito candles while Cindy started the fire.

My phone was a-buzz with messages from all my friends. Curled up on my side, I checked in with everyone while I listened to Georgie play in the other tent. With all our adventures I had to catch both Bevin and José up on what was happening in Florida. They had their own adventures in Wisconsin as well. As I was finishing up about Orlando, Cindy called us to dinner.

We had brought hot dogs, with all the fixings, and marshmallows—an all-American camp out. We found sticks and started roasting dinner over the flames.

Flinching in disgust, I squinted at Sarah in disbelief. "You put what on your veggie dogs?"

"No ketchup, that's for sure. Wisconsin heathen."

Margot started to laugh at us. "Don't you two live in the same place?"

My gaze shifted from Sarah to Margot, and I shrugged.

Sarah stuck her tongue out at me and, with her nose in the air, she turned her back to me. She made it clear she was talking to Margot. "In Chicago, where I'm from, we know how to eat a proper hot dog. Mustard, onions, relish, tomato, dill pickle, celery salt, sport peppers, the works. Never ketchup." She shuddered, actually physically *shuddered* at the word 'ketchup'. "That's just gross."

Shaking my head, I sighed and grabbed some of the chips we brought to have with the dogs. American chips, not fries.

Margot and the rest of the group were trying not to laugh at us, but I heard the snickers.

After dinner, we sat and talked to let the food settle. This was the parents' idea. We kids were eyeing the marshmallows and chocolate bars, ready to pounce. Though, that may have been just me.

"Jade, stop acting like a cat who's seen a mouse." Cindy was putting away the hot dogs. "You can wait five minutes for dessert." She laughed at my crestfallen face.

"Yeah, Jade, it's only sugar," Sarah teased.

"But marshmallows." I gazed at Sarah with big hopeful eyes. "So, you don't want any?"

She threw half a hot dog bun at me.

Tom snapped his gaze towards us then towards the food. "Hey, clean that up. We don't want any critters around in the middle of the night. Nothing ruins a campout more than critters."

Margot intoned seriously, "Especially alligators."

Sarah and I just gaped at her, dumbstruck. My heartrate quickened at the thought.

"Alligators. Here at the park?" Sarah gulped as she tucked her legs under herself. She swung her head around frantically.

Margot kept her face blank for another minute before she burst out laughing. "Nothing to worry about in this area, we should be fine. But Sarah, your face. Thanks for that."

Counting to five to calm my heart, I confirmed with Cindy. "Five more minutes 'til dessert?"

Cindy was still chuckling. Apparently, we were the only chumps who didn't know alligators wouldn't be in this area. "About that," she agreed.

Grabbing my phone, I updated my dad on the camping trip, the bike ride, and all the adventures of the day. By the time I was done, it was time to roast marshmallows.

Margot and her family had never roasted s'mores over a campfire.

Margot shrieked and Georgie squealed in delight. "But it's on fire. The marshmallow, it's burning."

Snorting, I helped her out. I loved roasting marshmallows. "It will be okay." Grabbing her stick, I blew out the flames. "See, it's all good."

I snatched a few graham crackers and a block of chocolate, assembling the perfect sandwich. "Take a bite."

She did, and her eyes grew. "Oh, my. That *is* delightful."

Another convert. My job here was done.

After dinner we cleaned up; the remark about critters, at least, was no joke.

All too soon, it was time to get settled and into our tents. Sarah and I took the half of the tent on the outside. I tended to be the first one up in the morning, and I could make coffee. My family had been camping since I was little, and I had proven myself capable. We stayed up talking for a bit, playing on our phones, and reading.

Despite my attempts to fall asleep, something kept me up. It was dark outside at two a.m. Slipping out of bed, I tried not to wake up Sarah. She wasn't having any trouble sleeping. As I found my shoes, phone, and a small flashlight, she stirred a little and rolled over, but didn't wake up.

I slipped out of the tent to sit by the fire pit. Sarah's parents were sleeping soundly, as were Margot and her family. As quietly as I could, I moved towards the RV and the coolers and found my water bottle. The flashlight's beam was just strong enough to cut though the dark, but not bright enough to wake anyone up. Thankfully, my water bottle wasn't empty, and I drank the last few sips. At the fire pit area, I sat on a camp chair, and tried to relax.

An itch in my body told me I had to move, not just sit there staring at a dead fire. Usually, I could control my need to move, this irritation under my skin, but tonight I couldn't. The camp site wasn't big enough, I would wake someone up. That said, I couldn't really explore the woods, that wouldn't be safe. The area was unknown and dark.

Vibrating with need, I gazed at the tents and the surrounding woods. Contemplating the hours of sitting here, I debated waking up Sarah and dragging her on a walk with me—anything to make this night not quite so long.

Then I saw a movement. I squinted to see better. What was that?

Georgie waddled out the door flap of his family's tent.

What the hell? I didn't see anyone with him.

I grabbed my phone and flashlight and quietly followed. Pausing at his family's tent, I planned on waking up Georgie's parents, but when I checked, I couldn't see him. Where did he go? Find Georgie first. Maybe he just needed to go to the loo, as he called it. He shouldn't be alone.

Pulse racing, I ran around the tent in the direction I had seen him headed.

Behind the tent there was a small path. I quickly sent a text to Sarah telling her what I was doing and set off after Georgie. I mean, how far could he go? He was three and small, I was fifteen. Finally, I saw Georgie entering the tree line ahead of me. Darting to him, I quietly called, "Georgie, wait." No reason to wake up the camp if he just needed to pee.

He didn't stop.

When I finally got to the trees, I couldn't see him at all. I grabbed my phone and sent a second text to Sarah quickly stating where I was. I snapped a couple of pictures for good measure, though, even with the flashlight, it was probably too dark to show much. I followed, trying to catch up with the toddler.

Hearing a yelp, I took off. Georgie was about a hundred feet away, face-to-face with a black panther. I froze. How was I looking at a black panther? Black panthers didn't live in Florida. The Florida panthers, or cougars, weren't black and lived in the southern part of the state.

Talking softly so as not to scare the panther, I tried

again to get Georgie to come to me. "Georgie, back up. Just walk back to me."

My heart jumped into my throat. It was beating so fast I could barely breathe.

He screamed again.

I didn't blame him, I wanted to scream, too, but I didn't want to scare the big cat into attacking. As slowly as I could, I approached Georgie to grab him.

When I was about ten feet away, the cat gazed at me with intelligent green eyes. My first thought was that those eyes were almost the same color as mine. *Stop being distracted, Jade, you and Georgie are in danger.* The cat continued to watch me.

Slowly, I crept forward, reaching out to the boy. Slowly, ever so slowly.

The cat looked smart. If I didn't know better, I would think the cat was trying to tell me something.

"I can't leave him," I told the panther. "He's only a baby." The panther cocked its head as if listening. "I need to bring this kitten back to his parents; they'll be worried." Somehow, I don't know how, the panther seemed to understand.

Was I going crazy? I was talking to a wild animal in the middle of the night. I just had to get Georgie out of there and safe.

Georgie turned back to me, sobbing. I inched toward him, gently. The panther watched me for a few seconds, allowing the movement. When I got to Georgie, the panther and I continued to stare at each other. An understanding seemed to pass between us. Okay, I must be over-tired, if I imagined communicating with a wild animal in the woods of Florida in the middle of the night. My one goal was to get Georgie home. Just as I was about to pick him up, I heard a noise.

"Jade, where are you?" It was Sarah, and she was crashing down the trail, making enough noise to scare every creature around. There was the flap of birds' wings, and my heart skipped a beat. My breath went staccato. Instinctively, I moved my head in the direction of the sound and then snapped back to the panther. Eyes wide. The panther still hadn't moved.

The panther stood frozen. Our gazes had us locked, both of us scared. What was it afraid of? Finally reaching him, I grabbed Georgie and was about to run when suddenly the world shifted around me and I was on the ground with severe pain in my leg. I didn't understand. The panther's gaze was still locked with mine. It hadn't moved.

What happened?

Georgie was safely with me, but everything was skewed. I looked over and there was a second panther. Maybe the first panther's mate?

That panther had attacked me.

That panther had bitten me.

I was on my side. Oh, gods it hurt. There wasn't a lot of blood. Not a bad bite.

Why hadn't I woken up Georgie's parents?

I felt woozy. I couldn't faint, not with Sarah and Georgie out here with wild beasts. Sarah!

Sarah came crashing towards where I lay on the ground and the second panther went after her.

She saw me and screamed, "Jade, oh, God, are you ok?"

"Sarah! Go get he—"

The panther attacked her.

It clawed down her arm and torso and bit her thigh when she fell. The first panther was licking the blood from the bite on my leg. When had it approach me? Distracted by Sarah and the second panther, I hadn't seen it move. I was so scared for her. I had to keep Georgie safe.

A shot cracked, the sound crashing through my head. Avery stood there. He had a gun. Where had that gun come from? Both panthers fled. I fell back and away from Georgie, glad someone else was there to help. But no, I was the medicine person, the healer, I had to help Sarah. Sitting up, a wave a dizziness overcame me. Tom was hovering over Sarah, his eyes wild.

"What? Talk to me. Tell me about her." Through the pounding in my leg, I began inching towards Sarah.

"I don't know if she's alive." He was touching her forehead, then her neck.

Dragging myself over, I managed to get to Sarah. "Tom, listen to me. In my stuff there's a black bag. Go get it."

He looked panicked. "What, why?"

"Please, just trust me. It's an emergency medical kit. Go get it. Run! Hurry!"

Tom left. As he ran off, Poppy and Cindy arrived.

Georgie ran to his mom.

"Avery, can I have your shirt?" He seemed a bit dazed but handed it to me. "Did you hit either of the black panthers?"

"There was more than one?" He swung his head around as if they were still there for him to see.

Nodding, I took his shirt and started to tear strips. The first strip was used for my leg. If I passed out, I wouldn't be able to help Sarah. Then I started to triage Sarah. First, I checked on her vitals. Though she was bleeding from a few places, there was only one severe wound on her arm where the panther must have dragged its claws across her skin. Her pulse was thready but present.

Once Avery decided the panthers were gone, he finally answered my question. "No, I shot up into the air. I couldn't tell where you three were. I just wanted to scare it…them off. Your flashlight wasn't giving off enough light."

"It was a panther?" Cindy asked. "I didn't think panthers were this far north."

"Did you say black?" Avery pulled out his cell phone and used it as a flashlight, lighting up the bushes. "The cougars in Florida aren't black. Are you sure you weren't mistaken because of how dark it is out here?"

"No," I said, "it was a big black cat, I'm sure of it." Their argument wasn't helping my focus, Deciding I didn't care about the debate, I continued working on my friend.

Just then, Tom came up with my bag.

I heard Georgie's voice off to the side. "Black kitty was scary…"

I couldn't get distracted. "Someone hold up a light, I need to see."

Cindy held up a flashlight.

I put on some gloves and started my examination. My first priority was cleaning out the wounds. As I did this I asked, "Have you called 9-1-1?"

"Yes, of course we did," answered Cindy. She was fully focused on Sarah, and not the color of the panther I had seen. At least one adult had their priorities straight.

Sarah's pulse was getting weaker, but it was still steady. Once her wounds were cleaned out, I could quickly bandage the smaller ones. I used the remainder of Avery's shirt on Sarah's leg. One gash was gaping. Surveying the four adults, I needed to determine a potential helper. Tom and Cindy watched me closely, kneeling next to Sarah, holding on to her other hand and the light so I could see. Avery stood watch in case the panthers returned. Poppy held Georgie's hand.

"Any of you able to assist?" Poppy turned a bit green but nodded.

"I need you to hold this together, like this," I put my hands on either side of the gaping wound on Sarah's arm, "so I can sew it closed. This is the worst injury, and a simple bandage won't do anything to stop the bleeding."

Cindy's eyes widened. "What do you think you're doing?"

My breath was ragged. "She needs stiches. Normally a wild animal attack wouldn't be stitched, but her arm wound is gaping. I've disinfected it."

"Do you even know what you're doing?"

"Yes."

She continued to stare at me, waiting.

Gazing up, I wanted to growl, but this was her daughter. "I've been training for a couple of years. I've stitched my brother up and a few other family members as well. Please. Please let me help."

Tom grabbed Cindy's arm. "Let her. She's losing a lot of blood."

Finally, Cindy gave a single curt nod.

Poppy's face remained pale, but she assisted me.

Tom and Cindy waited and watched, and Avery held on to Georgie's hand.

The stitch work was slow, but Sarah was better off than she had been. The bite on her thigh should have been deep, but like mine, it wasn't. It was like the panthers were trying to scare us as much as we scared them, not really trying to hurt us.

Once I was done stitching Sarah's arm, I wrapped it in an ace bandage, and I changed my gloves. Finally, I cleaned out the wound on my thigh, which hurt, but not as much as I predicted. Then I slapped a bandage on it.

My breathing was shallow. I was fighting shock.

"Jade," Cindy exclaimed, and the light wavered. "You were attacked, too? I didn't even know. What do you need?"

"We've lost blood and are probably dehydrated. Think about the times you've donated blood and what they give you afterwards to pep you up. That's pretty much what I need." My voice was softer than usual as I explained. I was getting dizzy and was tired of being the adult.

"Were you bitten anywhere else?" Tom started looking me over critically, noticing the blood on my clothing.

"No, Sarah started screaming as soon as the panther got to me. She saved me." My body was getting weaker.

Shakily, sounding distracted, Poppy said, "Thank you for saving Georgie. I don't even know why he came out here."

"Kitties, mommy. I wanted to play with the kitties," Georgie explained.

Poppy looked down at her son in horror. "Oh, God."

In the background I heard emergency vehicles.

Giving in to the dizziness, I lay down. Why was it I couldn't go on vacation without visiting the ER?

CHAPTER 13

As soon as I heard the emergency vehicles, my brain snapped into working order. Rolling to my side, I patted the ground until I found my phone then texted my dad. It had taken time for the emergency vehicles to get to us and it was now nearly four in the morning in Florida, which would make it three in Wisconsin. Nothing would stop him from responding. Someone in the pack was always on call, and he had taken this week. If I called, he would hear how tired and stressed I was, and he would come. That couldn't happen, not yet. There were enough adults here to figure out what was going on.

If I sugar-coated anything he'd see through it and be more upset. I'm okay, don't freak.

The response took a few seconds, but I was right. He responded: What happened?

Okay, so far so good.

I woke up and had to pace. You know. I sent that first. He would know I was typing, and I didn't want him to have to wait for a long block of text. I saw Georgie head to the woods. I chased him down.

Dad answered: What happened? You go into the woods all the time.

There were panthers.

Georgie okay? What happened to him? Should I call in Tilly and Rory?

No. I got that out quickly. The rest I wanted to get out in in one big chunk. I was bitten. Sarah saw. She screamed. She was attacked. Avery came out with a gun and scared them off. I patched Sarah up. The EMT are almost here.

My text was almost as frantic as my breathing.

Pulling down my sweats, I sent him a picture of my leg to prove I was fine. It was bandaged, but you could still tell that it wasn't bad. That is my only injury.

His reply was a bit slower in coming. I could imagine him studying the picture. That's not bad. Not much blood.

Finally, the analytical Dad; he must be calming down. That's just it, the attack seemed more a warning than anything else. Dad, it was weird.

That's it, I'm coming down. Even his text sounded fierce.

No. Again, I got that word out fast. We're fine. I'll be home in a couple of days.

Breathing hard, I lay on the ground waiting for his okay. My good foot was shaking with nerves, and I kept gazing up through the leaves at the stars. *Come on Dad... agree.*

Keep me informed. I may still come.

Closing my phone, I flopped back and took a huge breath. *Phew!*

Eyes closed, I concentrated on the adults talking near Sarah. Cindy hadn't left her side. She had been focused on her to the exclusion of everything else for a few minutes. "Tom, where did you go?"

"Jade asked me to take her bag back to camp after she put everything away. She didn't want it mixed up with the stuff going to the hospital. I also grabbed some clothes for the girls for when they get released."

"Was all of that really necessary?"

"I don't know. I just know that when we leave here, I want to be able to stay with Sarah and not have to think about clothes."

Cindy let out a sigh. "You're right. I'm sorry for snapping at you."

A rustling sound had me checking out what they were doing. Tom took a seat on Sarah's opposite side. Each of her parents bookending her. Cindy held her non-injured hand, but everything else was bandaged so Tom just sat close.

The paramedics finally arrived and made a beeline to Sarah. Pushing myself up to my elbows, I watched.

She was still out of it. They got her up on a gurney, took her vitals, and checked over her injuries. Full onsite triage. After a few extra minutes on her arm, they got her into the ambulance.

I heard them compliment the adults on a nice job patching her up, like always. They asked which adult had medical training. They all pointed to me, still on the ground with an obvious wound to my leg.

One of the paramedics came over to me and looked over my leg. He removed my bandage and checked out the bite. They got me on a gurney and strapped me down.

"You did good work on your friend there. Where did you learn to do stitches like that?" one of the EMTs asked while checking out my leg.

"I've been working with a family member for a while, learning the family trade." My elbow gave out and my shoulders slipped to the ground, stopping the interrogation. This was probably for the best since I wasn't sure, beyond that, how to answer these questions. She packed me into the ambulance.

Well, it had been a pleasant stay in Florida until now.

Sarah and I were given a room together at the hospital. The doctors didn't have much to do for her besides pushing fluids. They were impressed with what I had done. Most of them assumed it really had been one of the adults since the stitches were so neat and I was injured, which was probably for the best.

I could see the news: "Fifteen-Year-Old Girl Patches up Friend after Panther Attack in Florida Woods." Then there was the question of what we were attacked by. Well, I knew what I saw, even if no one else believed me.

We were finally in a room and secure by eight, and I could sleep. Sarah woke me up about an hour later, so, sleep was getting further away from me. She was in a lot of pain and had no idea what had happened. I filled her in while the nurses got her medicine. The pain medicine helped her with the distress enough that she finally fell asleep. Somehow, I managed to fall back asleep until someone asked me what I wanted for lunch.

My eyes were gummy, but I got out some words. "Um, is there a menu?"

My stomach growled and I realized I was starving. Holding my hands in fists, I stopped myself from snapping at them to hurry.

"Here you go." She handed me a menu. My eyes were blurry with sleep, but I finally got them to focus. Nothing sounded great, but hunger was the best spice.

"Can I have a burger and a pizza? Sausage?" The orderly laughed at the pitiful sight I must have presented.

"It isn't allowed, but I'll see what I can do. You haven't eaten since you got here, and you seem half-starved."

Unsurprisingly, a half-hour later, a tray with a burger, fries, and ice cream appeared in front of me. Disappointed in the quantity, but eating like Owen, I dug in. It wasn't the best food, but I was starving, and somehow it tasted divine.

After lunch, I paced the small room. With the medicine, my leg didn't hurt at all. Whenever a nurse came in, I plopped down as if I were a good patient, but I needed to move. I had too much pent-up energy. Boredom set in. I wasn't tired, and I didn't have anything to do. Sarah was out and the nurse said the medicine would keep her asleep until dinner.

Sarah's parents came in after I had finished eating. Tom looked me over. "You look better. Are you okay? Is that a dumb question?"

Smiling brightly, I shook my head. "I'm fine. Bored. Starving, but being a teenager, that's part of the definition. But I feel peachy."

Cindy came over and felt my forehead. It was such a motherly thing to do that it warmed me to my toes. "No fever. Do they have you on meds?"

"Antibiotic and a rabies shot, like Sarah. I was up to date on everything else."

Cindy gave me a warm smile. "Well, we can find entertainment if you want. We've been hanging out down in the lobby. Maybe they have Monopoly." That last part was said with a pinch of snark as she wiggled her eyebrows.

It made me laugh, who knew *that* was possible?

The room was quiet, except for a machine in the corner. "You two should go out and get some real food. If the food in the cafeteria is anything like what I just ate, then someone in our group deserves better. The nurse gave Sarah enough medication that she'll be out until late this evening."

Tom patted my hand. "We know that. We're the parents. Believe it or not, they do keep us informed of these things."

Flopping back on my pillow, my face split in a genuine smile. Both Sarah's parents were making me feel better. "Anyway. You two should go get some real food. I'll text if anything changes here, promise."

They exchanged a glance and nodded. Cindy rubbed my shoulder and then my cheek. "Okay, but make sure you let us know if anything changes. She's our daughter…and we worry about you too, hon."

A little over an hour later I was sitting on the edge of the bed starting to go stir-crazy when a stranger walked in.

"Do you want company?" She was an older teenage, taller than me, but not by much. She had dark skin, dark hair, and green eyes, kind of like mine. In some ways she was a weird combination of me and Sarah.

"Whoa… your eyes… they're, um… hi," I blurted, then blushed. "Sorry, that was rude. I don't know you. Is this some sort of volunteer program? Sit with the bored for so many hours and earn school credit?"

"Not really." She walked in and leaned against the closed closet door.

"If not for credit, why are you here?" A stirring in my stomach was giving me a bad feeling about her. My hand inched towards the nurse call button. I almost had the controller in my hand.

"I wanted to talk to you. You smell weird, and I wanted to find out why. See, we can both be abrupt and rude."

What she said totally threw me, as did a bit of an accent. My hand dropped away from the controller as I cocked my head to the side.

She seemed pleased with herself.

"I'm in a hospital. Maybe that's why I smell weird. I was attacked by two panthers last night, and my friend may not survive." I was frustrated and taking it out on her. She didn't deserve it, but I didn't care.

"She'll be fine, and I think you know it. And only *one* panther attacked you."

That stopped my ire. My breathing sped up a bit and I tried to slow it down. "How do you know that? Who are you?"

"Don't you know?" She just looked at me, calmly.

Something about her eyes.

"No, why would I?" Something was nagging in the back of my mind, but I refused to listen. This was not happening. This was not allowed. "What are you?"

"Now *that* is a better question. My name is Dayo. We met last night. In the woods. You still smell weird. Wolf? Panther? A stream in a wooded forest? A cup of tea?"

She shook her head as if trying to order her thoughts. Then she continued. "Tonight is a full moon, and you and your friend need to get out of the hospital before sunset. We need to find a way to get you out. My dad will try to help. He may be able to explain things to your friend's parents…if you don't want to."

Her eyes narrowed a little. She wasn't sure if I knew what she was talking about, though she was betting I did. It was a challenge. My turn. Would I take the next step in this game?

Staring at her, my head slowly moving back and forth in denial, I tried to think this over. My brain could not comprehend what it had just heard. A panther. *A werepanther.* No way. Not a chance. I was a child of werewolves. That was what I was going to become, one way or another. My path was set, and I was going to be the healer for my family. This could not be happening. This could not be happening to me right now. No.

"Jade, who is this and what is she talking about? Are my drugs really that good?" It felt like a punch in the chest as I quickly turned to Sarah. She was groggy from the drugs and wasn't supposed to be up yet. My eyes widened. *This wasn't happening.*

Deep breaths…

The medications had worn off? Of course they had. If she was now a werepanther, medication levels had to be a lot higher to have any long-term effect. If werepanthers were anything like werewolves, she would also heal faster.

Damn, damn, damn, damn, damn.

Slowly, I got out of bed and went to her. "Can I see your arm?"

She held her out arm to me. I removed a bit of the bandaging and, sure enough, the healing appeared days old.

Breathe, in and out, I told myself. My mind started to spiral, but I had to get it under control. First, there was the escape and getting in contact with Sarah's parents. As for my dad and clean up with the hospital, that could happen later. "Sarah, I need to call your parents. We need to have a long talk. This is going to be…well, this isn't going to be easy."

Grabbing my phone, I walked to the corner of the room. Sarah and Dayo watched me curiously. It took a few seconds to get my heart slow enough to make this call calmy, then I dialed. "Hi, Cindy. Can you and Tom please come back to the hospital? We need to talk."

CHAPTER 14

Because of Owen, I had been to the hospital many times. Their procedures were well known to me. The miracle of werewolf…*wereanimal* healing couldn't be seen by doctors or medical staff.

Thankfully, I'd insisted on Tom grabbing clean clothes. Right now, Sarah and I needed to look like visitors, not patients, and having our own clothing was the first step.

"Sarah, I know this is going to sound strange, but you're just going to have to trust me." Sarah was awake, but still groggy. She nodded. Dayo had a satisfied smirk on her face as she leaned on the closet door again. "I want you to change into your street clothes. We're going to go meet your parents by the front doors. I've let them know that's where we'll meet them."

To speed things up, and avoid some of the drama, I'd texted them that last part.

"Are we leaving? Don't we have to check out or something?" Sarah's eyebrows come together as she searched the room. "Where's the paperwork?"

"Sarah." I willed her to listen to me. "We need to go meet your parents, they're almost here. I promise you, it will all be okay."

She wasn't convinced, but she got out of bed. She gathered her clothes and went to the bathroom to get dressed.

Once the door was closed, I turned on Dayo. "Why did your partner—friend—whoever—bite us?" All my anger finally erupted out, and I could feel my blood warming my face. "Are we changing tonight? Am I a…" Too angry to form words, I waved my hands around demanding answers from her.

She blew out a breath. "I don't know. That baby came to play with me. I wasn't going to hurt him. Then you came out. My dad saw you and thought you were the babe's mum and were going to attack me, but you were so calming, he couldn't do more than the one bite."

She paused as if in thought.

"Then that one," she inclined her head towards the bathroom, "started yelling, and Da freaked. He thought she was attacking. After the first scratches and bite, he realized she wasn't. He was about to run when the gun went off. Then we both ran." Her eyes narrowed as she considered me. "What *are* you?"

She kept asking me that. I wasn't a werewolf and I'd been told I smelled strange my whole life. If Dayo just scented wolf she wouldn't be asking me anything. Not knowing how to answer her, I continued to ignore the question.

We both heard Sarah finishing up in the bathroom. The water turned off and the lock disengaged.

I gathered up my stuff. "I have to change."

As soon as Sarah was out, I bolted into the bathroom, washed up as best I could and quickly put on clean clothes. Once I was out, I found Sarah and Dayo sitting in the room staring at each other. They weren't talking. It was like I could smell their animosity. It made me want to sneeze.

Focus, Jade, one thing at a time.

Time for my plan. "Here is what we'll do." Both their glares turned to me. "We need to make it past the nurses, then it should be pretty easy to get out the front door. Sarah, grab your bag. Dayo, distract the nurses at the nurses' station. Sarah, follow my lead."

Dayo seemed hesitant.

Grumbling, I explained, "This isn't the first hospital I've snuck out of." The room wasn't big enough to pace, but I was doing my best as I tried to get them both to see why we needed to hurry.

They both just gaped at me.

Waving my hands to emphasize our rush, I snapped, "Not now."

Sarah sat on her bed. "But why are we leaving? I'm so confused. And hungry. What's going on?"

It didn't appear Sarah was going to move.

I stopped my circling to face her. Holding back a snarl, I calmly said, "I promise, I'll tell you everything, but we have to get out of here first."

I went back to walking. Dayo and Sarah just sat back, observing me.

"We need to get out of here," I insisted. My body vibrated with the need to escape.

"No," Sarah said. "I was attacked by a wild animal last night. This is the safest place for me. Why would I leave?"

My heart raced, and I was starting to get frantic. I wasn't used to feeling frantic. "We need to get out of here. You're healing too fast."

Hearing myself, I knew I sounded like a crazy person.

Dayo shook her head with a half-smile.

Sarah's eyes bulged. She stared down at her bandaged arm and up at me. "Too fast? What does that even mean? How can a person heal too fast?"

"Sarah, please, trust me. I can't explain it here. It isn't safe." My heart was beating too fast, and breathing was getting harder. We had to leave. If a nurse popped in to check up on us now, we were toast. I started to panic.

"Jade, I don't get it. If coming here means healing, wouldn't staying here mean healing faster?" Sarah was talking slower, as if trying to talk me down. Great.

My mom had taught the kiddos how to handle panic, slow down breathing, control the heart, and organize thoughts. Plan, I needed a plan, I had to find an escape route. Could we escape through the window? The window was locked and at least eight floors up. No way. I stuck my head out the door. The hall led to the nurses' station, but wait, there was also a door to the stairs that was clear. We could make it. But there were nurses in the hallway. I ducked back in.

Sarah watched me and looked worried. "Jade, what's wrong with you, you're freaking out. Just sit back down. And who is she and why is she still here?" She pointed at Dayo.

My eyes shifted to Dayo. Breathing deeply, I dropped onto the bed, and gazed at the ceiling. Next on the list, think calmly, relax, and escape. Think. Plan.

After a minute to calm myself down, I sat up and looked at Sarah. "Listen, Sarah, you were attacked last night and shouldn't be awake. You're not only awake, but not in pain. What does that tell you?"

"That I have killer meds in me? That I heal fast? That I'm a rock star?" She flashed her hands out with the last sarcastic remark. "I don't know, what?"

She glared at me, starting to get as frustrated as I was.

I spoke slowly and calmly. "It means there is something

going on which modern medicine can't explain."

How could I convince her to listen to me and not the doctors and nurses? Somehow, she had to believe her fifteen-year-old friend over the experts. Yeah, right.

"Oh, but you can, Jade?" she hissed out, mockingly. "The great and powerful Jade can explain what the doctors here can't?"

She flopped on her side, turning her back to me.

My head began to pound. "Yes."

"Maybe you should tell her more," Dayo added unhelpfully.

Pound, pound, pound. "Not here. Not now."

"You may not have that choice," she added.

Sarah jerked up to a sitting position, faster than humanly possible. I blinked. "Why are you even listening to her? Who is she? I'm your friend. You should be listening to me." Sarah sounded hurt.

Grumbling under my breath, I massaged my temples. Not here. Not now. This was not how this was supposed to happen. This was *never* supposed to happen.

"What?!" Sarah almost yelled.

Jerking up with the noise, I ran the few steps to the door and checked for people. The hallway was blissfully clear. No one had heard us, no one was running down the hall. I closed the door, turned, and stared at her. Wanting to scream and cry or just sink through the floor, I gave up.

"Okay, I'll make a deal with you. I'll give you five minutes of an explanation if you agree that after that we leave. Your parents must be close, and I really want to explain to everyone, not just you. This won't be easy, and I don't want to do it over and over."

"Fine. But if I don't like what you have to say, I'm staying." She flipped her legs up onto her bed, got comfy, and prepared to stay there all day.

"Five minutes?" Looking over to the stranger in the room, I asked Dayo a silent question. She shrugged. "Fine, pull off the band aid. It was Dayo's dad who bit and scratched you last night."

They both gawked at me in utter shock. Sarah had just turned her head, and Dayo's mouth dropped open. I don't think she expected me to be quite that blunt.

My mouth curled into a half-smile at their expressions.

Sarah sputtered as she sat up and swung her legs around to face me. "Um, what?"

"Too fast of an explanation?"

"That doesn't make sense, I was attacked by a panther, and Dayo is a teenager."

"No, I'm a werepanther." Dayo said, standing tall and proud. "My family comes from a long line of werepanthers."

Sarah eyes narrowed and her face turned red. She was pissed. She shot out of the bed. "That isn't funny," she hissed out. "I took it on good faith that you would tell me the truth, and here you are messing around with me with this stranger?"

She started to pace the room. "Did you come up with

this while I was in the bathroom?" she demanded.

This wasn't going well. I needed to calm everyone down, but things were getting out of hand. "This isn't a joke."

"The hell it isn't." She stopped pacing and squared off, glaring at me. "This is the sickest joke I've heard. Werepanther? What the hell? We're friends. Why would you try to trick me like this?"

She was starting to sound hurt.

"Sarah." I reached out to her, but she glared at me, and I let my hand drop.

"Don't, just don't." She turned away. She grabbed her bag from the ground and tossed it on the dresser with such force, it cracked the mirror.

We all just gaped at the shards.

"What...just...happened?" Sarah choked out quietly. She stared down at her hands which started to shake.

I took a deep breath, went over to her, and gave her a big hug. She clung to me and started to cry.

"I don't want to be different. Am I a freak now? What the hell happened?"

Her shaking stopped when I squeezed tighter. "I don't know, but can we please get out of here?"

She nodded. When she pulled away, she took one more look at her hands before slowly walking over to pick up her bag. Her movements were painfully slow, as if afraid she would break something else.

The path out of the hospital wasn't bad. We took the stairs.

They weren't expecting patients who were supposedly knocked out on drugs to be walking out under their own power.

Once we were down a few flights, no one knew us from any other visitors. We wound our way through the maze of halls to the front door.

Outside, we waited for Sarah's parents. Dayo and I exchanged numbers.

I tuned to Dayo. "I don't know where we'll end up. Back at the campground from last night, I hope. That would be best. It would be a private place for our conversation. I'll text you. You'll bring your dad, right?"

"Yeah, we'll meet you. He'll want to talk to you, Sarah, and her parents." Dayo left as Sarah's parents pulled up in their rental car.

Tom jumped out of the car. He was breathing hard, and his face was set. He was pissed. "What are you two doing outside? Where are the doctors?" His thunderous gaze turned towards me. "I know you play at knowing medicine sometimes, but this is going too far!"

Cindy, who was driving, didn't seem much happier.

"Let me explain. You have to hear me out first in private. Also, Sarah needs food, lots of food. Have you broken down camp from last night?"

I thought the change of subject might make Tom's head explode. Thankfully, it had the effect of confusing him enough that he just answered me. "No."

"Perfect, can we order pizza and pick it up on the way?"

Shoving Sarah into the backseat of the car, I climbed in behind her before they could stop us. "Three large should do it. Let's go out to the camp site and stay there one more night. I know you think I'm crazy, but I'm not. This is important."

There must have been something in my voice. Inside the car, Cindy had her phone out. She found a pizza place on the way out of town and called in to order the food.

There was a sparkle in Sarah's gaze that made me worry for my body parts. "At least two with meat, please."

Cindy was absently putting together the order. "But Sarah's vegetarian."

"No, Mom, I think Jade is right. Sausage. I want sausage." There was a growl in her voice.

That last bit may be what put her parents over the top. Pizzas ordered, conversation came to a stop as we found the pizza place, picked up the pies, and headed to the campsite.

As we drove, Tom glanced back at me. "I don't know what has gotten into you, but after this talk, I'm planning on putting you on the next plane back to Wisconsin."

CHAPTER 15

It appeared the campsite had been ransacked, especially my stuff. Numbly, I stared at my things strewn everywhere.

Tom saw where I was heading. "Sorry, Jade. First, I had to find your medical bag, and then your clothes. I was a bit frazzled."

A pair of Sarah's shoes were mixed in with my stuff. "No worries. I don't have much here that matters." Taking stock of my belongings, I got the necessities organized. Most of it could wait until after we'd eaten and discussed matters.

Dayo had let me know she knew our campsite when I

had texted her about where we were heading. The text to my dad about leaving the hospital was both easier and more complicated. He knew about hospital disappearances and understood even I sometimes healed too quickly. Letting him know we headed out so he could fix the issues was a great way to cover our bases.

Tom started a fire, lit the mosquito candles, and we gathered around the pit. Before the first log caught, we were eating pizza. Sarah was on her fourth slice when I was on my second. Neither of us had eaten enough.

"Wow," Tom said. "I don't think I've ever seen you eat that much."

"Huh?" Sarah counted the crusts on her plate. She hadn't realized how much she had inhaled. "I'm just so hungry. I feel like I haven't eaten in days."

"Okay, we've been patient enough. What's going on?" Tom snapped, still angry. He was glaring at me like I was an errant child who had to be disciplined for endangering his daughter.

Considering the facts at hand, I decided to start with the folklore most people knew. "What do you know about werewolves?"

Three sets of eyes stared at me like I was crazy. I expected it. This wasn't a conversation I had ever wanted to have…with anyone.

I lifted my hands placatingly. "Hear me out. Not everything you think you know is true." Moving to Sarah,

I knelt and tore off the bandages on her arm. As I did, her parents gasped, and Sarah tried to stop me. She almost succeeded. She may have been stronger than I was now.

Desperately, I looked up at her. She knew part of the story. She had to help me.

She nodded slightly and relaxed, letting me work.

The bandage removed, I quickly peeked over my shoulder. Everyone watched, eyes wide, mouths wider, shocked. Her arm was almost healed. The stitches stood out on her mostly pink, barely scarred arm.

After a bit of a medical examination, I realized the skin was almost completely grown over the stitches. If they didn't get out now it would take a knife.

"Oh, no!" Jumping up, I grabbed the scissors and tweezers out of my bag. Returning, I started removing the deep stitches. "Sorry if this hurts," I mumbled.

Sarah's eyes were huge. I could hear her halting breath, it almost stopped. If I focused, I could feel her pulse under my fingers as I worked, and it was thumping fast.

"What are you doing?" Cindy moved to stop me. Her eyes were equally wide. "The stiches need to stay in for longer. The doctors said three to five days. I know you put them in and think you know what you're doing, but Jade, you are only fifteen. You need to stop!"

I didn't stop. The longer I waited, the harder it would be to get the stiches out.

"Is her arm healed?" Tom came closer to watch me

work. "My God, it is," he whispered. "How is that possible?"

Cindy started to pull on my shoulder.

"Cindy, love, look at Sarah, really look. Her arm doesn't need the stitches. The skin is pink and healed. The blood is from them being removed. Go ahead, Jade, finish what you're doing…but really, how *is* this possible?"

Half my life was spent ignoring questions, but I knew I couldn't continue ignoring his. It was time. "It's one of the benefits of being a were…panther." I sighed. "Here it is: last night Sarah and I were bitten by a werepanther. That means tonight, at the full moon, there's a better than good chance we'll turn into werepanthers. Wereanimals have some advantages, like advanced healing."

Waving, I noted the arm I was trying to fix. "Seeing as how you don't believe me, you can imagine how hard the werecommunity has worked to keep their existence a secret. That's why we had to get out of the hospital. If a nurse or doctor had seen how quickly the medications had worn off, or how fast Sarah healed, we would've been in trouble. That had to be avoided. So, we left."

Sarah watched me, brows knitted. "How do you know all of this?"

Another deep breath. My alpha had made me promise to never tell our secret, and that was law. Alpha law. Werewolf law. I couldn't tell them everything, but I had to tell them something.

"I've met a wereanimal before." Her stare turned from

terror to hurt then betrayed.

"Sarah, this isn't anything to play around with. It's a big secret. No one can know. I can't even tell you who or what. But I also won't tell anyone about you except for my parents. I'll wait until I get home, though. This isn't anything that should be discussed digitally. Again, secrecy. My dad's in IT security. I know how easily email and texts can be read by those who shouldn't read them."

A rustling had us all turning out heads. Dayo walked up with an older man.

"Kal?" Cindy stood up, smoothing down her pants as if trying to look professional. "What are you doing here?"

Kal seemed shocked to see Cindy.

Suddenly, I was on less firm ground as well. Standing, I gazed between them. "You two know each other?"

"Kal works in a similar field as me. He's attending the same conference I am."

What?

"This complicates things. Or this makes things easier. I'm not sure yet. Dayo, these are Sarah's parents, Cindy and Tom. Apparently, your dad knows Sarah's mom." Facing Sarah, I said, "Sarah, you can remove the rest of your bandages, I'm pretty sure you're all healed."

Kal took in everyone around the fire pit then turned to Sarah. "Yes, you should be fine."

Cindy and Tom's heads snapped to him at that comment.

In a nervous voice, Cindy asked, "Kal, what do you

know about what happened to my daughter?"

He sighed, sat down, and watched the fire.

Cindy sat down as well, but still seemed uncertain. Dayo and I sat as well.

Kal spoke to her. "My family is from Africa. I moved here when I was twenty-five, when my clan decided there were…" His gaze shifted from Cindy to me.

Resigned, I nodded, figuring he was asking how much I had told them. I wasn't sure why I was the unspoken leader, but it seemed it was the role everyone wanted me to play.

He continued. "There were too many werepanthers for the land to support. Panthers live in Florida, so it seemed this was the smartest place for us to land in the US."

So many emotions crossed Sarah and her parents' faces. I didn't know if they knew what to feel. Scared, mad, wonder, shock, it was all there playing over and over.

"Did you do this to my daughter?" Tom decided to settle on anger.

Kal's eyes dropped. "Simply put, yes, I did. But I didn't do it on purpose. I thought she was attacking my daughter. I did not mean to hurt her; I was in protection mode and I'm sorry."

"Sorry? Sorry! Is there any way to undo this? Did you make her like you? Is there any way to make her normal again?" Tom leapt up, waving his hands, and started to pace. "I don't know anything about werewolves, but I don't want my daughter turning into a freak every time there's a full moon. She doesn't need to spend her life howling at the moon."

He was so mad he was spitting.

"Werepanther," Dayo whispered.

Sarah went from looking shocked to looking slapped.

Staring at his reddening face, I said softly, "Stop."

Tom kept going, waving his hands, spitting mad. He finally whipped around, facing Kal, legs apart, one finger pointing at Kal, glaring. "Is she going to be a monster? Is there any chance for her to be the same person she was before?"

"Stop!" This time I yelled. Sarah was turning paler with every word her father spoke.

Everyone turned toward me. "She isn't a monster. Of course she's the same person. And if you don't want to lose your one and only daughter, you may want to reevaluate the words you are using out of ignorance and fear."

Tom's gaze snapped to Sarah. He blanched then glared at me.

"Who are you, Jade Stone?" Tom stalked towards me. "You demand we get you and our daughter from the hospital without a word. You expect us to believe your story about knowing a werewolf but don't give us any details. And now," he paced away frothing at the mouth, "and now," he yelled, "you tell us how to react to this ridiculous story!"

His pacing took him to one of the RV's and he began to punch it in frustration.

Cindy got up and went to him, trying to get him to

stop. Suddenly, he spun around and glared at me again. "Why are you the expert?" he yelled.

I froze. Everything in the clearing went silent and everyone stared at me.

"I'm not," I choked out.

He needed to calm down and the only way was if I stayed calm. "I just know more than you do. I know that tonight is going to be scary for all of us. I'm trying not to be scared about how much my life has changed. Don't you understand, this isn't what I want either? It isn't just Sarah who was bitten."

A tear rolled down my cheek.

He just gazed at me, as if seeing me for the first time since they left the hospital. A scared fifteen-year-old.

Shaking my head to move on, I reminded him, "We need to be ready for tonight, which is going to be here very soon. We need Sarah to be ready for the change. I may need to be ready as well, I don't know."

"You smell strange." Kal took stock of me for the first time tonight. "Why is that?"

"I don't know. I have never had anyone tell me this before you and Dayo." Thinking about Owen's description of me smelling like a Christmas tree by a stream, I pushed those thoughts away. Now wasn't the time. "Do I smell of panther?"

"Yes."

Not what I wanted to hear. Everything had changed.

Organize your thoughts. "Well, there you have it. We

should hang a blanket so that Sarah and I can be ready for the change. Are you two going to change as well?"

"I will." Dayo gazed at the fire. "I'm new to changing. I don't have the control to deny the moon yet. My first full moon was just three moons ago."

That pretty much matched up with Owen.

"I will stay human to watch over the camp and protect this area. Dayo will run with the girls." Kal turned to Tom and Cindy. "I will also be able to answer any of your questions."

"One last thing before we change, or possibly change." I smiled at Sarah's parents who were weary, not really wanting more new news. "You should call the hospital and tell them you took us out before they get worried."

They seemed relieved that my words were so mundane compared to everything else they had heard.

We set up a blanket as a barrier. As the sun set, the three of us, Sarah, Dayo, and I, went behind the barrier. Stripping, I didn't feel like ruining any more clothes, I saw Dayo stripped as well. Sarah was hesitant, but finally mumbled something about dressing rooms and started taking off her clothing.

Florida weather was great; I couldn't imagine doing this for the first time in a Wisconsin's sub-zero winter. A thought of Owen's shift in the freezing cold garden behind the school made me chuckle. This was so much nicer.

Thinking of his transformation reminded me of his first fall, so I got down on my hands and knees. Like I had done for Owen, I laid out some basic ideas for Sarah. "Relax. It will be hard, but the more you relax, the easier the shift will be. Don't forget to breathe."

She just looked at me blankly.

Then I moved to Bevin's advice to Owen. "Once you change, you won't be able to reconcile who and what you are for a couple of seconds, maybe minutes. That may be different with me here, but with me changing, I don't know. No biting. You are not allowed to bite people. That's the biggest rule. Got it?"

Sarah, who had also gotten down when I did, finally broke her remote look. "Relax, don't bite. Got it."

Dayo watched me. "I've never heard rules before. They make sense, though." She seemed to think about it for a few seconds before getting down herself. She may have been more attuned to the moon and when the shift would start.

A few minutes later, I started feeling weird, queasy, dizzy. Breathe. In through my nose, out through my mouth. My body changed, bones moved, hair grew.

Sarah gasped. In fear? In shock? I repeated my mantra loud enough for her to hear. "Breathe in through your nose, out through your mouth, deep meditative breaths."

Her breathing seemed to even out.

Everything changed.

Soon, I couldn't speak my mantra any longer.

Thinking became impossible.

I couldn't see.

Could I scream? No.
It hurt. I hurt.
This was all wrong.
What was going on?
Pain.
Pain.
Pain.
Everything stopped.

CHAPTER 16

Lying on the ground, I had no idea what was happening. The smells, oh gods. Pizza. People. Animals. Trees. Water. Food.

What was going on?

Who was I?

What was I?

The trees, green and lush all around me. Green leaves, green…jade green. Jade.

That's right.

I tried to stand up.

Where were my hands? My heart began to beat faster.

Four legs. Four feet. Four paws.

Shaking myself out, I investigated. Black fur…right…I was panther. Where was Sarah? There was another panther. Was that Sarah? The panther looked up with dark brown eyes. Sarah's eyes. She looked scared.

Panther Sarah was beautiful, sleek and black.

Did I resemble her? Were we similar?

Water. I needed to find water. I padded around the cloth hanging to shield us. Walking was weird. I stumbled and fell. Sarah made a sound I thought was a laugh and nosed me. Pushing myself up, I tried again.

This time I made it around the curtain and turned my gaze to the people. The first person I saw was Tom. His eyes bugged out and he backed away, scooting his chair with him.

The sweet scent of candy wafted to me. Was that the smell of people?

Shaking my head, I closed my eyes and shifted my gaze to Cindy.

"Sarah?" Cindy asked, pale, her breathing shallow, eyes at my paws. She stood with her hand out, but she was backing up. Mixed messages.

I shook my head.

She finally met my eyes. "Jade?" She took a steadying breath and stopped her retreat.

Though it felt odd, I did my best to nod.

"Sarah?" Tom's voice trembled. He had stopped backing

up, too, but he was still trembling.

Shifting to check behind, I saw Sarah pad out and stop beside me. My eyes narrowed in annoyance; she had figured out how to move faster and better than me.

"They look like twins. Are they safe?" Cindy asked. That sweet smell filled the air.

Kal approached us, hands out. "Jade, are you okay?" His scent cut through the sweet scent. Huh, sweet must not be all people.

Gazing into his eyes, I gave another attempt at a nod.

He approached Sarah. "Sarah?"

I glanced over. Her tail was tucked, scared.

She nodded as well.

"She is safe, but scared. I would say, give her time. She may accidently hurt you and that would do more harm to her than you."

Taking everything in with my new sight, I saw a panther by the woods. Dayo must have shifted before us.

Nudging Sarah, we padded towards Dayo and into the woods.

"Where are they going?" Tom's fear seemed to have turned to ire.

Kal's calm voice was the last thing I heard as I ran into the woods. "They need to run. Don't worry. Dayo is with them. I'll follow for a bit. They won't get lost. They'll be able to find their way back. This is what they need right now."

Picking up speed, moving faster towards the woods

and the lake I remembered, I didn't know how much more he said. When I got to the water, I just stared. Sarah came up next to me. We did look like twins, except for our eyes. Mine were green, hers brown. Dayo followed us, keeping us safe, making sure we weren't afraid of our new selves.

There were other differences. Sarah was a bit bigger than me, both in her body and her ears. Dayo was the smallest of the three of us.

After a minute of watching our reflections, I dove in and swam. Sarah and Dayo quickly followed. It felt so good. It felt like my body was made for swimming. Eventually we got out and roared at the moon.

The three of us spent a few hours playing like kids in a new playground.

The scent of rabbit reached me. The human side of me recoiled, but I was more panther. I saw the rabbit ahead of me and froze. Sarah froze next to me.

Dayo launched herself ten feet and pounced on the rabbit like a silent shadow of death. She quickly killed it and shared the meat.

Afterwards, we went to drink some water and clean off.

Curious, I pounced, but didn't quite make it ten feet. Dayo showed Sarah and I her technique but soon enough we got tired. We returned to the campsite.

All the adults were asleep.

When we got close to Sarah's parents, Sarah crouched down, ready to pounce. I thought she was playing.

Dayo silently ran between her and her parents, sensing something I had missed.

Sarah's lip snarled up from her teeth, and her muscles bunched, ready to fly. Did she think her parents were other animals? Was she going to attack them?

I ran at Sarah and leapt when she leapt, slamming into her in the air and we tangled as we landed. She snarled at me as she got up, ready to attack me. Her claws raked my side.

Ouch.

Standing, I stood between her and her parents. Dayo came up next to me.

Sarah snarled low in her throat. She stood tall and proud.

Dayo and I tried to stand up to her, but slowly we crouched.

"Sarah," came a low command.

Kal came up from behind me. My hackles rose, but I recognized his scent.

Sarah growled, lowering herself to the ground, ready to attack.

"Sarah, you must remember who you are and where you are." Kal's accent was thick as he approached her. He reached her and put a hand on her snout. He looked her in the eyes, playing for dominance.

Sarah's eyes flashed and her body vibrated with anger. Her growl grew louder, but Kal did not let go.

Dayo and I whined and fell to our bellies, burying our snouts in our front paws.

They stood there staring at each other for several

minutes until Sarah finally dropped her eyes. Her body was still tense, and she let out a low growl before relenting.

"Good enough," was all Kal said.

Sarah huffed out a snort, backed up and stood up proud. Dayo and I slowly followed suit. She swung her head in our direction before surveying the campground. She lifted her head, scenting the air in the direction of her parents before turning back to Kal.

He continued to watch us for a few minutes before deciding things had calmed down. "Off to bed, you all need some sleep."

Though I was keyed up from the attack, we all followed his instruction and went where we were told. As soon as we lay down, I fell asleep quickly.

The next morning, I found we had all shifted and had been covered with blankets. I assumed this was Kal's last action before he went to bed.

We quickly got dressed.

Cindy was tending the fire. "What did you three do last night?"

Yawning, I grabbed a box of left-over pizza and dug in.

Sarah grabbed a slice, and after swallowing a bit turned to her mom. "Coffee?"

Tom handed us each a cup from a local café along with a chocolate pastry. I gazed at him questioningly.

He shrugged. "You do know it's after ten. I was up early. Kal warned us you may sleep in after being up late.

I figured good coffee and sugar, the sustenance of teens."

The first sip hit my system and I started to feel alive again. "I think I love you." I didn't know if I was talking to the coffee or Tom.

Bacon hit the pan over the fire Cindy was tending. My brows hit my hair line. "Bacon?"

Cindy chuckled. "Kal came prepared. Now if you want any, you'll start telling us about last night. What did you do? What was it like? Where did you go?"

We moved to the fire pit and sat down.

Sarah and I stared at each other. I shrugged and tilted my coffee cup to her.

She took one more swallow before trying to explain. "It was weird. First we had to figure out how to walk on four feet."

"Paws," I interjected.

"Right, paws." She laughed. "Paws, good lord. Okay, yeah, paws. Jade led us to a lake, so we got a bit of a view. Did you two notice how similar we looked?"

Her parents nodded.

Kal, who was following along but letting us figure things out, added, "Your look is that of my people. Sleek and deadly."

Sarah smiled slightly before continuing. "We swam and climbed some trees. Dayo started to show us how to pounce. It was pretty cool. Nothing like long-jump in gym class."

Snorting, I almost lost some of my dark ambrosia.

"Maybe the first time I've ever enjoyed running."

Sarah laughed at that. "I mean, you did start off falling on your face, if we're going to be honest."

"Darn it! But after that I didn't fall!"

That garnered laughs around the fire.

My stomach grumbled.

Cindy looked at me in shock. "How can you be hungry? You finished off the pizza and the pastry."

Kal coughed softly. "I have some eggs to go with the bacon…and some bread. We can make some breakfast sandwiches. Hopefully, that will sustain the girls until lunch."

Tom's eyes bugged out. "Lunch? When did my daughter's appetite grow to that of an Olympic athlete?"

After breakfast Cindy and Kal agreed to stay in contact, and we all headed our separate ways.

We decided to spend the rest of our stay in Florida close to home.

The next night we did most of the cleanup of our borrowed house. Our flight out of Gainesville was at nine Saturday morning. I mentioned to Cindy that the herbs that they had given Sarah wouldn't be a good idea. Not knowing if they would have the same effect on a werepanther as a werewolf, a confined airplane wasn't a great place to find out. In the end, she decided on sleeping pills. Though they put a norm out for hours, with a wereanimal's higher metabolism, they would probably only work for two to three hours, which would be about right for getting us home to Wisconsin.

When we got to the airport, the building was mostly empty. We were early and we got through security and to the gate without seeing many people.

My body started to tingle as I sat next to Sarah at the gate. People were filing in the other gates, and I was feeling boxed in. My skin started to itch. My breathing came faster. My eyes started to water. It was almost like I could feel the other people around me.

What was happening to me?

"Tom, Cindy, I need to use the facilities." They were both reading books and just nodded, barely noticing.

Searching for the nearest bathroom, I ran, bumped into a man looking for his gate and almost knocked him over. "Sorry," I mumbled and darted through the door labeled, 'Women'.

Once there, I splashed water on my face and tried to breathe. What did my mom always say, boxes, breathe, compartmentalize?

It seemed like too much. Too many people.

Someone came towards the bathroom, she was talking to a friend about freshening up her make-up.

Her heals approached, click, click, click.

Heart pounding, I ran to the last stall in the line and locked myself in.

I perched on top of the toilet trying to hide from people. *Breathe.*

This was panic. Logically, I knew this, emotionally, I was lost.

Calm down and get ahold of yourself, Jade. Breathe.

There were calls for different flights, but none of them were ours. There was a lot of time left. So many people.

I had to get a grip.

Opening my phone, I tried to distract myself. Social media. Funny memes. That took up some time, but not enough. I couldn't focus.

Text messages. I couldn't think of anything to tell Bevin or José that wasn't a security risk. There were demands about the ER, couldn't explain. That would have to wait until we were all in person.

The phone went back into my pocket. How much time had passed? Was that the call for my plane? Did I miss my flight? No, wrong carrier. Mom's breathing exercises again.

Too many people were coming in and out of the bathroom. I could hear them, feel them, practically taste them.

What was happening?

"Jade?" Who was that? So many people.

"Jade?" I glanced up.

Breathe.

"Are you in here, Jade?"

Breathe.

My eyes were closed.

"Jade, honey, are you in here?"

Cindy.

That was Cindy.

"Where are you, dear?"

There were footsteps down the aisle.

My arm moved, and I unlocked the door. It swung in.

Cindy looked at me perched on the toilet, shaking. "What's wrong?"

"Too many people." It was all I could get out. They were everywhere. I couldn't see them, but I could hear them, smell them, feel them, taste them.

Cindy grabbed my hand and pulled me off the toilet. She helped me to a water fountain and gave me something to take.

I reluctantly put it in my mouth and swallowed it with a drink of water. "What was that?"

"A sleeping pill."

"I don't know if that was a good idea." But it was too late.

She got me to a seat next to Sarah. After that, I didn't remember much.

There was Cindy helping me onto the plane. I remember some of being on the plane and starting to breathe erratically, but Cindy gave me another pill.

I vaguely remember Tom helping me into the car.

Somewhere between the airport and home I finally truly woke up.

"I'm hungry," were my first words when waking.

Sarah laughed. "Those were my first words, too, about an hour ago."

"How are you feeling otherwise?" Cindy turned to look

at me from the passenger seat.

"Fine, but those pills usually make me queasy." Breathing, I took stock of how I was feeling. "Next time give a girl some warning."

Cindy just smiled. "Couldn't help it. You were panicked and in the bathroom over an hour. We would have missed the plane if I allowed for discussion."

My mouth dropped open. Over an hour? I shook myself and got my priorities in order. "So, about that food?"

Sarah handed me a wrapped sandwich and a juice. It was in a hard-plastic container shaped like a triangle and had a gas stations logo on it. I turned it over in confusion.

Laughing, Sarah grabbed it from me. I shook the bottle of apple juice and opened it for a large gulp. Done with that, Sarah handed back the weird container with the sandwich in it, opened. The sandwich was cut in half, middle bits hanging out.

Sniffing, I smelled ham and cheese. I took a bite. Ambrosia. Okay. It didn't taste that good, but my grumbling stomach seemed to agree with my mouth that I had waited too long to eat.

Cindy watched the two of us suspiciously. "How long is this larger appetite going to last?"

The side of my mouth quirked up as I thought about Owen. "Well, think of it as now having a teenage son."

Both of Sarah's parents grumbled.

Cindy turned to Tom. "I think we should get that

membership to Costco. We need to stock up on, well, everything. Sarah is going from a light vegetarian eater to a teenage omnivore. This will take some getting used to."

"At least we can go back to having steak once a week," Tom sounded genuinely excited.

"I thought you both liked being vegetarian." Sarah sounded hurt.

"Honey, why do you think we have a weekly date night?" Cindy turned back to us.

Sarah's eyes popped. I laughed, and her parents smirked. How many times can the parents scandalize the teen?

We arrived at my house. Pulling into the driveway, my palms began to sweat. My parents were going to smell the change on me. Despite deflecting and ignoring the questions, I knew why Dayo and Kal thought I smelled weird. My question avoidance was at an official end.

As we drove up to the house, Sarah grabbed my hand. "Do you want me to come in with you?"

Gods, what a horrible idea.

"No, it's okay, I can go in alone. I'll see you in school on Tuesday."

"Are you sure? I can help explain things to your parents. Don't you think you'll need help explaining things? My parents could help, too. You're not alone."

"No. No. I'll be fine. It's fine."

"You're going to tell them, aren't you?"

"Yeah. I'll tell them." *If they can't tell on their own.*

CHAPTER 17

The door swung open smoothly and no one was waiting for me. Perfect!

Though I had kept in contact with my parents for most of the trip, I didn't tell them my exact arrival time. Thank the gods I couldn't see anyone, but I could smell that they were home. It confused me for a second how weird that was. Shaking it off, I darted towards safety. "I'm going to throw my things in my room!"

Hiding wasn't a permanent solution, or even a good one, but I needed time. Mind swirling, I needed to think and figure this out.

When I got to my room, I shut the door and dropped my bags. Nothing had changed. How had I changed so much and for such a bizarre reason, for my room to be exactly the same, it seemed wrong somehow. Filled with pent up energy, I started pacing.

As fast as it came, it left, and I collapsed on my bed. Overwhelmed, nervous, scared, and confused, I took stock of my surroundings, wondering how long this room would stay my room.

What would my parents do?

Would they kick me out?

Would they disown me?

Would the pack run me off?

Would Sarah's parents take me in?

What was I going to do?

There was a knock on my door, and I jumped. "Pumpkin, everything okay in there?"

Dad sounded worried, loving. How long would that last?

"Yeah, I'm fine. Just a long day of travel. I'm resting." *Yeah, right.*

"Can I come in?"

Breathe. "Um, not right now. Please."

"Are you okay? Was the attack worse than you told me? Should I get your mother?"

Perfect. "I'm fine, but, yeah, get Mom. I think having both of you would be better." Doing this once would be better than twice, theme of the week. I knew I was confusing him, but that was okay. I was confused, too.

Dropping an arm over my eyes, I tried to slow down everything in my body. A few minutes later, I heard them approach. My hearing had improved. My sense of smell had improved. Everything had changed.

I stood up.

When they were close, I just said, "Come in."

My dad opened the door. He took a step in and froze. I saw it, the look on his face. Shock. Anger.

He growled.

Mom's arm shot out or he may have pounced. Building up the nerve, I shifted my gaze from my dad's glowing angry eyes to her. Hers were calculating, angry, sad.

"What happened?" Dad growled, his voice more wolf than man.

"I think you know what happened." Slumping back on my bed, my face dropped into my hands. My worst fears were coming true.

"Why didn't you tell me?" His voice demanding, I heard him step closer. He was the alpha, not my dad.

Slowly I raised my head up to him, my eyes hot with unshed tears. "How? How could I tell you? You always say electronics are not safe. I had to wait until I was home…I waited."

"There was a full moon," he accused. "You're certain." His voice dropped with each word. This only happened when he was furious.

"Yes."

He turned and walked away.

A tear rolled down my cheek as I watched him retreat. I tried to control my feelings, but I was losing my dad.

My heart dropped at the thought of losing my family.

My gut clenched for the loss of my pack.

My soul died a bit for all my loss.

I tried to take in a breath to calm down, but my breathing was too ragged. My throat closed.

My mom watched Dad walk away, her face no longer angry, just sad. "Oh, honey, I am sorry this happened to you. How is Sarah?"

Choking past the blockage, I finally managed to get some air.

"She's figuring it out. She and her family are taking this better than Dad." Gazing at my hands, I had to get the next bit out. "I had to tell them about wereanimals."

She stiffened up. "What did you tell them?"

A knife in my chest. More tears burning my cheeks. The sharpness of her voice made me think somewhere in the house Dad was probably listening, too. This answer was too important to the pack.

"I didn't tell them about the pack, Mom. I know the alpha rule. I told them that I had met a werewolf in the past, and through that animal, I had learned some things. That's it. I know the rules."

Gulping, I shifted my gaze from my hands up to her.

She needed to understand. "The rules helped Sarah. The rules helped her family. It helped them start to understand. They also got us out of the hospital before anyone saw how fast she healed." I ran out of things to say.

"Can I see what you look like?" Mom asked.

"What? My injury?" My head spun from such a change in direction. My world was ending, and she wanted to see a panther bite? This wasn't what I had expected.

"No, not your injuries, silly, your animal. I have never seen a werepanther, or even a panther in real life. Also, you smell weird. Weirder than normal, that is."

"I wish people would stop telling me that."

Mom's eyes narrowed at me. "What people?"

We finally got to the bits about Dayo and Kal, about what had happened, and about the fact that they may be relocating to the area, but probably not that close, to finish up their research with Sarah's mom. She learned that they thought I smelled calm at first and weird after the bite. They said I smelled both of panther and of wolf.

"That's it. You smell of many things. You have always been the odd duckling, but now, I don't know, we'll have to have a pack meeting and warn them, and then present you. Everyone will have to get a good smell of you. You may have to be presented in both forms. I don't know." She shook her head and looked to the ceiling, as if there were answers there.

She shot me an intense alpha gaze, then softened it

with a smile. "But first, I want to see your panther. I have a few steaks in the refrigerator for once you've changed."

Mom seemed so calm, so organized. For a second, I just watched her, then I started moving towards the backyard. As I headed out, she went to the kitchen to get the food.

The backyard had privacy walls; I ducked behind one and tried to calm down. I stripped down, but thinking of Dad made it hard. Closing my eyes, I found my center of calm, but I was hurting so much.

Finally, Mom came up to me and gave me a big hug. She could smell my emotions; she could probably taste them, I was emoting so strongly.

"Don't worry so much about Dad, he will come around. You will still be our healer. He knows that deep down. Just relax." She backed away and headed to where she had left the steaks.

So, thinking about healing, I closed my eyes and relaxed. Eventually, I felt all those wrong body changes. It was faster, but not by much. It was still weird and no less uncomfortable. It hurt. Bones shifting, hair growing, body parts elongating, and a confusing moment of nothingness. And pain.

The world was different and felt cold. Why was the world cold? What were these odd smells? Shaking myself, I smelled wolf. Enemy. Bunching my muscles to pounce, I got ready to defend myself. I was stalking forward when my brain caught up with my actions, and I remembered who and what I was.

Mom, not enemy. I froze.

Full of pride, I stood up tall on my four legs. I trotted around the corner and faced my mother.

"Dear gods, you are big. You're also stunning." She approached and scratched my ears. It felt oddly wonderful. She pointed at the steaks; they smelled dead, but edible.

I ate.

"Jade, do you feel like yourself?" Mom asked.

Again, it felt weird, but I nodded.

"You still smell of wolf. It is the weirdest thing; you smell of calm, but it's changed. Before you smelled of a pine forest and chamomile tea. There is more water in your calm smell now, maybe a lake or a stream. You also smell of the pack, and of our woods. You smell of Florida, and panther. You are the oddest creature I've ever smelled."

She smiled at me. "You are rather wonderful, my daughter. We will get this all figured out. Do you want to run or are you tired?"

To answer her, I rubbed up against her legs to say I love you and turned to trot away.

CHAPTER 18

There was a blanket on me when I woke up in the treehouse the next morning, and there was a pile of clothes neatly stacked next to me.

After I'd left my mom the previous night, I'd run. For some reason, both shifts had made me want to move. It was somewhat ironic, since I'd spent my life avoiding running. Maybe it was all the shifting of the body parts needing to loosen up.

When I'd returned home, I was too tired to change so I'd leapt up into the treehouse. It had always been a safe place for me. There was an enclosed area in the back, but most of it was just an open platform surrounded by low benches. It was open to the stars. I had curled up and fallen asleep.

April in Wisconsin was cold. Covered in fur I was fine, covered in skin, brrr. Dressing, I wrapped myself in a blanket someone had thrown over me. The sunrise was beautiful and made me feel at peace. If all else sucked today, at least the start was lovely.

As cold as it was, it wasn't as cold as I was used to it being. Werepanther. Right. Okay, so I was awake, I was dressed, next I needed my phone. In my pocket. And text messages.

Sarah wanted to know if I had told my parents and how they reacted. I didn't know what to say to her. Bevin had texted. José had texted. Everyone wanted to know how I was and how Florida had been. Not knowing how I was or what to say, I turned off my phone and put it away.

Sitting in the treehouse, I just held my head and thought about my dad, who now hated me. Then there was Owen, who usually followed my dad. He would probably hate me, too. Well, I guess Brooke would win after all. And then there was Mom. She was so supportive. I smiled.

There would be a pack meeting. How would that affect my future? My smile faltered. Today was going to suck.

My stomach grumbled. Needing food, I climbed down slowly and banged my shin. Getting up and down as a panther was so much easier than as a human. I trudged across the lawn and entered the house. It was quiet.

First, coffee. While the coffee brewed, I started on

an omelet. Onions sautéing with ham, I chopped some peppers and got the eggs ready. As everything was cooking in the butter, I quickly checked the fridge…veggies, meat…cheese! I ran back to the stove and added the last ingredients before flipping out the omelet onto my plate.

Yum.

I sat at the kitchen table, eating, when my mom walked in. "Smells good. Were you outside all night?"

"Yeah, I don't know when I shifted back, but I guess I was more tired than I thought. When did you cover me up?"

Her brow furrowed. "I didn't."

Huh?

"Who, Dad?" Confused, I stared at her.

"I don't know, dear, but I'm glad you found your clothes. I left them out when you left for the woods. Waking up naked and confused has never been one of my favorite aspects of being a shifter."

"Does everyone know?" My path had always been clear, and this brought shame to the alphas of our pack. Holding my coffee, evaluating my feelings, I realized I didn't feel ashamed. I felt powerful when I was a panther, but I knew who I was supposed to be, what I was supposed to be—a werewolf. My life had been mapped out for me from the moment I splinted Owen's leg. Now my path was gone.

"No." Mom poured herself a cup of coffee with milk. "Dad and I know this story is yours to tell, not ours. We also wanted to let you tell Owen first. He shouldn't find out with the rest of the pack. He was out late with his friends, and you were asleep when he got home. He'll be up soon."

Early to Owen was about noon so I was dubious about her claim.

She cleaned up my mess in the kitchen. "We told him today was important, and that if he didn't get up by seven, he would be out of the loop. He whined, but we told him that this was from his alphas, not his parents."

I looked at the clock. Six fifty-four. Noticing my mug was empty, I decided I needed more coffee.

"Is there going to be a full pack meeting today to discuss me?" My voice came out rough and quiet, not sounding like the fierce panther I wanted to be. I hated how dejected I sounded.

"Yes." Mom grabbed my coffee mug and filled it up. "We've called the meeting for one this afternoon."

No wonder I had received texts from Bevin and José. They were probably trying to figure this out. Usually, I let them know what the meeting was about as soon as I knew one was being called.

"Isn't that early for a meeting?"

"What meeting?" Owen said from the living room. He got halfway to the kitchen, still waiting for an answer when, like Mom and Dad the night before, his eyes got wide, and he froze.

My stomach dropped. I didn't want to lose another family member. Not my brother. Not Owen.

"Do I smell a cat?" Owen asked tilting his head and looking confused. "Do we have a cat? When did we get a cat? I don't know that I've been around many cats, but that's a cat, right? Did you bring one home from Florida? Is that what the meeting is about? I vote no."

I groaned. "Do I have to tell him?"

Mom smiled at me.

Owen's need for food and coffee won out, and he came into the kitchen. To get to the food he had to pass near me. When he got within a few feet, he stopped again and just stared at me.

"Jade, did you bring home a cat from Florida? Because you *really* smell like a cat." He continued to the kitchen as I closed my eyes, hiding my nerves.

Finally, bracing myself, I stared back at him.

"You also smell more like a wolf than you did before. And calmer. And weirder. Jade, you smell really weird." His nose twitched a few times. He kind of looked like he needed to sneeze.

My head hit the table. I groaned again, louder. "Mom!"

Coffee. That was going to be my salvation to make it through the day.

Mom chuckled.

With my head still on the table, I mumbled, "Get your coffee. I'll try to explain slowly enough for you to understand."

Once he got his coffee, he took a long drink, and sat down. He grabbed for some of my food and my head snapped up. I snarled. His eyes widened, he dropped the food, and his hands shot up like I was holding a gun at him. He appeared halfway between shock and wanting to pacify me. I was normally willing to share.

"Owen," Mom said, "I'll make you something of your own. Jade has had a trying day. Let her eat."

"Day?" Owen replied. "Trying day? It's seven in the freaking morning, how can she have had a trying day? She snarled at me. Snarled? What the hay? I need more coffee."

Well, at least he felt the same way I did.

Mom made eggs, bacon, and toast for us, and I told Owen about what happened in Florida.

Laughing hard, he said, "Can't you ever go anywhere and not end up in a hospital? And I thought it was me."

"Wha—I ca—really?" I sputtered. "I tell you I turn into a black panther, and all you get out of it is that I ended up at a hospital again? That's it?"

"What did you expect? Do you want me to cheer? Pet you? Give you some catnip?"

Mom was trying hard not to laugh. It wasn't working.

He gave me an infectious smile. Quirking a half smile in response, I took another sip of coffee to brace myself and then ruined the mood. "Dad hates me."

Owen stopped laughing. He looked at my face. My eyes burned from holding back tears. His gaze swung over to Mom, whose previously laughing face had turned blank. "Really? Are you sure?"

"He smelled me, heard my story…and walked away. You know what he expected of me. I failed him."

"Can't you still be the pack's healer?" Owen asked, sliding over to touch his shoulder to mine. "Has anything changed besides the animal you shift into?"

His touch helped me to breathe.

"Not for me. I mean, I was hoping to become a wolf. I've done a lot of research on wolves."

At the word 'research,' Owen snorted.

Glaring, I continued. "I know nothing about panthers. If the pack decides I can't be in pack territory, then that's that, I'm out."

Owen's eyes grew wider as he seemed to understand my situation.

Leaning into him, I sighed. "That's what the meeting is about. Full pack meeting at one o'clock today. The pack is going to decide my fate." I hid my hands under the table so he couldn't see them shaking.

"Is it killing you that you haven't done your research yet?" Owen bumped his shoulder against mine, trying to cheer me up.

When I didn't smile, he put his arm around me. "You said Sarah is a werepanther, too?"

I nodded.

"That's cool. I mean, she's going to take one sniff of me on Tuesday and know what I am, so it's good I know about her. You told her you had run into a werewolf, so now she'll think it was me. Your story will make sense. She'll also think that this is why you weren't worried about telling Mom and Dad."

Gaping at Owen, my eyes and mouth hung a bit wider open. He was never this smart. But what he had just said was clever. It fit into what I had said in Florida so well that I didn't have to worry about the pack or any of the other werewolves being outed.

"That was actually smart." I widened my eyes in mock wonder.

"You don't have to sound so surprised," Owen said, rolling his eyes, and taking his arm back. He looked a bit hurt.

Finally relaxing a bit, I laughed and knocked my shoulder against his.

He smiled back at me.

"I knew you two could figure it out," Mom said, sounding certain. "Now we need one more member of the family on board, and then we can face the pack."

Dad came in from a side hallway. "Do you think it will be that easy?"

With the tension Dad brought to the kitchen, I needed to move. Restless, I got up to fill my and Owen's coffee mugs.

Mom, moving out of my way, stepped towards Dad. "No, I don't. But I think we're alphas and that Jade is our daughter. She still has a lot of wolf in her smell."

She took a breath as if presenting arguments to the pack. "I think she can be our healer, even if she isn't a werewolf. She can start doing more intensive work now, since we no longer need to worry about her getting bitten. Most importantly…"

Mom stopped for a second and glanced at me. She turned back to Dad and her body got very still. "I think you need to start acting like the father who has loved his daughter for fifteen years," she ended with a low snarl.

My dad gazed at me with dead eyes. I felt the weight of his disappointment. All his hopes for me dashed in one moment. He hadn't had enough time to figure this out. In a neighborhood of werewolves, time wasn't on our side—not unless I went away again. We just looked at each other, both of us understanding that everything had changed.

Finally, Dad shifted his gaze to Mom. "She'll need to go outside while we air out the house. I don't want her stench to be in here when the pack starts to arrive. Not until everyone understands what's going on." He took a deep breath. "Shower, change, go back outside to the treehouse." That last was said to me, though he was still facing Mom.

Mom let out a guttural yell and returned to cleaning the kitchen.

Dad spoke as if I hadn't been dismissed and Mom was still listening. "The meeting starts at one with a few general announcements. Then Jade will come in and tell her story at a quarter after."

He started to pace between the living room and the kitchen, thinking things over aloud. "The pack needs to know about her and Sarah. They will smell her, and they need to know that, if they aren't careful about proximity, Sarah will smell them, too. We need to decide as a pack if we want to formally introduce ourselves to Sarah and her family and make the pack known to them."

Owen gaped at this. Introducing a new family to the pack was a big decision. I was numb. Sarah was my best friend, but if I was being kicked out, then none of it mattered.

Dad continued in a flat voice. "After Jade tells her story, we're going to let the pack smell her in both her human and panther forms, to let them get their base reactions out of the way. Then she will go back outside. Finally, a vote will be made as to her future."

"What will you do with your daughter if the pack votes that she has to leave?" Mom sounded furious. Her eyes were glowing.

"We will send her to my parents. Since they're norms, they won't know the difference if she's a werepanther." Dad still sounded dead inside.

Mom's head snapped to Dad and a low growl left her. "No. We will not uproot our daughter. The pack will not do this to us or *our daughter*. If they vote her out, I am moving out of the neighborhood with her, and she will stay in the school district. Or I'll disband the pack."

She spoke with such intensity that I knew she was speaking truth.

"You would leave the pack?" Owen asked.

"No, I am the alpha. *I am the pack*," Mom spat.

"Technically," Dad said, "you don't have to live in the neighborhood to be part of the pack." He was starting to realize just how mad Mom was.

"If Mom doesn't live here, does that mean you two are separating?" Owen asked. I could smell his worry.

I wasn't sure if he was purposely poking at Dad, or genuinely asking these questions.

Neither of my parents spoke for several minutes. Dad's eyes were lowered. Mom's eyes glowed with fury.

Finally, Mom said, "If your father will not fight for Jade, then he's not the man I thought he was." And with those words she turned and left.

CHAPTER 19

Again, I sat in the treehouse. The air was chilly, so I made a nest of the blanket between the benches under the tree branches. Sitting back, I watched the clouds chase each other across the sky.

The pack had raised me; thinking about losing them made me sad.

Mom was super dominant. When she turned, I guess everyone knew she would run the pack one day. She decided to leave the Midwest for college to avoid conflict. When she was in college, she met Tilly, one of the now Floridian alphas. Instead of fighting, as dominant wolves sometimes do, they became friends.

There had been a lone wolf in the area. A lone wolf wasn't always a bad thing, but this one was attacking people. Lone wolves that start killing and tasting people can never integrate back into normal society. They become rogues. Mom and Tilly decided to take care of the rogue wolf. They would have to kill him.

One of the survivors of the attacks was River Stone, the child of some very hippie hippies—just look at the name.

At first, River had a hard time believing werewolves were real. He was like Tom and Cindy. Once he accepted the idea of werewolves and the fact that he now was one, he and Mom became inseparable.

That rogue left a few other victims alive. One of them was Rory Wall, who ended up with Tilly. They became the alpha couple in Florida.

The other victims were Clare, Janet, and Allison, a trio of friends who had been out clubbing together when they were attacked. All three came back to Wisconsin with Mom and Dad. Mom's dominance attracted other wolves to her.

Clare was José's mom and Janet was Bevin's. Both were dominant as well. Allison, my aunt, was the only submissive in the bunch. It was impressive that my mom and Tilly could take out that wolf alone considering how many dominant wolves he'd produced. And two alphas to boot.

My future depended on everyone in the pack, but the alphas and the ones ranked just beneath them held a lot of sway. My parents were split on the issue of my staying in the pack. My heart skipped at the thought. My hope was that the rest of the pack would follow Mom.

As I sat there in my nest, my mind circled, thinking about pack, family, and what would happen to me in a few hours.

Gazing at the house, I saw Owen peer out the window towards me. His eyes were sad, and I saw his shoulders rise and drop with a gusty breath. I don't know if he saw me watching him. We fought at times, but we'd always been close. We'd always had each other's backs.

Slowly raising my hand, I waved.

His head shot up and he glanced over his shoulder. Dad must have called him. He nodded and moved off.

If the meeting was called for one o'clock, then the pack members could start showing up any time after twelve-thirty. It was such a weird time. Usually, a meeting was either called for late morning, and brunch was served, or it was called for mid- to late-afternoon and then dinner was served halfway through.

By calling the meeting for one o'clock, my parents were making a point to tell the pack that they should not show up early. They were also saying that food might not be part of the deal.

It was a cold start to a pack meeting.

It guaranteed that everyone would be a bit off. It would also ensure that I didn't have time to talk to Bevin and José. They would be in the basement with the kiddos.

That was probably the biggest reason for all of this. My dad wanted me isolated. I wondered if he knew how hard this was for me and how much it hurt.

I wondered if he even cared.

CHAPTER 20

Mom brought me lunch, a few boxes of takeout Chinese food and some soda. My belly grumbled as I wolfed it down to counter all the coffee I'd had since breakfast.

Between bites I asked Mom, "Would you really move out with me?"

"Yes."

Such a simple answer to such a complex, messed-up situation.

"It would complicate so many lives. Mom, I'm not worth it."

She smiled at me sadly. "Yes, love, you are."

Shoulders slumping, I shook my head. "Don't make this decision. I could probably stay with Sarah and her family. That wouldn't mess up the pack, the family."

Imagining how this would affect the pack, Owen, even hurt Dad, my mouth ran off without me. In the end, it was just me. There were so many other people to think about.

She took my food, put it aside, and grabbed my hands. She looked into my eyes as if trying to see something. "You are always so worried about everyone else. Do you ever worry about you, Jade?"

My brows came together. I was confused.

"I didn't think so," she continued with a sigh. "You have to understand that you're worth it, too. You've always been worth it. I'll think about what you've said if you promise me, you'll think about what I've said."

Touch was a new comfort to me. Intrigued and a bit sad about the whole situation, I dropped my focus down to our hands. After a few seconds I steeled myself and met her gaze. Her eyes were moist. She was holding in a world of emotions. They were bombarding me. "I'll try."

"I am sorry you are all alone out here. Have you been texting with your friends?"

Swallowing past the lump in my throat, I shook my head and quietly said, "No."

Her eyes widened in surprise.

"I promised Sarah we'd tell Bevin and José together, and what could I tell Sarah about all of this?" I waved my hands at the house.

She nodded in understanding and gave me a quick hug.

Another bite of beef and broccoli and a swallow of soda. "Sarah doesn't know about any of us. I can't tell her about werewolves, I can't tell her about the pack, and I can't tell her that I may be getting kicked out because of a group decision...It's not even a parental decision." I gulped in air, trying to calm myself.

My voice dropped to a whisper. "It would be too hard to explain, I wouldn't even know where to start. It's too much."

"I know, love," she rubbed my arm, "but hopefully after this meeting it will get easier. You've kept the secret of werewolves your whole life, but now you have a secret you can share with Sarah."

Sadly, I gave her a smile, then my phone buzzed.

Grabbing it, I checked the display, and sighed. "She keeps texting. I just don't know what to tell her." Frustrated, I opened my hand, dropping the phone to the blanket. "I know she's worried."

Mom gave me a big hug. "I'll come out and get you when it's time." One more big hug and she left me to finish eating.

And so, once again, I was alone, isolated, and left with my mind spinning.

After a while, I heard cars pull up out front. I watched through the windows as pack members come into the house, but no one saw me. No one expected anyone to be in the treehouse, so no one was looking. The house was obviously aired out since no one seemed confused by my werepanther scent.

Maybe they had cooked bacon.

I felt my phone buzz and saw a few texts from Bevin and José.

Chica, where are you? Why aren't you in the basement? José demanded.

Bevin was not much better. I don't know why I'm trying, you haven't responded to my last million texts, but really Jade, where are you?

Flopping on my back, the sky was so open and blue. Too bad I couldn't just fly away. This was too much. I sat back up. Grabbing my phone, I had to tell them something before they started searching.

I started a group text. Don't worry. I'm in the backyard doing stuff for parents. Explain later.

OMG, you're alive!! Bevin's reply was almost instant. It made me smile.

Yeah, I've been busy. I'll fill you in soon. TTYL.

That wasn't good enough for José. That's it. You've been ghosting us for days, and that's it??? Chica!

The more I text now, the longer it will take. BUSY. No worries, k?

```
Fine.
Fine.
```

What a lie. Worry was all I had.

How ironic. I lived in a pack where Bevin being transgender was accepted, José being gay was accepted, but my being a werepanther? Egads, never. There was always a new concept that one's parents needed to cross to be more open-minded and accepting.

Should I have started with telling them I was a lesbian?

After everyone had arrived at the house, and I knew I didn't have long to wait. Standing up, I cleared everything from the treehouse, throwing out the boxes, and stacking the coffee mug and fork by the back door. The base of the structure made a great place to stretch—I was stiff from sitting so long. Mom found me hanging, stretching out my back.

"We're ready for you."

My heart sped up. Was I ready?

"None of that, hon, stay calm. You'll be in a room full of people who can hear and feel your heartrate. Your anxiety will only make things worse. Calm, you know how to do it. We've been practicing this for years. Now it's go-time."

My mouth dropped open as I gaped at her, disbelieving for a minute. And then I started the breathing exercise to slow down my heart.

"Better. Stay in that mind space. It's time to face the wolves."

Did she just say that? I glared at her and then giggled.

The meeting room was like a private den, or second

living room. It was secluded, with extra couches and comfy seating. The floor was slightly slanted like in a theater so that people in the back could more easily see the front. There were bean bag chairs if people wanted to sit on the floor and tables for drinks or writing pads. Just because this was a meeting room, didn't mean people couldn't be comfortable.

The door was set into the corner of a side wall and opened near the front. That way, when you walked in, you were walking onto the "stage." There was another door in the back of the room that exited into a hallway with a bathroom. This hallway led back to the main part of the house. If someone needed to leave the meeting, they didn't have to walk across the stage. They could use the door in the back.

We joined the meeting through the door at the front of the room. The first thing I saw was a divider wall set up on the far side of the stage. I knew they wanted me to shift, but right here? On stage?

When I walked in, everyone turned towards me. A shiver flowed through me as I imagined the information they'd been given. The wave of reaction as they caught my scent could be tracked. One by one, they froze for a few seconds. Then they became confused. There were mumbles.

"Is that a cat?"

"What's going on?"

"Wow."

"Why does Jade smell weird?" Uncle Jackson demanded,

coming up to sniff me, brows furrowing. He loomed over me, his scent invading me. It wasn't unpleasant. He and Mom always smelled safe, but now there was a layer of bafflement.

I groaned.

Mom laughed, entering behind me. "Jackson, unhand my daughter."

Dad's face hardened.

Aunt Allison seemed oddly excited. Eyes bright. She followed my uncle up and gave me a hug. Hugging her back, I relaxed.

"I don't know what's going on, but I'll always love you dear," she whispered.

She grabbed my uncle's hand and dragged him back to their seats.

Owen flashed me a supportive grin.

"What have you told them?" I asked Dad darting glances between him and the rest of the room.

"Nothing," he said.

"Nothing?" Shock almost knocked me on my butt.

His eyes softened. "We were going over some basic pack business. Your story is yours to tell."

He sounded less angry, almost like my dad again.

He turned to the room. "Jade will now tell you her story. Please stay in your seats until the end." He said this last to my aunt and uncle.

Dumbfounded, I searched my parents faces and they both smiled encouragingly…both of them.

It took a second to shift my attention to the pack, these people who had been my family my whole life, and from them I saw confusion. They no longer felt like family.

"Um, hi." Darn it, I sounded soft and scared. Not good in front of a pack of werewolves.

Breathe.

Okay. Standing taller, I started again. "Hi, everyone. As you know, I went to Florida over spring break. While I was down there, I was bitten by a panther, a black panther. A werepanther."

Everyone looked at me in a strange way, like I was speaking a foreign language. We all knew there were werewolves, but any other type of shapeshifter had to be a myth. Werepanthers sounded like a crazy joke, even to me. Some people started to laugh, as if they thought I was joking. Others started to scowl.

"I know this sounds sensational," I said in a rush, needing to get through this, "but they have werepanthers in Africa, apparently. A lot of them. One of them relocated to Florida. When his area in Africa became overpopulated by werepanthers. He chose Florida because there are panthers there."

My chest hurt as I ran out of air. *Slow down. Take control.*

There were so many wolves in the room. They were family, but something about their smell was off. I felt weird, like I was surrounded by foe. Before my nerves took over, I started to prowl around the stage.

"He married and had a daughter, who is also a werepanther. Sarah's family and I were out camping with another family. They have a three-year-old who wandered off in the middle of the night. I went after him."

Family. Pack is family. I forced myself to stop moving. "I saw the panther and thought the little boy was about to get hurt, maybe even killed. I tried to protect him. The panther didn't attack. Apparently even to werepanthers I smell calm?"

That last was a question. I wasn't sure about this last part, but apparently the pack was. Several people nodded. That was good. "A second werepanther thought I was the kid's mom and was going to attack the first werepanther to protect the kid…my kid…and he bit me on the thigh. My friend Sarah saw and started to scream. The panther attacked her next, scratching and biting her."

"Two panthers and only one attacked?" T.J. questioned with a sneer. "Why wouldn't they help each other out?" His disbelief hurt.

"Not now, T.J.," Mom reminded him. The Alpha, with a capital 'a', shot him down.

Staring at him, my soul hurt. Then my gaze shifted to Aunt Allison who was radiating love and continued peace. "One of the adults caught up with us and scared off the panthers. I bandaged Sarah's leg and stitched up her arm. Then we waited for the ambulances to arrive."

Comments filled the room.

"Of course, you did," said Fred, Bevin's dad.

"Can't you travel without ending up in the ER?" asked Clare, José's mom.

"Do you do this to help yourself learn about doctors and hospitals?" asked Alejandro.

"I always thought Owen was the accident prone one," joked Aunt Allison.

"Hey. I resemble that," said Owen, leaping up to give a bow.

Laughter broke the tension in the room.

"Did you have to bandage yourself, too?" asked Tanner, Dad's right-hand man.

My gaze shifted to him. I tried to be serious, but then I started to laugh. "Yes."

"Okay." Mom got up and came to me. "I want Jade to walk around all of you so you can really get a good scent memory of her." She gave me a push toward the assembled pack members.

Clare pulled me in for a deep smell. "Is that what a panther smells like?"

"I think so," said Andy, Chris's partner. They were both submissive wolves.

"Get over here," said Aunt Allison. "I knew I recognized that smell. I love the big cat area of the zoo and spend a lot of time there during the workday. Yes, that is definitely panther scent. Panther...also wolf...and pine trees...and the forest...oceans...and calm?"

Uncle Jackson grabbed my arm for another smell.

"How can anyone smell like an emotion? I mean, I can smell emotions people feel, but you just smell like 'calm'."

Aunt Allison shook her head and chuckled. "Jade, next time I have a bad day, can I come and just sniff you? Or when I have a crazy animal at the zoo, can I call you in? You are like sniffing chamomile."

I relaxed as I returned her smile. My aunt was so cool. How many wolves could work at a zoo?

As I passed by T.J., his hand flashed out and grabbed my wrist. He was oozing so much disdain I just wanted to recoil, but this was T.J., my brother. My whole being yearned for support from him. His voice slipped out, invading my body. "I don't know what happened to you, but this changes everything."

My heart stopped, and I just stared.

After a minute Owen came over and put his arm around me whispering in my ear, "Ignore him, sis. You *are* still you."

Pulling away, I turned from a person who may have no longer been my family.

Returning to the stage, almost everyone still seemed weirded out, but the room felt much calmer to me. I think Aunt Allison's acceptance helped the most.

Mom turned to the room, taking control. "We are now going to have Jade shift so you can meet her in that form."

Several people were fidgeting, uncomfortable. Chris started to stand and then sat down. He gazed around the room then his eyes landed on Mom. "Can I ask why we're doing this?"

"We have to decide what to do about a non-wolf wereanimal in pack territory," answered Dad.

Everyone in the room stopped fidgeting and shifted their attention from Mom to Dad.

Clare finally broke the silence, face reddening, she growled, "What do you mean, decide? Jade is your daughter. She is family and she is pack. What decision is there left to make?"

Dad started pacing on stage. "It isn't that simple. We all love Jade. I love her; but you haven't seen her as a panther, yet."

"Have you?" asked Clare. Waves of ire came off her, filling the room. The people around her were starting to shift in agitation.

"No, but Hazel has. I'll admit, I didn't take the news well." He turned to me. "No matter how this concludes, you will always be my daughter, and I love you, pumpkin."

Heart beating loudly, I almost missed what he said next.

"When Jade shifts, your animals will react to what they see and that will tell us what we need to know. As humans, we all love Jade, but as wolves, do we love her enough to accept her as a panther? If the answer is no, then this meeting will be much longer because things around here will have to change."

Andy grabbed Chris's hand. The two of them stared at each other, then up at Dad. "If the answer is no, what will happen to your daughter? Will you kick her out? What about our next healer?"

What? Could I be losing my position, too?

"No." My voice shot out of me before I knew I was speaking. "Please, no. I want to be the pack's healer. Please don't tell me I've lost that, too."

Ignoring me, Dad continued, "That will be part of the discussion. We must figure out how we feel after our wolves get their eyes and nose on a panther in their den. We also have to discuss what to do about Sarah being a werepanther in our territory and whether we want to invite her family into the circle of information about werewolves and our pack."

"Jade didn't tell her all that already?" asked Tanner.

Everyone looked at me. "No." The offense I felt came out clearly in that one word. "I told Sarah and her family that I had run into a werewolf in my past, but I didn't say anything about any of you, specifically. I told her it wasn't my place to say who. I explained that the secret was too important to ever tell anything about anyone else."

Facing Owen, I gave him a smile. "Owen told me that he would tell Sarah he was the wolf I was referring to so that we can keep the pack a secret. That is, until she runs into one of you. Her nose is really good. As good as a wolf's," I teased.

"Yeah, right." T.J. got up and moved towards his sister, Candice, and sat down. The two of them started to whisper together.

Hurt all over again by his sudden animosity towards me, I forced my gaze to Owen, who shrugged in confusion.

I thought I heard a few other doubters about Sarah's sense of smell, but I wasn't sure who made the comments.

Likewise, I didn't understand why so many in the room were surprised that I had kept the pack a secret. All of us knew the rules. None of us would tell on purpose. It was alpha law.

"Okay," Dad said. "Jade, it's time."

Nervous, I knew I had to do this.

Breathe in through the nose, out through the mouth. Mantra set.

I went behind the wall.

Mom and Dad joined the others in the audience so that no one was in view.

Stripping, I got down on my hands and knees, let my head hang down between my arms, and softly whispered my made-up mantra. *In through my nose, out through my mouth, slow calming breaths.*

Breath set.

Next, relax.

Bigger hurdle, forget the room of wolves behind the wall. Not wolves, I told myself. Family. Room with *my family*.

And then it happened. Bones, muscles, pain, hair. Pain. Pain. Pain.

Everything was different.

Where was I?

Who was I?

Wolves—the enemy—all around me. Barely enough cover. Hunkering down, I was ready to pounce. Sniffing, I tried to figure out how many enemies I had. Could I take them all on? What would be the best angle of attack? I stalked forward.

Calculations. There were too many of them.

And then the scent of family penetrated the fog of my fear and aggression. Mom. Owen. Dad. Aunt Allison. Pack.

My whole body shook, and my thoughts cleared. Pack meeting room, not the wild, and I was surrounded by family. Rising from my attack position, I shook my body and slowly padded out from behind the partition.

The first person I saw was Mom. Her eyes softened with love as she smiled at me in pride. I stared at her for a full minute, knowing that this pause gave everyone else time to figure me out without me having to see their reactions.

I let my other senses, mainly scent, emotion, and hearing, roam the room, and what I perceived was fear, disgust, and hate. The taste of their emotions overwhelmed me. They were invading me. They were so thick. Finally, I looked around at their faces. It only took half the room before I knew the outcome. It made me shiver. It made me want to cry.

They weren't going to accept me.

It was all too much.

I had to escape.

I turned and ran.

The door handles in the house were handles that push down to open, perfect for animal form. Within a heartbeat, I was out of the room and running for the front door.

There were yells for me to stop, but I couldn't take the rejection. Once outside, I ran through the backyard, into the woods, and up a tree. Being black, I disappeared.

Where would I go now? Sarah's? I had to get to Sarah's house. She would understand. She would help.

"Jade?" That was Mom. I could hear her yelling from the front door.

"Where did she go?" Dad.

Their voices were so clear as a werepanther, even though they were still in the front of the house, and I was in the back.

The path between my house and Sarah's was mostly wooded areas, parks and backyards without anyone seeing me. When I needed to cross streets, I made sure there weren't any people around. It was a Sunday afternoon and cold, so people were inside. Once I arrived in Sarah's backyard, I pawed at the back door with my claws sheathed and then laid down on the lawn to wait.

Sarah's mom answered the door.

She screamed.

CHAPTER 21

Sarah came pounding from somewhere inside the house. "Jade? Oh, my god. Can I bring her to my room, Mom? If she shifts back, I don't want her out here." Sarah put her arms around me in a hug.

Her mom's eyes were huge, and her hands were shaking. She didn't answer.

Tom came up a few seconds after Sarah and wrapped his arms around his wife's waist. He put his head on her shoulder. He seemed much calmer than his wife. "That makes sense. Jade, please be careful."

I padded to Sarah's room as carefully as I could. When

I got there, I collapsed on her floor.

Sarah sat on her bed and eyed me. "What can I do to help you? Are you okay? You haven't been texting me. You smell more like a wolf than you did in Florida." She blew out a breath and smelled confused at her own comment. "I wish you could answer me."

Collapsed on her floor with my head in my crossed paws, I looked up at her. As much as I knew I should shift back, I didn't know how to approach her questions. Staying a panther seemed easier. This wasn't fair, but nothing about the day had been fair.

Sarah's mom approached the bedroom. She knocked then spoke through the door. "Sarah, Jade's parents are on the phone. They say she ran off and want to know if she's here. Have you seen or heard from her?"

Wow, Sarah's mom was being awesome. She was giving me time before telling my parents where I was.

My eyes widened in fear. Giving Sarah a pleading look, I tried to convey I didn't want to deal with my parents yet.

"No, Mom. I've been texting her since last night, but she hasn't answered any of my questions." The frustration in Sarah's voice was real. Her answer was practically a growl, and she was glaring at me. She sighed as if she wanted to yell more but realized now wasn't the time.

A few minutes later, Sarah's mom stuck her head in the room. She seemed much calmer. She glanced over to me. "I'm not going to cover for you forever, but you can have a bit more time. Please shift back soon. I don't know what happened, but I can guess. I really hope my guess is wrong. Your parents sounded really worried about you, Jade. They didn't sound mad."

Staring up at her, I realized if I were human, I would've been crying. Finally, I nodded, and she left.

Sarah watched me expectantly. Sighing, I knew I couldn't put it off any longer. I had to change. Closing my eyes, I focused on the shift. It hurt as much shifting back.

Sarah handed me some clothes once I was human again. After I dressed, she gave me a huge hug.

She let me cry.

She didn't expect me to talk. She just held me and let me release as much grief and sorrow as I could.

When I calmed down, she met my gaze and stated matter-of-factly, "Food."

We left her room to raid the kitchen. Her parents joined us. Having just returned from Florida there wasn't much, but we made some sandwiches and they tasted great.

After we ate, Sarah and her parents just sat there watching me, waiting for an explanation. I could tell they all wanted to know what had happened, but they didn't want to push.

Sarah's phone rang. She looked at the display and took the call. "Yeah... Hi, Bevin... Huh, let me ask."

She had been listening to Bevin for a few minutes. She held out her phone to me, somehow making the motion an accusation. "Bevin is at Jade's house."

They all glanced at me. I sighed again. This was getting complicated.

Sarah turned to her parents. "He wants to know if we could all come over. He says Jade's family has something they want to discuss with us. He thinks Jade is here, and Jade should come, too. He doesn't know why Jade ran away, no one tells the kids anything — his words not mine — but he wants this resolved before someone's head explodes."

That made me chuckle. Classic Bevin.

Sarah glared at me and covered the mouthpiece of the phone. She lowered her voice. "Do you know what he's talking about? Is José there, too?"

"You made me promise not to tell them about us without you being there… Yeah, José is there, too."

Guilt. There were pack rules about outsiders, but I felt bad that she was the only one of my friend group who wasn't at my house. She was the only one out of the loop.

My head dropped to the table. "We should probably go to my house. It will clear a lot of things up."

Lifting my head as if facing a firing squad, I added, "It'll also explain a lot of my secrets, if this is about what I think it's about."

Rubbing my temples, my gut clenched thinking about what I'd felt at the pack meeting. Going home was not what I had in mind. The disgust and the hate still filled a part of me. At the same time, I knew it was safer if Sarah and her family knew the full story. A story I couldn't tell without the alpha's permission.

We all did our part, gathering the dishes to put in the sink. "I don't know why Mom didn't call personally, but maybe she's still in the meeting. Although maybe that was why she called before. Maybe she thought Bevin would get through where she didn't."

The last had been said softly, in a whisper. Sarah could hear me, but I wasn't sure if her parents could. Tom, who had been helping with the cleaning, stopped. "What meeting?" My head swung to him, and I gave him a half-feral glance. I guess he had heard me after all.

Getting up, Cindy got ready to leave. "Tell Bevin we will come."

Sarah removed her hand from the phone's mouthpiece. "Hi, Bevin, we'll come. When should we get there… Okay…Yep…Nope…Okay…See you."

Sarah ended the call. We all just stared at her questioningly. "He said to get there as soon as we could. He asked if we'd eaten. He asked if I knew where Jade was. He asked me to stop lying. That's it." Shaking my head, I snorted. If anyone knew Sarah and me, it was Bevin.

We gathered up what we had to gather. For me, that would be exactly nothing. We piled into the car and were off.

Not ready to go back, I had a big decision to make: did I want to go in with them or not?

A block from the house, I told Sarah's family to drop

me off. "I'll be in the treehouse. You can tell my mom."

Slipping through the woods to the back of my house, I probably made it there before Sarah and her parents got to the front door. I climbed into the treehouse.

The treehouse, my safe place. For a minute or two I could mentally lick my wounds.

Mom came out to join me.

"What happened?" She really didn't have to explain what she was talking about.

"I saw you and I knew I had your support, so I just let your love flow through me as the rest of the pack got their fill." Tears filled my eyes. I hated that my emotions made me do that.

"I started observing the room. I could see and feel the hate, and disgust, and anger. I didn't even get halfway. It was too much, Mom. I just…it was too much rejection. I had to leave. I could see how the pack would vote and couldn't handle the people I love the most telling me I wasn't wanted."

"So, you left before they could tell you to leave?"

"Yeah. Seemed safer. Less hurtful. Easier. I just couldn't take their rejection. Not from my family."

"I don't know what you saw, or what you thought you saw, but most of what you saw was shock. I've told you, honey, you're beautiful in your panther form." She gave me a hug.

In her embrace, I started to get my emotions under control.

She pulled back and looked me in the eyes. "Right now,

Dad is talking with Sarah's parents, meeting them for the first time. Not the first time but paying attention for the first time. Sarah's eyes are a bit wild. I think you were right about her sense of smell. I think it would be best if you were there for her right now."

She was right. Sarah needed me. I was being selfish not being in there for her.

We both climbed down. "Can José and Bevin join the meeting this time? I really want them to be part of this."

"I think later is best. They're with the kiddos, and there isn't anyone else who can be with them right now. I want all the adults to be in on this discussion. I want everyone, even the non-wolf pack members, to recognize each other. It's just that important. Sarah and her family are going to be learning a lot today. They aren't pack, but maybe one day they will be."

Mom sounded slightly upset, but I didn't think it was directed at me.

We entered the house, and I immediately gave Sarah a hug. "Don't worry, just breathe."

"But danger, wolves, oh, my God, Jade, what is going on?" Her voice was quiet, for now, but she looked really spooked. The whites showed around her eyes, and she was shaking. Guilt filled me and I knew why Mom had wanted me here.

Sarah's anxiety was spreading to her parents.

My decision to abandon them to the wolves, quite

literally, had been beyond selfish. Finding my center, I tried to do what I could to calm her.

Mom spoke to everyone. "Let's get to the meeting room."

Squeezing her, I kept my arm around Sarah's waist, and tried to help pacify her. We headed to the meeting room. The closer we got, the stronger the scent of wolf was, and the slower Sarah walked.

I hugged her encouragingly. "Don't worry, Sarah, it will be okay. Everyone here is safe, I promise. It will be okay. Breathe through your mouth. It will help."

Grabbing Sarah's hand, Cindy looked at me, concerned. "What's wrong with her?"

Mom smiled warmly at Cindy, guiding her towards the door. "We will explain everything. Just give us a couple of minutes."

When we entered the room, everyone was still there, milling about and talking. It got quiet as everyone headed back to their seats. Glancing around, I didn't know if they were still my pack, still my family, or if they were now something different and new. It made me sad.

Knowing they could all sense my emotions didn't matter, I couldn't stop feeling.

Owen waved from a big couch he had to himself. "Sarah, Jade, come sit by me."

Sarah relaxed a little when she recognized a face in the crowd. Behind the couch was an empty loveseat that Sarah's parents took.

Dad took the stage. "Welcome. First things first. Jade, I wish you hadn't run. I'm sorry if we scared you off. None of us meant for that to happen. I don't know what you saw, but we'll deal with that later, maybe on a one-on-one basis. I, for one, thought that your panther form was stunning."

Around the room there were sounds of agreement. I was astonished by what my dad said. Stunning? Could I keep my dad, even if I was a panther?

"Holy crap, Jade." Sarah thought she was being quiet but didn't realize that wereanimals had excellent hearing. "You told all of these people? What happened to not telling anyone?"

I was torn between amusement and chastisement. She would understand soon enough.

My dad smiled down at her. "That's an excellent question."

Sarah's eyes shot forward and I could hear her heart rate jump. *Wow.*

There were sounds of confusion from the norms in the room who hadn't heard Sarah, including her parents.

My dad shifted his gaze from Sarah to her parents. "Sarah, Tom, Cindy, everyone in this room is part of my pack. We are werewolves."

Sarah's hands fell to her lap, and when I looked at her, her jaw had dropped. Checking over my shoulder, Tom and Cindy's eyes were huge. I knew that if I could smell their fear, so could most of the others in the room.

My dad continued, ignoring their emotions. "Hazel

and I are the alphas of the pack. Tanner is next in line, and then Clare, José's mom. I could go down the line, but I think you get the idea. All the kids in the basement belong to the pack."

Sarah's eyes widened and she looked between Dad and Aunt Allison. "Is Annie a werewolf?" Annie, Dillan's older sister used to babysit Sarah.

My mom turned and smiled warmly at Sarah. She knew the connection. "No, she never changed naturally, and we don't force people to change if they don't want to. She decided it wasn't for her. She went off to college instead."

"One of the biggest rules we have is secrecy. The kiddos in the basement, down to the youngest, know never to tell anyone about the pack. Jade wasn't allowed to tell you about the pack, even after you were changed. That's Alpha law number one."

Desperately, I looked at Sarah to see if she understood why I had been so secretive. She was transfixed by what was happening on stage.

"Hazel and I are the alphas. We are also Jade's parents. When we learned about what happened in Florida, we knew we had to let the pack know about Jade, but we also had to let them know about you." Dad pointed to Sarah.

Sarah's eyes were huge. She sank down into her seat as if she didn't want the attention. She was in a room full of strangers who smelled and felt like the enemy. I knew the feeling. They were my family and even I was still fighting with my panther side. I put an arm around her. Owen leaned in to give her his support by taking her hand.

Dad, for his part, gave her a quirky smile. "Your nose is too good. We either had to be excessively cautious around you or introduce ourselves to you formally. We chose the latter."

Cindy tapped me on the shoulder to get my attention. "You were brought up knowing about werewolves?" She still sounded scared, but she seemed determined to get things figured out.

Shrugging, I gave her a small smile. "Yeah. I have seen people turning into werewolves my whole life. It's never been that big of a deal to me."

Her voice was still shaky. "Has everyone here been brought up this way?"

"No." Tyler spoke up first. "My wife and I were both attacked only three years ago by a rogue wolf. My wife died. My daughter is downstairs. Thankfully, she didn't get bitten."

After the attack, my mom and dad had approached Tyler to see if he was changed. When they knew he was a werewolf, they invited him to join the pack and he agreed. He had too many bad memories where he had been living and having a pack to help out made being a single dad easier. He worked in IT. My dad offered him a job right away, so the move was seamless.

Cindy started to tear up. "I'm so sorry about your wife."

Tom stared at me. "Why did you end up on our doorstep if you have such an understanding…family? Pack?" He seemed to be trying to steer the conversation back on track.

Shivering at the memory, I tried to explain. "I'm not a wolf, and panthers and wolves don't necessarily mesh. I was introducing my panther to the pack. I shifted behind that wall," I pointed, "and came out. When I took in my surroundings, my..." I didn't know if I should say family or pack, so I just waved my arm around randomly and continued, "...searched the faces, all I saw was hate and fear. I figured I should leave before they were forced to kick me out."

The shock that went through the audience was palpable. I could taste it, and I heard Sarah sneeze with the intensity of it.

"Oh, honey," Clare exclaimed.

"No," came Fred's deeper voice.

Tanner jumped up. "It wasn't like that." He recovered himself and sat back down.

"What?"

"But..."

Owen took my hand and squeezed it. "I told them you misread everyone. As soon as you left, I looked around and guessed what you must have seen. They said I was young and didn't know what I was talking about."

He got off the couch and knelt in front of me. "You just took in the wrong half. You should have started with me, Chris, Andy, and Allison. I think Allison is ready to adopt you. Chris and Andy have been trying to figure out how to adopt a cat, and you're my sis. Also, Dad's eyes were filled with pride. Get it? Panther, pride, heh." Of course, he would laugh at his own joke.

Huffing out a small laugh, I smiled with him.

He gave me a quick hug and sat back on the couch on the other side of Sarah.

The support from Chris and Andy shouldn't have come as any surprise. Chris had been a member of the pack for years. He had been married and had a daughter, Chloe. His wife, Connie, started cheating on him, probably because he really wasn't interested in her, or any woman really. She never even learned that he was a natural werewolf.

They divorced, and Connie said that Chris could have full custody because, if he was gay, then their daughter would probably turn out to be a freak just like him, and she wanted no part of it. Now who was the monster?

When Chris met Andy, it was love at first sight. Andy was very perceptive and quickly figured out about the werewolf side of Chris. He asked if he could join the pack. There was a pack meeting—much like what we were doing right now—and the pack decided this would be acceptable. Usually, the change wasn't allowed in anyone over the age of twenty-two or so. However, they relented for Chris, one of our submissives.

Submissive werewolves were the heart of the pack. Often packs will do more to keep them happy because their happiness spreads to the rest of the pack. They monitor the emotions of everyone and keep the pack healthy.

I searched the room. Everyone was staring at me. This time I didn't see hate. This time I saw concern and love. I saw family.

Tanner stood and paced the room. "I'm sorry if we scared you off. My wolf saw you as a major fighter. I don't know if you know how terrifying it is to see a black panther for the first time. You are beautiful, but terrifying."

Tanner was the one I figured would be the most against a werepanther joining the pack.

There were nods from many of the others around him.

He continued pacing. "My wolf was trying to decide if there was any way to take you down. The look you saw was my inner fight. I had to let my wolf know that we didn't need to take you down, that you were Jade, that you were pack, and that you were safe."

He ended his pacing near me, he knelt in front of me, took my hands, and stared in my eyes. "It wasn't hate for you. It was hate for my own insecurity about you. You know you're like a daughter to me."

I was shocked. He shot up and headed back to his side of the room.

"That pretty much sums it up for me, as well," explained Clare. "Your panther is dominant. I can feel it now, but not as much as when you are in panther form. When you're human, you have so much wolf and calm mixed in, you're more confusing than anything else. Now, that lady next to you, Ms. Sarah, she puts all of us to shame. Did she heal in, like, an hour? She is as dominant as your mother. She needs to learn how to put up shields."

Mom chuckled.

Sarah gaped.

"So, you aren't sending me away?" I asked.

Chris shot up. "Not if we have any say. We may be bottom of the lineup, but we know the heart of the pack, and that includes you."

Dad smiled. "No, you're staying. You are family. We'll have another meeting about if our pack will include you and Sarah in your panther forms on full moon nights if she wants to run with us. Sarah has always been part of your pack, one of your closest friends. The choice about you will also have to include her."

He came over and gave me a hug. Something inside finally clicked into place.

He then returned to the front of the room and addressed Sarah's parents. "You now know about us. If you want to be part of the pack, you will have to learn the rules, agree to what it means to have alphas. The pack still needs to have a final closed-door meeting. That being said…do either of you cook?" Dad ended hopefully.

Everyone in the room laughed at just how hopeful he sounded, even Sarah and her parents.

Allison started to gather her stuff. "Panthers are usually pretty solitary, but I think you two could handle being in a pack, if it were the right one."

Mom stood and took the stage to wrap up the meeting. "I also think we need to schedule those of you who were really struggling to come over next weekend and have you and Jade shift together, maybe with Allison present, so that everyone can acclimate before the next full moon."

She moved from the center of the stage over to where we were sitting. "Sarah, if you want to join us then you will be welcome as well. I know you've just been given a lot of information, so take some time to think it over before you decide."

The meeting broke up. Cindy and Tom stayed to talk with the adults. Tanner, Clare, and Allison went to cook. Sarah, Owen, and I made a beeline to the basement.

"Okay, Jade, what the hell have you not been telling us? You have too many secrets," José sulked.

Sarah put on a valley girl accent. "This is, like, so cool. For once, I'm not the one in the dark."

"I can't believe you're here, and that you were at a…" Bevin's voice dropped for the last word to a whisper, "meeting."

Owen laughed. "She was in the pack's meeting room for an hour, with her parents, and you still aren't sure if you can say the word 'pack.' You are the most paranoid person I know, Bevin. Say it with me, 'pack.' It's okay, 'paaack.'"

Trying not to smile, Bevin punched him in the shoulder.

Owen laughed harder. He was having way too much

fun. Compared to me, he'd had fewer emotional ups and downs. He'd learned about me right away. He'd supported me quickly. He'd had confidence in the pack accepting me right away. He was simply having fun at this point.

Before I could answer, Allison came downstairs. "Jade, I know you're tired, but sometime this week could you and Sarah come over to my place? I would really like to do a full checkup on the two of you in both forms."

"Both forms?!" Bevin and José bellowed, almost in unison. It was cute, although completely unfortunate in timing.

Allison blushed with embarrassment and started stammering. "I'm so sorry. I should have thought before coming down. I didn't give you enough time."

"It is alright, Auntie." In my peripheral, I saw Sarah. Her eyes were twinkling. She was ready to bust out laughing. She nodded in agreement. "I'll text you when we can stop by your work."

Allison skipped back upstairs, presumably to continue cooking.

Slumping, I leaned on Bevin. "Okay, Sarah, I've had to do this way too many times. I've had to explain it to everyone. I've had to take crap from everyone, I think it's your turn to explain."

Deciding standing was too much, I crashed on a couch to listen as she explained about our trip to Florida and our run-in with Dayo and Kal during our camping trip. She went on to explain my lack of communication and how I showed up at her doorstep this afternoon.

Owen piped in with what he knew from the meeting—both parts—and what our parents had put me through. In the end, the full story came out. I didn't have to say a word. José and Bevin were sitting on either side of me, giving me all the comfort they could.

Owen started to laugh at the end of the story. "Look, José, you now have the two cats you always wanted."

Sarah and I glared at him, even though I secretly thought it was hilarious.

Bevin gazed at me with absolute seriousness. "Just one question. Jade, can't you ever travel anywhere without ending up in a hospital?"

I hit him with a pillow.

CHAPTER 22

Tuesday. School. Had it really only been a week?

It was warm for Wisconsin, forty-six degrees, a veritable heat wave. Compared with Florida, though, it was freezing.

Being a werepanther, the effects of temperature were muted for me. The cold didn't seem as bitter as it used to. I wore jeans, a t-shirt, and a zippy sweatshirt that read, "It's more fun in Gainesville."

It felt wonderful not to be bundled in so many layers. My arms actually went down. Sarah and I met in the usual place.

"Did your parents decide?"

Sarah's head dropped back as she searched the clouds, then she soldiered on. "Yes, and then no, and then yes. It keeps going back and forth. The problem is this isn't a game. It's real life. They don't want to get caught up in something they can't get out of." She sounded lost and threw her arms up in frustration.

Huffing out a laugh, I snorted. "They were told that they can leave the pack at any point, right?"

"No," Sarah said, looking confused. "We thought it was like the mafia." She changed her voice to sound low and gruff. "Once you're in, you're in for life."

"Sarah, we told you about Annie. She left, went to college, may or may not return. Did you think we were lying about that?"

"Well, no. Honestly, I kind of forgot about her. Okay, so it isn't something you have to join for life. That's good to know. I'll text my parents when we get to school."

She sounded like her normal self again.

"Do *you* want to join the pack? Are you flipping out about all of this? Do you hate me for never telling you about any of this?" My fingers were getting numb, and my heart skipped a beat as I asked that last question. Trying to breathe, I was terrified the answer would be yes. I didn't know what I'd do if I lost her as a friend.

"Do I hate you? No. I'm impressed, really. You've kept this from me for, like, ten years. That's impressive. You're even more like a sister to me now."

There was a pounding on the pavement behind us and when I looked, it was Bevin.

"Hey, kitty cats."

My eyes narrowed. "No."

"Fine. Although, you are missing out on some prime nicknaming potential," he said, waggling his eyebrows.

Sarah didn't look any more amused than I did. It occurred to me that we hadn't thought at all about school and all the people we were about to see, and my hand shot out and grabbed Sarah's elbow. "Stop. Before we get to school, Sarah, we should talk. You are most likely going to be overwhelmed."

Her eyes narrowed and then she raised an eyebrow in question.

My memory of the airport made me shiver. "Scent, sound, even vision. You need to find a headspace for peace. Close your eyes, breathe. If you need to cover your ears, do it. You can be subtle about it, but you need to protect your senses. There is going to be a lot of information flowing in, and you'll have to try to control it."

Sarah's jaw dropped, then she snapped her mouth shut and her eyes closed in concentration. She wasn't happy. "Crap, I hadn't thought about any of that. I mean, the airport and plane were crazy, but everything was so new, and we were so rushed and medicated I really didn't notice anything. Is that why Mom gave you all those sleeping pills?"

I hadn't realized she hadn't gotten the full story. I nodded.

She looked a bit nervous and turned like she was thinking about heading home. Then she turned back to me, and her confidence had melted away. "I thought that we would just go back to school, and everything would be normal. Maybe we should've practiced going into crowds unmedicated…like the mall or something. Damn."

"That would have been smart." I definitely surrounded myself with brilliant people.

Bevin wrapped his arms around us both. He turned to Sarah. "It will be fine. You'll be great. You are amazing. You'll go in there, kick butt, and take names. It's Jade here who will probably mess things up. Too confident and all that."

"Geeze, thanks." Sarcasm dripped from my words as I raised an eyebrow. "Just be conscientious, Sarah, and you'll do great."

We looked at each other, nodded in encouragement that we could do it, and continued on to school. As we approached the parking lot, we encountered more and more people. Sensations overtook me, scent, taste, audio, there was so much. Sarah must have been having similar sensations. We both began to shake.

"Wow," Sarah said, "I don't know what to do with all of this information. Remember that Superman movie? When he was a kid, he freaked out at school, and ended up in a janitor's closet?"

When did we start holding hands? "Yep."

She squeezed. "Yeah, I'm not even inside the building

yet and I totally get it."

Sarah stopped halfway across the parking lot, dropping my hand. "See that kid over there, Jared, his heart is racing. I had no idea he had a crush on Tiffany. Tiffany could care less. I can smell how disinterested she is. I can smell it from here. We are, like, three car rows away, and I can smell it. This is both disturbing and wicked cool."

Bevin just stared at her. "How do you know he has a crush on her?"

Sarah dragged her eyes away and focused on Bevin. "Jared's heartrate spiked when he approached her, and he got awkward. It was obvious, trust me. And you can smell all sorts of emotions, it's…"

"Interesting? Fun? Horrible?" Summing this up was almost impossible.

Sarah evaluated all the students and pointed at another group. "I can hear their entire conversation."

She pointed to a group of kids near the door of the school. They were talking about what they had done over spring break. It didn't sound interesting.

Bevin watched me. "Are you getting all of this information, too?"

Overwhelmed, I nodded. "Yes."

Bevin's eyes grew.

We had been told that werewolves took in a lot of information, but experiencing it was a completely different matter.

"I may not have all of Sarah's superpowers, but I'm with her so far. There are, what? Twenty or thirty students out there, and I already know more about them than I've known in years, more than I want to know. Okay, into the building." Pushing on their backs, I herded us all in the direction of the door.

We got about five feet into the hallway when Sarah and I froze. Too much information. Bevin pulled us over to the side so that we didn't cause a traffic jam. Sarah's back slammed into a locker, and she slid down to the floor. Was she having a panic attack or just overwhelmed?

Leaning against the lockers, I put my hands to my head and breathed slowly.

"We can do this. Breathe," I whispered, hoping Sarah could hear me. "Breathe…in and out, deeply, through your mouth. Separate your senses in your mind. Take each of the scents, put them in a mental box, close that box, and save it for later. Take another breath, deep, in and out, through your mouth. Close your eyes."

Glancing down, Sarah's eyes were wide. She didn't seem to understand.

"Close your eyes," my voice snapped out. Once they were closed, her breathing seemed to even out. Following my own directions, I closed my own eyes. "Again, take the scents and pack them away. Now take what you hear, imagine you have earmuffs on and nothing you don't want to hear gets in. Breathe in deeply, and out, only through your mouth…"

Almost centered, I heard Alyssa, one of Sarah's friends from all her sports teams come up to us. "Oh, my God, Sarah, what's wrong? Did you fall? Are you okay?"

Sarah moaned softly.

Bevin intervened, "Hey, Alyssa, how was your spring break? Did you go anywhere?"

"Do I know you? Why are you blocking Sarah? Get out of my way." There was a scuffling sound like she was trying to push Bevin, but he was stronger than he appeared.

Feeling calmer, I opened my eyes to check on Sarah. She no longer seemed like she was about to bolt. Speaking softly, I asked, "How are you?"

"Holy hell, how am I going to do this? How did you do that? How did you know?" Her eyes were still wide.

She shifted her gaze to Alyssa. "Hi, Alyssa." She spoke slowly and grabbed my hand so I could help her up. She plastered on a huge fake smile. "I'm fine. I was just tired after such a long trip to Florida over spring break. Let's talk later, 'k?"

Sarah dragged me away at practically a run. I heard Bevin trying to keep up with us.

When we got to the lockers, Sarah's gaze bore into me. "How did you do that thing with the earmuffs and boxes? It was good until Alyssa showed up."

Bevin started getting his bag ready for classes but glanced over at Sarah. "Jade's mom has been leading us through meditation and headspaces since we were five. Jade always took to it, we figured it was because she had to live with Owen. Can you imagine?"

Sarah laughed, relaxing more.

Bevin went over to Sarah and gave her a hug. "The important thing in all of this is to remember that you control what is coming into your head. I know what she just said sounded weird but do your best."

Bevin had just boiled down years of meditation into a one-sentence lesson. Cool.

"Sarah, if you get overwhelmed, go to the nurse's office, tell them you feel sick. If you need to go home, do that. Text your parents now, about the pack and about possibly coming home if you get overwhelmed. Also, if you don't mind, let's visit Allison after school."

"That sounds good. We have English together first period, so you can help me through that. Lunch—if we really need it—we can eat outside? Okay…if Owen can do this, so can we." Sarah was ready to soldier on.

José came down the hall from the stairs, hearing the last bit of Sarah's statement. "That's the spirit. How's our first morning back?" His eyes twinkled with amusement. He seemed to know the answer.

Giving him scared eyes, I plopped on the floor as if I were being dragged down to hades.

"This is awful, José," Sarah sat beside me. "I can smell emotions and unwashed teens. I can hear heart rates and other things. I know what people are saying. When people talk about me, I'm going to have to ignore it, won't I? This is going to be hard."

José looked sympathetic. "I hadn't really thought about that. If someone talks smack about you, let me know. I'll mess them up."

We all laughed.

Sarah's eyes were wild as she turned to me. "I know we usually hang out here, Jade, but can we go to class now? I think a room with fewer people will be an easier adjustment. We can text people from there and not kill anyone."

I thought she was kidding about the killing people. Probably.

CHAPTER 23

We made it to English class without killing anyone.

Our seats were on the far side, about halfway back. None of the other students were in class yet. First period didn't start for twenty minutes.

Our teacher, Mr. Sanchez, glanced up, nodded a greeting, and looked back down at what he was working on.

Once we were in our seats, we got out our phones and started texting.

My first text was to Allison about going to her work after school. She texted back that she thought that was a great idea. Next was Owen to ask if he could give us a ride to the zoo. He was awake and responded right away. I was shocked. He may not be late for school! He agreed so long as he could stay and watch. He said he'd missed the show since I'd run off.

I showed my phone to Sarah. Everything was set up for the afternoon on my end.

Sarah showed me her phone.

Sarah had texted her parents about the pack not being a lifelong commitment. They asked a few more questions to make sure she was certain, but after a few more confirmations, the communication seemed to get lighter.

Sarah and her parents didn't actually use the word pack, they used the word committee. They knew they had to be careful. They concluded by saying they would contact my parents and that Sarah should focus on school.

By the time we finished our business, other students started filing in. Ignoring all the extra sensory information was hard.

The increased heartrates and pheromones told me who was interested in whom by where people looked and how their bodies reacted. It was disturbing, especially when a boy—Jacob—looked at me and I realized he was interested in me.

Sarah stifled a laugh, and I knew she was sensing the same thing. My head hit my arms, crossed on my desk.

She was not helping.

"This will help me get through the day. Every time I get

stressed today, I'll just come back to this moment and laugh. All. Day. Long." It was the first time I saw her shoulders drop and her being happy since we'd gotten to school.

Despite my happiness for her, this moment wouldn't help me. I groaned.

Mr. Sanchez started class. "Welcome back, everyone. I assume you all had a relaxing week off."

Relenting, I lifted my head.

"We are going to start by writing a twenty-minute essay on 'What I Did over Spring Break'."

The whole class groaned at this.

"Thirty minutes, then? Wow, you all want to make my first day back easy. Thanks for that."

This got a bunch of laughs, as he intended.

"Here is the fun part: it doesn't have to be real. You can write what really happened, or you can make up something fantastical. We are starting our unit on creative writing, and this is a great way to get the juices flowing."

Well, why not both? I got out some paper, and wrote the story of camping, panthers, a hospital, and a transformation.

Throughout class I could feel Jacob shifting his eyes to me. Yuck!

After English, Sarah and I separated until lunch.

Classes didn't get any better, but they didn't get worse, either.

Well, biology got better.

"How ya doin'?" asked Bevin before the bell rang.

"Overwhelmed," I told him. "I had to come up with a creative writing story about my spring break in English. So, I wrote a true story. I whispered softly so Sarah wouldn't do the same thing. Wouldn't that be a hoot, both of us writing the same story? After class, she said she just wrote about what happened without getting into a sensational story, so hers becomes the creative writing one, but reads real, and mine is the real one, and reads as fake."

Bevin chuckled. "That's funny."

The bell rang, and biology class started fast and intense. There was no time to talk. There was no time to worry about anyone else in class. There was only time to listen to Ms. White, take notes, answer questions, and try not to fall behind. My kind of class.

Then came lunch.

Sarah's skin was pale, and her eyes squinted. She sat hunched over her lunch. Her hands kept twitching like she wanted to cover her ears. She looked sick.

"What's wrong?" Sarah just shook her head, overloaded.

Trying to feel her out, I sat next to her. We were inside. She wasn't eating. "Let's move outside."

She nodded.

As we started packing up, Bevin and José joined us.

"We're going outside, Sarah needs a quiet space." Though I wasn't sure they would join us, we had to get away from the rest of the students. But they had brought their coats and were prepared for the cold outdoors.

When we sat down, Owen joined us as well. I was shocked. "What are you doing, slumming with sophomores?"

"Hey," both Bevin and José protested.

"Sorry."

"I told the gang that you were hurt over spring break and Mom and Dad said I had to check on you. They were all sympathetic. Brooke was extra sympathetic."

Gross.

Tilting my head, I stared up at him. "How can someone be *extra* sympathetic?"

He stole some of my fries. "You'll understand when you have a boyfriend."

Shivering, and not from the cold, I went back to my lunch.

"Sarah, you okay?" He sounded concerned. His transformation had been recent, and his shift from non-were to werewolf at school had been hard for him, as well. If anyone understood what we were going through, it was Owen.

"English was bearable, but Jade was there to help. You know, Ms. Calm. I hadn't realized what you all were talking about, but, damn, it's nice being around you again."

She said that last part to me. "My next two classes were rough, but I tried that breathing and boxes thing."

Owen chuckled.

Sarah narrowed her eyes at him. "What? You have a better idea?"

"Sort of. Later. Finish your story. We can discuss my strategy for navigating high school madness in the car after school."

José and Bevin's brows furrowed in confusion, but neither asked anything.

"Right before lunch, I have gym."

Owen groaned.

Now I was confused.

"No one warned you?" Owen asked, giving me an accusatory glance.

My arms flew up. "Warned her about what? I have gym this afternoon. What are you two talking about?" I was beginning to freak out a bit. This didn't sound good.

"Jade. Sister of mine. Genius extraordinaire. You are now a werepanther."

I jerked my head around to see if anyone was around to hear what he had just blurted out.

Owen just stared at me like I was an idiot. "Jade. You are a werepanther. Use your nose, are there any other people around?"

Focusing on my nose, I took in a long sniff. No. I relaxed.

Then I did smell something, and my head snapped towards the school. The door opened. Alyssa came out.

I groaned.

"Oh, my god, what are all of you doing out here…Hi, Owen." She gave his name some extra weight and gave him a flirty wave. "Sarah, are you okay? I heard you were hurt during gym."

She sat down next to Sarah.

We all just stared at her.

Bevin's mouth twitched a little. "Do we *know* you?"

Damn. Bevin was usually the polite one in the group.

Owen gave her a full-on smile. "Cynthia? Right? This is a bad time."

Alyssa's face reddened. "It's Alyssa, not Cynthia. And I can sit out here if I want to, even if it is crazy cold."

Sarah put her hand on Alyssa's arm. "Can we talk later? During math? I have an appointment, and I'm trying to convince Owen to give me a ride."

Alyssa seemed to understand. She gazed at each of us, like she was memorizing our faces for a police line-up, and then she turned and flounced off.

My shoulders had tensed up to my ears, slowly they dropped back down. "So, gym. Why was it tragic?"

Owen gave me the stare that all his teachers probably give him, a cross between exasperation and disappointment. "Okay, smarty pants. You now have enhanced strength, speed, and reflexes you didn't have a week ago. What's going to happen in gym class when you go to perform the way you did before?"

I thought for a few seconds and then my jaw dropped as it hit me, stunned. Then I turned to Sarah. "Oh, my gods, what happened?"

"What didn't happen? Today is a fitness test day. We had to run. We had to jump. We had to throw. We had to do a ton of stuff. About halfway through class, I pretended to twist my ankle."

She turned to Owen. "I just didn't know what else to do. I started off the run as a warmup, but I was going faster than everyone else, so I slowed down, and slowed down again, and then slowed down even more, and then the mile was over." Sarah sounded despondent.

Owen was laughing hard. "How fast?"

"What?" Sarah asked.

"How fast was your mile? Did you set a new school record? Do we need to worry about that?"

Sarah's face had gone blank. "I don't think so. Mr. Nelson said four and a half minutes. He sounded really impressed, but I don't think it was a record. I wasn't breathing hard, though, and when he looked at me weird, I started to breathe as if out of breath."

Owen couldn't hold in his laughter.

José and Bevin smiled at Sarah, eyes wide.

Sarah shook her head at them. "Then we had to do the long jump. Again, I tried to hold back. The first jump was too far, I just knew it, so I pretended my ankle twisted, and sat out the rest of class. Mr. Nelson was staring at me like I was a gift sent from heaven for track team. After class he gave me this." She threw the track and field paperwork onto the table.

Sarah put her elbows on the table and her head in her hands. "I can't join track. That would be totally unfair. I couldn't hold back enough to be realistic, either."

She sounded lost as she said, "Owen, what do you do?"

Owen had always been into sports, and after his transformation, he hadn't quit.

"Well, pretty much what you did. I pretend I'm just strolling through the park. I hold back. It's not as fun."

He grabbed more of my food. "In the barn next to our house, we have a gym and workout area. You can actually work out at full capacity and not worry. I suggest you do that. It will hone your abilities."

He paused as if he were considering something. "If you want, we can practice together, all three of us, so that you know what to do in gym class without thinking so hard. That's what Mom and Dad did with me, we practiced. Maybe after Aunt Allison's this afternoon, we can all go back to the house and do dumbed-down gym practice."

We all laughed at how ridiculous that sounded, but Sarah agreed. It didn't sound so bad to me either.

The barn was attached to the house via an underground walkway. The gym had a full workout area with weights and machines, an area for meditation, karate, or hand-to-hand combat. There was even a changing area with showers. Around all of this was a running track. It was set up so that the whole pack could be down there together. My Sunday had been spent cleaning it as part of the Florida agreement. That hadn't been fun, but at least it was done now.

"So, sis, gym this afternoon, huh? You going to call in sick?"

Scrunching up my nose, I considered. "No, I have my

big-girl panties on. I'll figure something out. Slow goes it. I'm not known for being very athletic anyway. If I need to get injured or see the nurse, I will."

"Isn't Jacob in gym with you?" Sarah teased.

Gods, not this again.

Perking up again, I thought, so was Piper. I wondered if she liked girls or boys?

"Who is Jacob?" Owen sounded curious, interrupting me from my musings. "Does Jade like a boy?"

Everyone laughed as I sneered.

"He doesn't know?" José sounded like a cat who had been given a bowl of milk. "This is so delicious. I love that you keep your cards so close to your chest, chica."

"What don't I know?" Owen looked confused and hurt.

My face flat at first, I gazed at him apologetically. "I wasn't keeping anything from you. I just didn't actually tell anyone. People figured it out and I confirmed, but I never really told anyone. Well, except José."

José smirked.

"Just talk, woman!" Owen demanded.

Frustrated, I relented. "Fine, I'm gay, okay? I like girls. During English, Jacob came in and both Sarah and I could tell he was interested in me. Sarah just about lost it. He kept watching me during class. It was weird. Ugh. Why me?"

"Oh, that. Yeah, you are pretty obvious. I've been wondering when you would come out."

"What? What are you talking about? You knew? Jerk."

I punched his arm.

"Sis, I'm your brother. I see what shows and movies you watch, and who you watch in those shows and movies," Owen confessed, laughing at me.

"Do Mom and Dad know, too?" This was becoming too much.

"Maybe. Mom probably does. Dad is oblivious to all things not pack, or IT and security, so, probably not."

"He's not wrong," piped in Sarah. "It's how I figured it out. Subtle, you are not. At least when a cute girl passes by."

I shook my head.

"Damn," said Bevin, "apparently I'm the oblivious one."

"Me, too, bro," said José.

"Yeah, but I've been hanging around her longer," Bevin said dropping his head down. "I have to up my game."

Owen stood to leave. "One last thing. Sarah, you just have to hold out for a few more classes. Then we'll talk on the way to Aunt Allison about dealing with high school drama."

"High school drama?" I questioned. "I thought you loved it here."

"Yeah, but not the werewolf part. It can be rough."

Laughing, Owen gave me a hug and a patronizing kiss on the top of my head, wished me luck in gym, and he was off to join his friends, having accomplished what he felt he needed to with us.

Sarah watched Owen walk away with a confused look. "Has turning into a werewolf made your brother more bearable? I mean, he just hugged and kissed you."

"I think so," said Bevin.

"No," said José, "he was always a good person—and understanding—just too straight."

CHAPTER 24

We met at Owen's car after school.

Sarah was reaching for the back-door handle when I stopped her. "You need to talk to Owen about how to deal with school stuff. I'll take the back."

"Are you sure?" she asked.

Owen walked up and unlocked the car. "My car, my choice. Sis gets the back."

We all piled in, buckled up, and were off.

"I know Jade told you Mom's theory about the boxes, and that's all great, but really, you just need exposure therapy. It sucks, but you need to build a filter, so you don't sense every damn thing that every person in that building thinks and feels."

He was right. Even with Mom's lessons, today was rough.

"I mean, don't get me wrong, dating Brooke is easier when I can smell her emotions, but I would rather have the doubt than be exposed to everyone's business all the time. Think of building a wall around yourself and not letting anyone or anything in."

"So," Sarah asked, "you don't use the mental boxes, you just use brute force to block the overstimulation?"

"Yeah. Probably not as sage as Jade, or my mom, but it's the only thing that's helped me. Over spring break, I went to the mall where I didn't know many people or to rom-coms where emotions in the audience ran high. I would try to get into a situation with a lot going on and do what I could to filter out the commotion."

"This isn't as bad advice as I had expected," Sarah mused.

Owen glared.

Sarah shook her head at him. "I mean it. The mental boxes approach is all higher order and hoity-toity and probably amazing if you have time to learn it, but I really need something down and dirty. Walking through the zoo, going to the mall, going to the movies, I bet those are all great ways to practice."

Owen seemed less put-out after Sarah's explanation.

Sitting in the back seat of the car listening to them discuss different ways to deal with big groups was nice. It had far less finesse than mom's method. It was more brute force, but in the end, it came down to what worked for each person.

That was one of the things Mom talked a lot about during her meditation sessions with all of us kiddos. It was probably why Owen had his own approach that worked out so quickly for him after his change.

My body sank into the back seat as they discussed. I was glad the two of them were figuring things out. From the moment we had been bitten, I had been a fount of information for Sarah and her parents regarding wereanimals, and yet we both had been bitten. No one seemed to remember or acknowledge that I was also new to being a werepanther. I had to figure out my place and my feelings, too.

It was helpful for Sarah to have a variety of resources. In some ways Sarah and Owen were more alike than she and I were. This was good.

Their voices began to wash over me, letting me get lost in my own world and I hadn't noticed when the car had stopped.

"Earth to Jade." Owen had opened the car door. "We're here, and I'd like to lock up the car."

A bit out of it, I focused on him with a blank stare, shook my head to clear it, and slowly exited the car.

Once out, I grabbed Sarah's hand and we were off.

We walked through the zoo. There weren't many people as it wasn't quite fifty degrees out yet. It wasn't big but there were enough animals to amuse and delight. We stopped to enjoy a few of them. The elephants ignored us. The lions were off playing with a toy beach ball, and one was curled in a huge box.

A few moms with strollers were taking pictures.

We walked by the gazelles, and they ran off as if scared. Glancing over at Sarah, she looked ready to give chase. Owen put his hand on her shoulder, and she relaxed.

We moved by the penguins who were happily swimming. The lemur and capybara hid when we got near as well. An older man said to his wife that he hated when teenagers came and scared the animals away.

It was rather disappointing. As we got further into the zoo and the small prey animals scattered, I realized I would be losing parts of the zoo with this change. I hadn't thought about the fact that I always came to the zoo with a non-werewolf adult. Mom and Dad never brought us. Now I knew why.

We rounded a corner and approached a group of people. Owen moved up beside Sarah, I stopped a step behind them. "Okay, this is it, let it all in. There are only twelve people there. Experience what it feels like."

As he spoke, I couldn't help but to follow Owen's directions as well. It was uncomfortable, to say the least.

There were some older people in the group, and I could almost taste their declining health. I could sense the hunger of a baby nearby, but the food its parents were feeding it was making it sick. A few college students. From the sounds of it, they were doing research for a class on animal behavior. The young woman was totally into the guy, but the guy was into the other guy. That wasn't going to end well. To top it all off, there was a man about to propose to his significant other. Here? Ugh!

The longer I was with the group, the more information I got. Their medical issues became mine. It felt like I was delving into them. The mom of the hungry baby had a cold. The dad had back issues, needing surgery. The college students were healthy, except for the gay guy, who had some form of cancer. It wasn't obvious, but I sensed it. As I continued to let it all in, I started to shake.

Owen directed Sarah. "Good, good. Okay, now imagine a wall, or a castle, or some structure that you can build around yourself to block it all out. These are not your people, your emotions, your feelings, so you have to learn how to block them out."

Owen said words and Sarah sighed, however I was already into these people's issues too deeply to build a wall. The more I let them in, the more I lost myself.

The hard sidewalk rushed toward me. Sarah called out my name. Owen's arms went around me.

"Idiot," he mumbled, as I started to black out. "Boxes, sis, put it in the damn boxes," he said, shaking me lightly to keep me conscious.

Boxes? What?

"Pull yourself out, separate, and save it for later. Or whatever Mom tells us to do." I heard him mumble that last bit.

Oh, stop letting it all in.

Gradually, I pulled back into myself, away from the group. Separating everything out, I filed it all away into the boxes. My breathing was ragged as I focused on Owen's piercing blue eyes. I thought I would see anger, but what I saw was concern.

"What the hell were you thinking?" he demanded.

Damn, he sounded like Dad.

"I was trying to learn your way. I thought knowledge was power, and if I could do what you did, I would be stronger."

"And how did that work out for you? Are you any stronger?" he growled.

Resting my head on his chest, I concentrated on breathing. I couldn't take his anger, or the concern in his eyes. It was too much.

His holding me seemed to help, though. After a few minutes I felt stronger and like myself again.

"Could we just move on?" I pleaded.

"Can you stand on your own?" he asked, more softly.

Owen was himself again.

"Yeah, I'm better. I got everything sorted out."

Lifting my head, I searched the area. The group was gone. "Damn, I wanted to tell that couple that they were harming the baby. The kid is getting sick from the baby food."

"Probably better this way," Owen said as he helped me

to my feet. "Having a teenage punk explain why your baby is crying rarely goes over well. They'll go to the doctor and get it figured out. You need to worry about figuring out you and your other half right now."

How was it he was suddenly the smart one?

But I knew he was right. We needed to find Aunt Allison.

CHAPTER 25

"Hey, Auntie," Owen boomed cheerfully as we entered her work area.

She met us in a private office in the back of the big cat habitat. She was working alone today so we had the place to ourselves.

Our Aunt Allison loved animals and was great with them, but she didn't like working on humans. She knew basic first aid and was willing to take vitals and triage patients, but she wouldn't have wanted to stitch up Sarah's arm as I had done in Florida. That was why she worked as a vet instead of as a doctor. She was one of the people who had taught me everything I knew as a healer.

Aunt Allison always had a soft spot for us kiddos. She came around the desk and gave each of us a hug, even Sarah. Sarah was a bit surprised but went with it, hugging her back.

Allison took in Sarah. "I know we just met, but we are going to get to know each other well, since you and Jade are pack no matter what happens, and I'm her aunt."

Her gaze shifted back and forth between me and Sarah. "I want to run a few baseline tests on the two of you. Jade, have you done that yet?"

"No, I've been sort of distracted, but I have a notebook and a flash drive here so that I can add me and Sarah to the database, if she's alright with it."

We both glanced over at Sarah expectantly.

She was staring at me with wide eyes. "Um. What?"

Snorting, I slowed down. "Sorry. I want to run or, actually, have Aunt Allison run some baseline tests and add you to a database I keep on the pack, you know, health records. Would you mind if I added you?"

Sarah's eyes were wide, her mouth hung open a bit, and she smelled surprised. Owen came over and put his arm around her reassuringly. Leaning into him, she smiled sheepishly, then turned back to me. "Yeah. That's fine. You keep the records? But you're like, fifteen."

Giving her hand a squeeze, I turned to Aunt Allison. "I'm also hoping you can download some of the chart information for me, then we'll both have the basics in our databases. I'll add our attack and the Florida medical information to the records that I keep, as well."

"Excellent. We want to make sure...."

Allison and I went on talking about medical records for about fifteen minutes. We discussed what would be done while we were human and what Allison would be observing during our change—which Owen would not be able to watch—and what she would examine when we were in panther form.

She got more technical, and I asked more questions when we got to the animal stuff. I had done my research about wolves, but I still had a lot to learn about panthers.

Owen ignored us, playing on his phone.

Sarah's stood gaping at us. She knew I had done some medical work, but Allison and I must have sounded like colleagues. I don't think she expected that.

"Can you email me the pertinent information on panthers? I feel so behind."

Still focused on his phone, Owen huffed and rolled his eyes.

Allison laughed and agreed to get me caught up on one of her favorite subjects.

Sarah walked over to us, blushing slightly...embarrassed? "If you have something dumbed down for me, I would love the information, too." She was never that hesitant.

Aunt Allison reached over and rubbed Sarah's arm.

"Absolutely. Getting you up to date on your other half would be my pleasure, and please make sure you ask questions. But don't forget, I don't know everything, but I love to figure things out. Jade, will you make sure we have each other's email addresses?"

Taking out my phone, I started a group email, which I found was the easiest way to share addresses and avoid typing things incorrectly. The email was about learning information on panthers from an expert. I gave it the subject: *School project help*.

We were ready to start, so I summarized what to expect for Sarah. "Okay, Allison is going to do a basic workup on us: vitals, blood work, and heart rate monitoring on the treadmill. She wants to watch us shift and then repeat all the tests on us as panthers. She has a couple of extra tests she wants to run that are animal specific. Does that sound acceptable to you?"

"Um, that sounds fine. That's what I was expecting, except for the treadmill."

Looking up from her paperwork Aunt Allison asked, "Have you shifted since Florida?"

I hadn't thought about that.

"No," she admitted.

"No worries," Owen said, being our role model with all his months of experience shifting. He gave her a winning smile. "You'll do great. It will take longer without the help of the full moon, but you can do the change at any time."

Sliding my eyes to Owen, I asked Aunt Allison, "I do have one question. As long as he's here, do you want to do the full set of tests on Owen, too?"

Owen shot me a dirty look. He hated having blood drawn and had avoided all his initial tests as a werewolf.

He glared. "Did Mom put you up to this?"

"Believe it or not, no. I'm the keeper of the pack's medical records, and I have nothing for the newest werewolf. What would make it worth your while?"

"Watching you shift," he said immediately.

Rubbing my eyes, I took a deep breath. "Me or both of us?"

"I just want to see someone transform into a panther. I don't care who."

"I kind of would like to see it, too," Sarah added.

Staring at the ceiling for inspiration…nothing. I shook my head. My grimace turned to a growl as I pinned Owen with my hardest stare. "Fine, but you both have to agree to behave and let Aunt Allison do any test she wants…on both forms."

As I tried to intimidate them both into submission all I got back were two giddy faces. I gave up with a huff.

Then Allison began. Even though she didn't usually work with humans, she had a great bedside manner. My guess was that she was used to being the only one who could talk. Explaining everything, she kept up a running monologue as she ran all sorts of tests.

Sarah was a bit surprised her heart rate was higher than

normal, but Allison let her know it was expected.

After that, Sarah followed Owen's lead and played on her phone instead of paying attention to the numbers.

The list of research question grew the longer we were there. My knowledge of wolves was so ingrained I didn't even know what I knew and what I didn't. This study was important for both me *and* Sarah.

Once Allison was done, it was time for me to change. Even though there had been a wall at the meeting, I felt no embarrassment shifting in front of the others. Growing up in a pack accustomed everyone to nudity. It was part of the change from human to animal and vice versa. We got to the point where the body was just the body. In the past, I'd found random naked people passed out on the lawn after they spent the night in wolf form. Usually, we would just throw a blanket over them. During the winter we dragged them to a warmer, drier place, and then threw a blanket over them.

When Owen first changed, he'd kept on his undies. That suggestion had been because he'd been scared and hadn't been certain about the transformation. Had he known for sure that he was shifting into a werewolf, he would've stripped.

Moving to a clear area of the room, I began to remove my clothes.

"Jade," Sarah said, eyes wide, reaching for my shirt to cover me. "Aren't you going to leave anything on?"

"Um, nope. I want to be able to wear all my clothes home, and trust me, you've seen it all, Aunt Allison has seen it all, and Owen could *not* care less. Honestly, he couldn't care less with you, too. Owen, are you scandalized?"

"Yes," he said, deadpan. "Absolutely."

His blasé answer made me laugh. "When you've lived with people shifting, nudity is just part of the process. I'm sure Allison will find a way to give you more privacy if you want it, or maybe have you stand back-to-back. But honestly, its nothing."

Owen looked so bored it was funny. "Can we get to the panther part now?"

"Yeah, warning first. Usually when I change, I don't know I'm not really a panther for a few minutes. Wolves seem dangerous to my panther. Sarah should be closer than you two. I think…maybe…I don't know."

Shrugging, I got down on my hands and knees, lowered my head, breathed deeply, and focused on the change. It was slower to start this time. Breathe, in through the nose, out through the mouth, over and over, and then it began. Bones shifting, muscles changing, face, hair, pain, pain, pain.

There were weird human smells all around. Pulling deeply from the human brain…medical smell. Then I caught the smell of panther: friend. Wolf: must protect my pack. Crouching, ready to pounce, I stalked towards the wolf who stood on two legs. He wore a weird, toothy challenge. The other panther put a paw on my muzzle to stop my ability to protect from this challenging wolf. The smell of brother entered my brain: brother, aunt, wolf, friend. My body shook as words formed.

"Are you…you?" Sarah asked.

My head bobbed in my best imitation of a nod.

"That was so freaking cool," Owen said. "I mean, I've seen wolves change, but did you see that? So much mass moving around. Bones, muscle, hair. So. Freaking. Cool. Allison, do they weigh the same?"

Sarah giggled.

"Before I continue with the tests, do you two want to pet her, maybe feel her fur? You both need to change, too, but I'll give you a minute while I take blood and get a few vitals. Just don't get in my way," Aunt Allison warned.

Owen leapt at the opportunity.

I rolled my eyes at his enthusiasm.

Sarah laughed so hard she snorted. "Jade, panthers are not supposed to roll their eyes."

Owen scratching my ears and petting down my back felt weird, but good. As kids, we were all given the opportunity to do this with the wolves, so I recognized the fascination. Being on this side was a new experience. This weekend was going to be full of this, so I guessed I was going to have to get used to it. Especially with the kiddos.

"You are just gorgeous, Jade. I know you are my sister, and I'm not supposed to say this, but, sis, you make a fine panther. You have these sleek lines and huge paws. Look at this, Sarah."

Sarah came over to peer down at me.

Owen's hand went under my chin. "Her eyes are the same as they are in her human form. They're perfect in this form, too. I can see why everyone has just fallen in love with her panther form."

Owen went on. Confused, I just glanced at him. Everyone loved this form? Who was this everyone he spoke of?

Aunt Allison finished up my labs and turned to Owen. "Okay, Owen, do you want to let Sarah see how a werewolf changes, or should the two of you change at the same time?"

"I almost forgot she's never seen a change. Have you ever seen a werewolf?" Owen asked.

"No." She sounded a little hesitant. She smelled a bit scared, sweet like candy. She squared her shoulders, took a breath, and said again more calmly, "No, I haven't."

"Dude, you have nothing to fear, it will just be little old me, only as a wolf. You are way more dominant than me, too. I haven't seen you as a panther, but I can tell, even as you are now, that you'll outrank me."

He gave her a charming smile. "You should watch. If you are going to be part of the pack, you should have some experience in watching different werewolves shift. Not all wolves shift the same way," he added.

"Okay." She sounded more herself. "But when I was a panther, I sort of lost it in the end. What if that happens again?"

Aunt Allison stared at her for a minute. "Were you

tired and overwhelmed that first time?"

Sarah nodded.

"Are you feeling that way now?"

"Not really."

"If you start to feel overwhelmed, I'll shoot you with a tranquilizer dart." She gave Sarah a sweet smile. "I'm not too worried. First shifts are notoriously hard, especially if you aren't from a were-family. You have more information this time."

Sarah's back stiffened and she smelled startled, but she nodded.

Now it was Owen's turn to shift. He stripped.

Sarah blushed.

We ignored it.

He got down on his hands and knees and hung his head. Did he have a mantra? Did he have a headspace that helped him shift? Eventually his bones began snapping and muscles began shifting. Thankfully, fur sprouted up, covering things I didn't want to see. Despite the number of shifts I'd seen, it always intrigued me, so I watched as his nose and face elongated and forehead area shrunk. His fingers and hands formed into paws. The next thing I knew, there was a gray wolf sitting there.

Fear flowed from Sarah. She gazed down at Owen. Then he wagged his tale and yipped, giving her a smile. She took a shaky breath and her scent slowly morphed.

"Oh. My." She dropped to her knees in front of Owen.

Sarah had always loved dogs, but her parents never let her get one. Not even pausing, she gave Owen a doggie hug, and then petted him and scratched him. His tongue was hanging out in a wolf laugh, so I knew he was fine with everything she was doing.

While Sarah was petting him and getting all doggie happy, my aunt ran her basic tests, including getting a blood sample. Yes!

She was so subtle, I don't think Owen even noticed.

"You were okay with watching the shift?" Aunt Allison asked Sarah.

Sarah, distracted by Owen, pulled herself away. "Yeah, it was weird, but awesome. Similar to what happened to Jade, but different. So, I guess it's my turn. Funny thing, since Owen and Jade are animals, I'm not as self-conscious about getting naked. Is that weird?"

Yes, I thought.

"No, dear, not at all." Aunt Allison, always the diplomat.

Sarah's shift took longer to start than either mine or Owen's.

Watching her, I wanted to tell her my mantra but couldn't since I had already shifted. After a few minutes, she glanced at me and said, "I don't know what to do without you helping me."

I whined a little.

"Jade, I'm going to hook you up to the treadmill now, I want you away from Sarah. She needs to learn to do this without you, love. You are …" She paused, trying to come up with a word. "Well, you're going to go to the treadmill, now."

My eyes dropped to the floor, I plodded after her. She hooked me up to the monitors. She had a list of tests for big cats, and I was in for a long hour.

About ten minutes into my run, I finally heard the sounds that said Sarah was changing and the yipping sounds that meant Owen was encouraging her.

After that, Owen ran on a treadmill, too, while our aunt took Sarah's vitals.

The rest of the afternoon passed in a series of tests.

Instead of having us change back, Allison suggested we run home. It was late and dark, so the chance of anyone seeing two black panthers and a grey wolf was small.

The zoo was part of the suburb which was filled with lots of wooded and private areas. The run would allow us time between shifts, which was a great idea. Aunt Allison promised to bring our clothes and bags to my parents' house. Uncle Jackson had dropped her off that morning so she could just drive Owen's car back.

Allison snuck us out the back to a hidden path into the woods. From there we could run home. We took the long way around, stretching our legs. I hadn't planned on a run, but it felt so good, like our first full moon night.

We ran out and into the woods. I started off by nosing in front of Owen, taking off and finding a tree to launch myself into. Sarah followed me. Owen tried, but couldn't make it up as high. He scratched at the bottom of the tree, whining.

Sarah and I jumped down and we all continued on our way. Finding a rabbit trail, instinct took over and I started down it. Sarah followed. Getting close, I made too much noise and the rabbits ran. Owen took off after the rabbits first, and caught one, snapping the neck quickly. We each took a few bites, getting some calories for our run.

Sarah and I showed Owen how we could pounce. At first, we could only get seven or eight feet. But as we played, we extended our length to closer to ten feet.

Finally, we turned towards home. When we rounded the last corner near the house, Owen pulled ahead of us. He ran around a tree to cross the last street.

Sarah and I ran a few feet behind him and heard a car's breaks and the squealing of tires on the road. Then there was the scraping of what sounded like nails on metal and a yelp of pain, followed by a loud thump on the ground and crashing of branches.

Sarah and I ran to a bush and saw the car come to a stop at an angle across the road. Owen's tail disappeared into the bush on the other side, but I could hear whimpers as he receded into the shadows. As much as I wanted to follow, I knew we had to wait until this car left. Sarah's vibrations next to me told me her desires were as great as mine but getting caught wasn't an option. We waited in the shadow of a tree.

The car that stopped was an older model Jaguar. A couple got out. It was dark enough that they used the flashlights on their phones to look at the claw marks on the hood of their car. They took a few pictures. The wind was blowing diagonally away from us, the wrong way for me to catch the scent of them. Lowering myself, a low growl from Sarah stopped me in my tracks.

The man looked around, flashing his phone's light into the darkness. The light got swallowed into the night, not penetrating the woods.

"Did you see that? That was the biggest dog I've ever seen," the woman observed.

"Dog? That was a wolf," the man snapped. He sounded angry.

"There aren't any wolves in this area," the woman insisted. "Should we call the police?"

"What would they do? That animal's long gone. Let's just go. We have pictures for insurance," he snapped, herding her into the car before he got back into the driver's side, and he slammed the door shut.

Once the car was out of sight, Sarah and I followed Owen's trail. He hadn't gone far into the woods. He was hiding in a bush, lying on his side, shaking. His tail was tucked.

He tried to stand but couldn't and let out a yelp of pain.

Sniffing and rotating my head didn't work to diagnose what had happened to him. To get to the problem I needed to see what was wrong, and I couldn't do that as a panther. After sniffing the air to make sure it was safe, I started my change.

Once human, I looked around. Owen was still lying

on the ground panting. Sarah was pacing, ready to protect.

"Owen, I'm going to feel your legs and body, I need to figure out what's wrong."

His head snapped to me. I don't think he noticed when I had become human.

Gently, I placed my hands on his neck and started to pet down his body. Everything felt normal. It was dark and I couldn't see very well, so I closed my eyes to help me focus on what I was feeling.

After I felt his chest and ribs, which seemed fine, I stroked down each of his legs. One of his back legs felt off, almost crooked. Taking a deep breath, I rubbed the leg a little harder and slower to get a good feel for what was wrong.

Owen started to pant faster.

There was a loud snap. My attention flew to Sarah, but she wasn't moving and hadn't reacted to the noise. She stared back at me. In my shock at hearing that noise, I had dropped Owen's leg.

"Sorry, Owen. Did I hurt you?"

His big eyes reflected the light from the stars as he gazed back at me unblinking. He rolled over to his side and slowly got to his feet.

"No!" I tried to grab him, but I was moving so slowly. Why was I so tired?

He ignored me. He started to walk towards Sarah and then back to me, nudging me.

Squinting at him and then Sarah, I got the hint.

Clueless as to what had just happened, I knew we had to go. Furthermore, remaining naked wasn't an option.

Shifting…again…took longer than normal. Once in panther form, I saw black spots for a few seconds before I shook my head and was ready to go.

The three of us made our way home.

When we got there, we all collapsed into a pile in the backyard to lick off any burrs or dirt. With the backyard lights, it was easy to see everything we needed to clean off.

Eventually Allison got there and placed our clothes and bags by the sliding door. It was getting late, and we had to face the human world. It was time to change back.

We each found our own piece of the backyard to shift. I couldn't seem to manage it. I was too tired.

Sarah walked over to Owen. "Has that happened to you before? With the car and the people?"

It was dark, but I saw Owen's face turn red. "No, I've never been seen before. I'll have to tell my parents. If you don't mind, I'm going to wait until you leave. I don't need to get yelled at with an audience."

Sarah nodded.

There was no way he was going to tell them, but I couldn't do anything in this form. I tried changing again. And failed again.

Mom poked her head out of the sliding door. "Sarah, your parents came to talk to us. We told them you were off with Jade and Owen. They're in the dining room. Once you've all eaten, they'll take you home. You should come in and tell us about your day and your adventures with Allison."

"Yeah, Sarah." Owen eyes sparkled. "Tell everyone about joining track team."

She groaned.

Focusing again on becoming human, the world went black as my snout hit the grass.

CHAPTER 26

Wednesday morning. My eyes were gummy, and my body was stiff.

Groan.

Pillow, bed, hands…Did I shift in my sleep? Could shifting happen during sleep? What happened last night? Rolling to a sitting position, taking stock of my body, I felt…fierce!

Yesterday was rough, but we had survived. The run was amazing. Something happened to Owen, and whatever I did had helped. Was that a healing? My panther was proud, with her I was strong and could do anything.

It was time. Decision made and heart racing…I was going to do it.

Over winter break, Sarah and I had been at a shop, and she'd convinced me to buy a shirt. After feeling Jacob's interest in me yesterday, I decided today was the day for its debut release. The shirt was short-sleeved, so I started with a black thermal. Then the new shirt. It was black with a rainbow circle over the chest with the word "Pride" written in purple cursive through the rainbow. In purple on the back were the words, "I Like Grrls!" To finish the look, I added black jeans and black shoes, and I was ready to face the world.

Reaching the door handle, my heart began a concert in my chest, and I froze.

Was I ready to do this?

Yes!... Maybe.

Pulling out my phone, I took a selfie, and sent it to Sarah.

She replied almost instantly, `Yes. Perfect.`

She knew what my statement was going to be today.

Okay, I can do this. Breathe.

Finding my center, I forced myself to the door, and got it open. Once through, I needed a bit of encouragement… *You can do this Jade!* When I got to the kitchen for breakfast, Mom stared at me.

"Turn," she said. I did. "That's new." Her voice was interested but bland.

Tingling erupted over my body, and I held my breath.

Gazing at her, I wasn't sure if she meant the shirt or the message. Exploding, I couldn't wait any longer. "And?"

"It's bold. I think the panther is making you stretch yourself. You're acting braver. I like that you're showing the world who Jade is. It's about time."

Finally, her face opened into a warm smile.

I deflated, my shoulders dropped, and my head sagged to the side. "How long have you known?"

I didn't like the whine in my voice.

She paused to take a drink of coffee before answering. "Since you were three, I think. Thanks for this, though. This means I win the bet with Dad about when you would start to tell people. He said you'd wait until college."

I groaned, sat at the kitchen island, and ate my breakfast. I was hungrier than usual and was scarfing my second plate before I heard Owen heading down the hallway.

Owen laughed when he read the shirt. "Man, Jacob's going to love that shirt."

"Jacob?" Mom prompted.

I told her about English class and my new ability to read people.

Mom nodded. "Ah, I get it. I think your desire to come out makes more sense now, knowing there's an interested party. There are ways to block out such interests that are more subtle, but this is probably faster." She laughed. "This *is* pretty direct."

It was warm enough that I didn't need a coat for school.

My backpack covered the message on the back of my shirt when I headed out. The "Pride" and the rainbow on the front were a common supportive message that anyone would wear.

Once by the lockers, both Bevin and José laughed at my shirt in delight.

I spun and then whipped off my backpack so they could read the back.

José whistled. "Damn, girl. You go from no one knowing to putting it up in lights. I feel like a gateway drug: once you tell me, you have to tell the world."

Hugging him, I laughed.

"I'm just glad I found out before you decided to tell everyone," grumbled Bevin.

As I gave him a hug in apology, I flashed the back of my shirt down the hall toward the majority of the students.

Although the school was mostly open-minded, I was expecting some pushback for the shirt today. What I wasn't expecting was that I could feel and taste the responses from everyone.

Everyone who saw and read my back as I hugged Bevin felt like they had a strong reaction. Where was the teenage apathy?

Coming to school, students only saw me from the front and the message that I support the LGBTQ+ community in general, but the message on the back was a personal statement.

Now I could feel the love and hate from people behind

me. The love was warm. It felt supportive and caring. The hate felt like acid, burning away from the inside. Too much acid. There were reactions from every direction that I could hear, smell, and taste.

Breathing hard, I moved away from Bevin. My back slammed against the lockers, and I sat down hard. Somehow my head ended up between my knees. The vibration of the locker behind let me know that I was shaking all over. Bevin stayed beside me, kneeling. His support helping to keep me from drowning. There was an ocean of emotion crashing into me and I tried to focus on the soft caring emotions, use those as an anchor in the hate, but it was so hard. He was my shelter.

"Jade, are you okay?" José asked.

The wash of emotion tore the voices from me. I clamped my hands over my ears…but the emotions were in me.

"It's everyone." Sarah's shoes paced in front of me like a mother cat protecting her kit from the other students. "No one is taking this lightly. Everyone who read the back of her shirt is a ten or a one, love or hate. I can feel it, but it's all directed at her. It's hard for me to breathe. I can't imagine what she's feeling."

Unable to respond, I could barely listen to her explanation. The waves threatened to drown me. I grabbed Bevin's hand to stabilize myself from the onslaught.

"Jade, Jade, Jade!" I couldn't tell who was calling to me.

My head shot up, my eyesight blurry. I tried squinting

to see better and finally got someone in focus. Sarah.

"Jade, let's go to class, put your backpack on." Sarah dragged me up. The boys helped me with my bag.

Once my bag was on, it covered up the back, and no one new could read the words. During class, people behind me could read the shirt. However, that wouldn't be a big crowd. A lake versus an ocean. That was something I could manage…I hoped.

We got to English class early again; I thought Bevin helped me navigate the halls.

"Two days in a row, ladies. Is this going to be your new morning hangout?" Mr. Sanchez asked.

"Maybe." Sarah shot him a glance and a half-smile as she helped me to my desk. "The halls feel more oppressive than usual lately. It's nice to have some peace in the morning. Do you mind us sitting in here?"

"Nope, not at all. You can sit quietly while I get my morning prep done. By the way, your papers yesterday were great. Obviously, you two took a vacation together, your stories were similar, but Jade, the creative angle you took was amazing to read. How did you come up with the idea of a panther attack?"

"Well, there were panther crossing signs on the roads down there. Sarah and I laughed about it. I thought, why not? So many werewolf stories, why not a big cat story?"

He beamed at me, no doubt pleased with my creativity. Sarah just kicked me under the desk and chuckled.

We played on our phones for a few minutes before the other students started to arrive, including Jacob.

It was weird feeling the changes in the air. Focusing on my phone, I heard him take his seat, which was on the other side of the room, and behind me. Despite trying to ignore him, I could feel him staring at me and I had the impression that he was hoping to get my attention. A chill ran through me the moment he read the shirt; despite trying to play a game, I felt him freeze. I took a quick peek over my shoulder and, sure enough, his eyes were locked on the back of my shirt. I don't think he was breathing.

Sarah, who could see him, smirked at me. She whispered, almost too low for me to hear, "He looks like a kicked dog, so sad."

A bit sad, I shrugged. I didn't want to hurt the kid, but I was definitely not interested in him. At least now he knew.

Having achieved one of my goals, I put away my phone and took out my notebook, ready for class to begin. English class was uneventful, and the next few classes went by quickly.

That said, lunch couldn't have arrived soon enough for me. In my eagerness, I arrived in the cafeteria before anyone else in my group, grabbed some food, and immediately went outside. I had had enough of people. I didn't even care if the rest of the gang sat inside.

Surprisingly, Owen was the first to join me. "You've caused quite the uproar around here, sis."

Taking a bite of my grilled cheese, I stared blankly at him. "I hadn't noticed."

"I had no idea how many boys wanted to date my pain of a sister. Did you?"

I threw my hands in the air in frustration. "No, and that's the thing. Even yesterday, only Jacob was interested. Today, people are coming out of the woodwork. More boys have taken notice of me today than ever. Why is that?"

My attempted to sound impartial was ruined by the whining.

Sarah swung in and joined us, plopping her bag under the table. "Forbidden fruit. Didn't you know? Once you are untouchable, everyone wants to touch you." She waved her hands, palms facing me, vibrating them.

Making a face at her I said, "That makes no sense."

José walked up to the tables, zipping up his coat. "Is our little Jade complaining about her newfound celebrity status? She's come so far in the world so quickly. Should we form a queue to get an autograph?"

Owen laughed and gave him a high five.

"I'm glad you two are enjoying yourselves. Can we please take these few precious moments to forget all that insanity? I mean, I wear a shirt proclaiming to the school I like girls, and not one girl takes note."

Sarah grabbed some of my fries, but before she ate them, she teased, "You don't want just any girl to notice, you want one specific girl to notice, and you haven't even had a class with her yet."

"Shut up." I went very still. I was opening up about a lot of things, but there were some things I still hoped to keep just between me and my best friend. Unfortunately, that wasn't going to happen in this group.

"What is this? Does my little sis have a crush?" Owen said in a mock-seductive tone. He was way too happy about this situation.

"Why are you even here? Shouldn't you be with Brooke and the jocks?"

Owen raised his eyebrows and held up his hands in surrender, but I was on a roll and didn't stop. "This is two days in a row, what the hell!" My voice was raising. "If you're going to hang out with us, the least you can do is not be annoying! Why is everyone suddenly interested in my business? Why can …" Not being able to finish the sentence, I started hyperventilating.

My brain was spiraling, and I was being unfair. My face burned and it felt like the fire was infusing my whole body. Was my body turning red? Was I emitting heat?

This day couldn't get any worse. My anger was out of control and there wasn't anything I could do about it. There had been too much stress today. My soul wanted to pounce.

I felt my inner panther stretching her claws and screeching through me. Apparently, she had decided it was time to protect me. She was starting to take control.

Owen backed up, hands still up, voice low and calming.

"Jade, your smell is changing."

"Thank goodness," said Sarah, "I thought it was just me. She smells more panther. Does that mean she could change? Like, here at school? I thought she had to be calm to change."

"It means the panther is taking over. It means human Jade is losing control. This is bad, we need to get her calmed down and under control." Owen approached me and I jumped up to swipe at him, as if I had claws. Since all I had was a hand, nothing much happened. "Well, hell," he muttered, stumbling back.

Sarah stood and stepped to approach, but I glared at her as well. She'd started this by blurting out my secrets.

Just then, Bevin showed up.

"What did I miss?" His upbeat voice cut through the tension.

José quickly summarized, talking quietly and serenely. He sounded like he didn't want to catch my attention. "Jade is more panther than Jade, she's pissed at Sarah and Owen, and we aren't sure how to calm her down. Look at her eyes: they're glowing. I mean, stunning, but terrifying. Probably not the best thing for school. Good thing her back is to the lunchroom."

The comment about my glowing eyes would probably shock me later when I had time to process, but right now I was trying to think of the best way to use this body to attack my enemies.

Arms went around me in a tight hug. A growl bubbled

up from my gut as my body began to shake. Needing to get away, I struggled.

"Jade, it's me, Bevin. Come back to me, sis. Ssshhhh. Jade, it's okay, we are not your enemies, you're safe. Today sucked, but you've been great. You are loved. Everyone here loves you. Close all the boxes. Clear your mind. Calm everything in your head. Remember, you are Jade."

Bevin kept talking. He was using my mom's technique. Jerking in his arms, I continued to struggle, but he just held on. As he kept talking, I took a deep breath. I smelled friends. I smelled family. I relaxed. After a few more minutes, I slumped against him. He was safe. When my struggles stopped, his arms got tighter, letting me know I was safe and loved. Tears wet his shirt as I came back to myself.

Finally, I pushed away and sat back down.

"You better?" he asked.

"Yeah." My voice was shaky.

Everyone else sat and we began to eat. No one was staring at me, which was good. Predators often perceived eye contact as a challenge or a threat. Simply staring at me could have set me off again.

"What happened?" Sarah continued to look down, speaking to her sandwich. She sounded hesitant and a bit sad. "Did I do something wrong?"

"No, yes, no, I don't know, maybe. I tell you secrets; you can't tell others. I know this group is close, but Sarah, I have to be able to trust you."

I didn't think I was really making sense, but this garbled explanation was the best I could do.

"I'm so sorry," she said, "I didn't even think. You never talked about liking people, or even being gay. And then, you come to school in that shirt, all fierce and bold, and I just took it one more step. That was one step too far."

Owen came over to me and sat down, straddling the bench facing me. He grabbed my hands. "Listen to me, sis, I'm allowed to poke fun at you all I want, it's in the brother's manual. I've read that sucker, like twice."

His touch helped, as did his goofy nature and I huffed out a laugh.

He shot me one of his quirky grins. "But you've had a hard day. Maybe even a hard week. Just tell me to back off. You usually don't have any problem doing that. Fierce swipe, by the way." He laughed. "I think it's great that you like someone. I've always told you who I liked. Even when it was Brooke, who you don't approve of. Nothing to be embarrassed about. You don't have to tell me…yet. Just remember that we're all safe."

"I think I did tell you to back off," I refuted.

He shrugged, and then gave me a hug. Not a school hug, but a home hug. A family hug, the kind of hug I needed.

After that, he looked me in the eyes long and hard to make sure I was really feeling better, that I was me. He kissed my forehead, I thought to get a bit more contact between us. Then he sauntered off to find his friends.

Finally centered in who I was, the atmosphere became relaxed again and I got back to eating. "I swear to you, if I had any idea the ruckus it would cause, I wouldn't have worn this shirt. There are so many 'out' people in this school, why is my wearing this shirt such a big deal?"

"Well," José put down his food and drink, his expression serious, "you don't give off the vibe. No gay-dar with you. More than that, you've always been so smart and quiet. I don't know. Everyone in the building knows who you are, but no one really *knows* you. You're such a mystery. And then you come in with such a bold statement. It's like you're suddenly real."

"I'm not real?" My gaze bounced from face to face, baffled.

Sarah laughed. "Nope, not even a little. I know you don't see it, but outside of our group, others don't really know you. You're a mystery."

"You know me. So do you two." I shot each of them an accusing look.

Bevin smirked. "Yeah, it gives us an air of mystique all our own."

My head dropped to the table. This day couldn't end soon enough.

The bell rang and I growled at it.

"That isn't going to help you," Sarah said. "You still have gym. It may not be so bad."

Gym. At least I could change my shirt for gym class.

Yesterday in gym, I told Mr. Nelson I had really bad

cramps. The same tactic wasn't going to work again without a note from my mom.

Since I wanted out of the shirt anyway, I decided to change and participate.

"Ms. Stone, you are feeling better today?" Coach Nelson said. Or asked, I wasn't sure from his tone.

Entering class, my answer was just as vague. "Not really, but not worse."

"Join the group who didn't get to do the base tests yesterday." His voice increased in volume, projecting loud enough to be heard a few blocks away. "As for the rest of you, if you want to retest, join us at the start of the running track. Otherwise, today we'll be doing strength and endurance testing."

He grabbed his clipboard and consulted it. Then he continued his directions. "Find a partner, and record for one another how many of each exercise you can do. So, one person does the sit-ups while the other counts, then you switch places. Work your way through each of the exercises. Not too complicated. Get to it!"

Waiting at the start line to run, I heard someone say, "Brave of you to wear that shirt today. I don't know if I could have done it."

Turning too fast, I started to lose my balance then caught myself before I fell on Piper. Normally she seemed so shy she almost folded into herself. I wanted to help her be bold and fierce, like I felt this morning. Despite her typical slouch, she stood tall, staring directly at me with her bright blue eyes. My heart started beating faster. I hoped no one could tell.

"You liked my shirt?" Suddenly shy myself, I felt unsure and hesitant. Her family moved to the district this year and I didn't know much about her. After the night Owen had become furry, we hadn't spoken much.

"Yeah. It was—" She was cut off before I knew what she was going to say.

"Okay, everyone," boomed Coach Nelson, "we will start with running the mile. I expect everyone to be able to run the mile in under thirteen minutes. If you can't, you'll be running and training regularly until you get that fast."

It was like a punch to the gut. Last time I ran, my mile was closer to fourteen minutes. The heat from lunch returned. What if I fell again?

"After that, we will move over to the long jump. I don't have any baseline for that. You may have to run for your lives one day, you don't normally have to jump for your life." He laughed at his own joke.

My hand covered my mouth before I could make a sound; if he only knew the truth, he wouldn't be laughing so easily.

Having no idea how running would go, I nervously squirmed while waiting for this torture to begin. Before class, I had decided that if Owen and Sarah were right, then I would try to stay about halfway back in the group. Owen had always been into sports, so his opinion was a bit sketchy, and Sarah liked to run. Again sketchy.

Coach Nelson blew the whistle, and we were off. At the last minute I decided to try to keep up with Piper. After a few seconds, she peered over and gave me a big smile. My heart flipped and I smiled shyly back. She ran decently fast, not the fastest in the class, but close to it.

She was just ahead of me. This would put me at a much faster pace than I'd ever run before, but, miraculously, it didn't feel very hard. A walk in the park, I could do this. My heart wasn't beating that fast. Could Owen and Sarah be right? Could gym not be the bane of my day at school?

Kicking it up, I caught up to Piper. We were running next to each other. My breathing was still even. This was doable, running was doable, I couldn't believe it. Somehow, I wasn't in the back of the class, and, more important, I was running next to Piper.

"Do you like to run?" she asked, huffing out the words. Her words almost landed me on my face. Shaking my head to snap me out of my thoughts, I had to get my head in the game. *No falling, Jade!*

Running, gah! "No." Realizing I was still doing well, I tried to sound winded. I probably failed.

She laughed. The sound lightened my steps; I had to slow down.

"I don't love it, but I run with my dad. We're training for a race this summer. You should run with us." Her smile turned slightly evil.

Yeah, I liked her.

"Be careful what you offer." Eyes narrowing in her direction, again, I tried not to fall. It was hard for Piper to talk and run, and I didn't want to draw attention to the fact I wasn't out of breath, so we mostly ran.

"I don't know," she continued between breaths, "you're keeping up, maybe we'll see." She gave me a quick grin, upping her speed at the same time.

Grunting, I upped my speed to catch up. It almost felt like the world was opening up under me as it hit me that running was no longer hard. It was confusing and thrilling all at the same time. Maybe this was something I should have expected, but so many other things had happened it hadn't occurred to me that it would be *this* easy.

Before I knew it, we were done.

"Nine minutes, twenty-three seconds," Coach Nelson told us with his normal disdainful sniff. "Ms. Stone, you've been training. You didn't even land on your nose this time. Ms. Schneider your time is a minute slower. You shouldn't slow down even to help a friend."

My jaw dropped. How the hell did that happen? Like Sarah, I tried to act tired, but I didn't do a great job at it. It didn't even phase me that Mr. Nelson was giving me guff again.

Plopping down next to Piper, I started to stretch out my legs.

"You are totally not winded." Piper turned on me,

breathing hard. "What gives?"

Leaning over to the side, my face burned. "I'm too distracted to be winded." I decided maybe flirting would redirect her from a question I didn't know how to answer.

Her face turned even more red. Score.

"Do you maybe want to walk home together after school?" she asked.

There may have been a bit of a squeal I swallowed before I tried not to answer too quickly. "Yeah, sure."

Acting casual appeared to not be my forte, but Piper didn't seem concerned.

The rest of gym class and the rest of the day flew by.

Following class, I checked my phone and Sarah had texted that she was heading home with Owen to train. I replied that I was walking home with Piper.

After much consideration, I decided I loved the shirt after all.

CHAPTER 27

Right when the last bell rang, I flew to my locker, barely saying hi to anyone, then made my way to the front of the school. Once there, I circled the lawn trying to figure out how to compose myself in a casual way. Should I sit on the stairs? Too cold. Stand by the doors? Too many students…

The tree! My bookbag settled on my back, I rested my arm against a tree where I could observe the flow of students leaving the building. The pounding of my heart in my ears was all I could hear.

It didn't take long before I saw Piper nudge her way

out amongst a crowd of student. She had her arms crossed and her head down as she made her way down the stairs. It looked like she was trying not to get noticed. She failed, I noticed her.

When she got to the bottom of the steps, I stepped into her path. Ironically, she didn't notice and knocked into me.

"Sorry," she mumbled before she looked up. Her blank expression transformed into a smile when she recognized me. My heart skipped a beat.

Returning the smile, I led the way off the school grounds. "Why do you hide in crowds at school so much?"

She looked up at me with her ocean blue eyes. Shrugging, she sighed, "It's easier. I've always been small. Blending in, not being noticed…it's easier than getting noticed by the wrong people. Don't get me wrong, if I have to, I'll stand up for myself, but I'd prefer to avoid the fight."

As we walked, she looked around the neighborhood. "How long have you lived in Stolzburg?"

It was such a silly question, I laughed. "My whole life. Have you moved around *that* much?"

"Yeah. My dad is a …" Piper paused, trying to find the right word. Her smell changed. She wore an artificial body scent that was flowery and a nice perfume, so I didn't really know her scent, but I could smell her anxiety. All the different scents she wore tickled my nose, so I didn't try to inhale too hard. Both the scents and the nervousness about the question were weird, but who was I to judge?

"My dad switches jobs…a lot." She gave me a half smile and a shrug, not seeming to know where to go with her answer.

Searching her face, I tried again. "Okay, but what does he do?"

She began to relax. She really was an odd duck. "My dad is a private consultant. He works mainly for different police forces. We move, he gets a job and then, after a year or two, he seems to get itchy and wants to move on. I don't really know why."

Slipping my hand into hers, I gave it a tiny squeeze. "How is he enjoying it here?"

Her focus shifted to the contact before continuing. "I thought it was good, but apparently my dad hit a dog or a wolf or some animal last night. I heard my parents fighting about it. Dad seemed weirdly upset about it, but cars, men, you know, weird."

I tripped over a crack in the sidewalk and would have fallen if Piper hadn't grabbed my arm.

"You okay?"

"Yeah. Just tripped." I shook my head to clear it. I didn't like that my school-life and were-life kept overlapping. *Why couldn't they be separate? Piper be separate?* "So, what about your mom? What does she do?"

Her shoulders dropped, and she got the cutest smile. "My mom's a nurse. Thankfully, there's enough jobs out there, so she's been able to get work easily. What about your parents?"

"My dad works in IT security. He owns his own business. My mom's a math professor. I live in the house my mom grew up in, so, very different from you."

There was a pause, then we both laughed at how dissimilar our upbringings were.

"Wow, I can't even imagine. The same house your whole life? I haven't lived in one place for more than two years running. That's so different. I'm torn between thinking it's cool, crazy, and a bit mysterious. Are you planning to live there when you're an adult, too?"

It felt like I'd be hit by a semi. Images poured through my head.

"Earth to Jade, hello? What did I say? Hello?" Piper waved her hand in front of my face. She looked concerned. Shaking myself out of my stunned paralysis, and having no idea how long I'd been frozen, I forced my attention back to her.

After a bit of awkward silence, I realized I had to say something. "Sorry. I don't think I can even explain what's going through my head right now and I don't really know. I'm really sorry. No, I probably won't live there when I grow up. Maybe my brother, Owen, will. I don't know, though. It's an…" Shaking my head to clear it, I was still stunned. "Interesting question."

Was I going to live in the pack house as a werepanther once I grew up? That had always been my plan. My life turned upside down! What an understatement. Things kept getting worse.

We walked for a bit longer and talked a bit more, but nothing really flowed well. "I'm sorry for turning into such a downer. I guess I've just got a lot on my mind. It's been quite a day. You were the highlight, though." Shocked at my own boldness, my face heated as my heart started beating faster again.

Piper smiled shyly back. "I agree. You've been my highlight, too. I'm really glad you wore that shirt today. I'm still mad impressed, by the way."

When we got to the next corner, we each went in our own direction.

When I got home, I went into the living room and crashed onto a couch. English became my best distraction…then biology. Once homework was done, my mind wandered as I sat and zoned out.

There was the option of starting gym for idiots with Sarah and Owen, but I admitted to myself, I didn't want to participate. The day had been long and rough, and I was ready for some alone time. So much had changed from the path I'd assumed for my life, I needed time to contemplate the changes and where my place was in the world. Where did I even belong?

Soon there was a herd of elephants on the stairs from the gym. Sarah and Owen were laughing and joking and making more noise than two people ought to be able to make.

"Hey, sis, you okay?"

"I've had a rough day, so, no. Just let me be."

Sarah plopped down next to me. "You sure? Nothing we can do?"

"Nothing will help, most of today sucked. There isn't anything you can do." Crossing my arms across my chest, I sank deeper into the couch.

"Nothing will help? Not even food?" Owen asked in a sing-song voice.

"No!"

He started to walk away.

Turning, I snatched his arm. "What kind of food?"

Sarah giggled.

"I'm guessing ice cream, chocolate fudge, and marshmallows."

My mouth watered and a moan escaped me.

"Two spoons? You willing to share with Sarah?"

Gazing over at her then back at Owen, I nodded.

Chuckling, Owen skipped off to the kitchen.

Once Owen left the room, Sarah asked, "Your walk with Piper wasn't so good?"

"No. Well, yes, it was nice, but she asked me a question that sent me reeling. I just froze. I probably freaked her out. I don't know, Sarah. She was like a small paddle boat of good in an ocean of bad. Knowing my luck, I sank that boat and now I'm left out to drown."

"Aren't you Ms. Sunshine?" she teased. "I'm sure it wasn't that bad."

Owen popped back in with the ice cream and the marshmallows. Just like that, I had my second positive moment of the day.

"What happened?" Sarah asked, scooping up some ice cream.

"We were talking about where we grew up. I told her that we lived in the house my mom grew up in."

"Wait," Sarah interrupted her brow hitting her hair line. "Your mom grew up here?"

"Well, yeah, this is the pack house. My grandparents were the alphas before Mom and Dad. Then, when Mom was so dominant, it was just natural that she would take control of the pack. She took over responsibility for both the pack and the pack house. But this *is* the pack house and belongs to the entire pack."

I took a few bites of ice cream. So gooey and good. The sweet fortification gave me strength. "I know my family has had use of the place for years, generations even, but it will never be my house. It was the first time I'd thought about it. My whole life I'd just assumed I would probably stay here. But I can't, can I? I don't even know if we'll be welcomed into the pack, officially."

"Not this again," groaned Owen.

"Stop, Owen. This isn't just me whining. You know as well as I do that packs are made up of a single type of wereanimal. We can all say that I'm welcome as a person, maybe even the healer, but that doesn't mean anything on a full moon night. Sarah and I might not be able to run with the pack. We might not *be* pack."

I was adamant. I had been doing a lot of thinking and I was beginning to realize my world was unraveling.

Being a werepanther and not a werewolf meant I would never *be* pack.

"Oh, and it was Piper's dad's car you hit, or hit you, last night."

His smile disappeared and he groaned. His weight hit the couch as he collapsed beside me, grabbed the ice cream and my spoon, and dug in.

CHAPTER 28

Saturday was panther day. Everyone was going to meet my panther form in small groups, the wolves, the non-wolf adults, and the kiddos. Parts should be fun, but the day would be long. Sarah and her parents were up in the treehouse with my mom, observing. My dad was in wolf form on the other side of the yard.

If all went well with my panther's introduction, then something like this might happen with Sarah, too. If she were to become part of the pack, her panther would need to be comfortable with the wolves of the pack. Most likely, this day of introductions was going to be dull, long, and tiring. In the end, we would all eat copious amounts of food. *Yum, food!*

As I lay in the grass waiting for the fun to begin, I thought about the rest of the week. Both days had gone by quick and smooth. Piper and I had spoken more during gym and exchanged phone numbers. That's as far as it had gone between us for now.

The chaos caused by my shirt died down when I wore average outfits for the rest of the week. Jacob showed no more interest in me, and Sarah and I were getting better at filtering out all the high school drama. We had a lot to learn, but we were on the right path. Mom helped by providing easier meditation advice for us to follow.

We were also getting better—or was it worse—at gym class.

While I was reminiscing, the morning of introduction had begun. The door to the dining room had slid open, perking me up. We started with the teens: Owen, José, Bevin, and Dillan, who came strolling out of the house. They all got to size me up, so to speak. I just lay there with my head on my paws watching them. This was going to be fun.

José approached slowly. "Dios Mio. Chica, you are lovely." He emitted the sweet scent of fear, and his eyes were wide.

I rolled my eyes.

Bevin let out a bark of laughter. "Sarah told me to watch for that. That is freaking hilarious. Jade, panthers don't roll their eyes. José, what are you scared of? It's Jade." Bevin came up and scratched my ears, petted my head, and then gave me a full body pet. It felt good and I stretched into it before lying back down. By then the others were there.

José relaxed and turned to my brother. "You're right, Owen, I would take her home and make her my cat. I now want a pet panther."

Gazing at José, I thought, *what a dork.*

His eyes shone with admiration. "Such beauty. Jade, can you show us how you can climb and jump?"

Sarah snorted up in the treehouse. "Don't forget pounce."

Chuffing in annoyance, I got up and started into the trees. Dashing back, I found a sturdy tree, and leapt. I caught the trunk and finished the climb to a high branch. A vibration began in my belly as I curled up and looked down, giving them a smirk.

Bevin squinted up at me. "She's smirking at us, isn't she?"

"Yep," Owen confirmed. "Someone should explain to her what expressions panthers do and don't have."

José watched in awe. "That was amazing, simply majestic."

Okay, I decided, I would cut him some slack. Leaping down near the base of the tree, I rubbed against José's leg. Eyeing Owen as prey, I lowered myself into attack position, back legs bunched, and sprang. My pounce was almost ten feet and ended just in front of my brother, whose eyes went saucer-sized. There was a chorus of gasps from the treehouse and the boys in the yard. Stretching my muscles,

I sauntered back to where I had been and laid back down.

Owen laughed, eyes still wide in wonder. "That was epic. I want to be able to do that."

My Mom stood in the treehouse and spoke down to us. "Enough, it's time to let the younger kids out to see Jade. We have them acclimated to the wolves, but Jade is a bit more… well, Jade is just more."

I chuffed in amusement.

The boys sighed and went back inside. Next on the Jade Tour were Tanner and Clare, in wolf form. They were two of the most dominant and seemed to have the hardest time when I had changed in the first meeting. They were escorting out their respective children: Easton, eight, and Estrella, thirteen.

Alejandro, José's dad, would come out, staying human in case a kid needed to be hustled out quickly. Sitting up for this interaction, and remembering Tanner's issues, I tried to center myself in my calm place. He approached hunched, head down, tail down. It surprised me that my panther was dominant. Lowing myself a bit, I licked his snout and he licked mine. The girls started climbing on me.

Clare just stood there, frozen. After a few minutes of her standing, Mom came up and told Alejandro to take the girls in. She grabbed Clare's snout and looked her in the eyes. Clare took a more submissive posture. Dad, in wolf form, came up next to Clare so that she wasn't alone. They approached me together. Clare licked my snout, and

I returned the gesture. She tackled me, but it was play, no teeth or claws.

Dad just sat with his tongue lulled out in a wolf laugh, approving.

On my back with Clare on me, I was about to flip when I heard a gasp from the treehouse. Ignoring it, I could smell Clare's scent changing from anger and attack mode to something more playful. This was more important than what was happening with the norms.

There was talking. Mom was probably explaining about everything that was going on. Maybe she was pointing out that, if I were in any danger, Dad would have intervened.

We play fought long enough for Clare to fully calm down. After our "fight", she gave me a headbutt and ran off.

The day continued like this with small groups of wolves, and humans. Everyone got to see me up close. All the kids got to play. They petted me and climbed on me. Most of the pack was fine in both forms, though there were a few others who needed help like Clare. The play fights made things interesting.

The last group to come out was T.J., Andy, and Allison. T.J. was the only dominant of the three. Andy and Allison were submissive, and Allison loved panthers. Allison had also spent over an hour poking and prodding me, so her being here was funny. Though her human-self had seen me in panther form, this was the first time she would meet me as a wolf.

With two submissive wolves and T.J., my almost brother, this group was considered the safest group after the first group with the boys.

Even so, my mom and dad were staying on alert.

The three wolves came out. I was standing, though I was tired. I had been sitting and standing for what felt like hours.

Allison practically ran out and headbutted me. Then she ran her head over my neck. If she had been a cat, she would be scent-marking me.

"That's Allison," I heard my mom say. "She's practically half panther herself. I think she wants Jade to know how much she is wanted."

Sarah, who had yelped at what felt like an attack, relaxed. "Did she scent-mark Jade?"

The air started to buzz. My awareness sharpened. Andy was sitting near me, head down, tail tucked. He wasn't looking towards me. T.J. was snarling at me. He was in full attack mode, tail down, legs spread wide, head down. I slowly shifted so that Allison was behind me.

"T.J., stand down," Mom commanded. His alpha demanded.

There was a thump as she landed on the ground. She wasn't in wolf form, so she was more vulnerable, but she was still fierce. She was alpha. He should've obeyed.

Why wasn't he listening to his alpha? Was this a dominance fight in T.J.'s mind? Dad, still in wolf form, got in front of Mom as they approached.

Before they could get to him, T.J. lunged.

I had only been a panther for a week and a half. There could only be one reason he was attacking, he meant to kill me. He was trying to eliminate me from the pack. This was my first fight in this form. *What do I do?* My heart jumped as I started to back up.

Out of nowhere, Andy tackled T.J. from the side. He was trying to help me, protect me.

When T.J. was close, I swiped his shoulder with my paw as hard as I could. He went flying but recovered quickly. He had been fighting in wolf form for years. He leapt towards my neck, and, though he missed with his teeth, he scratched my flank with his claws.

Hurt, pain.

All I could think to do was bite down on his snout. The crunch made me nauseous, but I pushed his nose into the dirt. Leveraging my weight so he couldn't escape, we each fought for control. He was tugging to break free, but everything was happening too fast. Lost and confused, I didn't know what else to do.

Suddenly, Dad was there. He seized T.J.'s throat in his jaws and yanked. I heard a snap and I leapt back, dropping T.J.'s snout. I stood immobilized, legs tense, vibrating in fear.

Breathe, Jade. Oh gods, was that blood? What had just happened? What had I done?

This was not what today was supposed to be about.

There was screaming and crying. It was coming from the treehouse. It broke me out of my paralysis. I tore my eyes from the dead body of the wolf, of T.J., my brother, up to the treehouse and saw horror on Sarah's face. Gazing back down, I saw blood and death.

Panicking, I ran. Branches hit my snout and leaves crunched under my paws until I decided on a tree to fly into. Climbing higher, my whole body shook as I hid.

I heard people calling for me, but I was terrified. The questions kept swirling in my head. What had I done? What had happened? Why had T.J. attacked me?

My worries and depression overtook me, and I sobbed. Who knew panthers could cry hard enough to shake a tree limb this hard? Would it break off and fall? Did I deserve the pain if it did?

It had been such a long week, such a long morning. All I wanted to do was curl up and disappear, but my heart was beating too fast. My side hurt; I was bleeding. I knew it wasn't anything serious, but it was just one more thing.

The day had started off so well, everyone meeting my panther form. What had happened with T.J.? Right before spring break he had hung out with me and Owen in the basement, the three of us playing a game of Settlers of Catan and eating popcorn. We'd been playing that since T.J. moved in with us when I was seven.

I knew his new job was stressing him out, but could it have changed him? Before I left for Florida, he'd mentioned the job, but not what it was. But this seemed different somehow, more.

Now he was dead. I would never know. We all knew that pack life…werewolf life…could be violent, short, but why did he attack me? When did he go from being my foster brother, my supporter, a close member of my family, to my self-appointed executioner?

I could feel the hot tears running trails through the fur of my face. Did panthers cry?

"Jade, Jade, Jade!" I heard Sarah calling for me. "You know I can smell you. I can smell your fear, your blood, and your guilt. I can feel how confused you are. I'm scared and confused, too. I need my best friend. I'm afraid of what my parents are going to do. Please, Jade, I need you, I need my best friend."

The flood of her emotions flowed through me. She was scared and alone. This, too, was my fault, I had done that. I had abandoned her…again.

She was crying. "I'm afraid of what I saw. I'm afraid of losing you."

The last part was quiet. She was hurting. This was all too much. Sighing deeply and knowing I had to be more, do more, I hopped down.

Sarah stared at me. She dragged her fingers through the fur between my ears. "I brought clothes if you want to change. If you don't want to change, I get it, but I could really use you right now."

Chuffing, which made her laugh, I focused on my human form, relaxed, and let my body shift. Being injured brought a new level of pain to the process.

My shoulder had a gash. Changing form had stopped the bleeding and progressed the healing. The guilt was eating me from the inside, and I didn't want to face food, but changing form took energy. Healing took energy. "Gods, I'm hungry. Please tell me you have food."

She handed me clothes and an energy bar.

I gave her a quick hug before getting dressed and eating. It wasn't enough. My stomach growled loudly, letting Sarah know as well.

"Wow, you *are* hungry," Sarah said quietly, more to herself. "Jade, I need you. I think my parents are going to leave the pack. They freaked out after T.J.," she faltered, "after he," another pause, "after."

"After I killed him." My voice was dead, and I felt drained.

"You didn't kill him, your dad did," Sarah said with some finality, defending me.

"No, Sarah, it was a pack kill, and I held him down. It was me. I don't know what I could have done differently, but Sarah, you don't understand, he was like my uncle, practically my brother."

She hugged me as tears flowed down my cheeks. I hiccupped, trying to control my tears. Overwhelmed with how much Sarah didn't know, I knew I had to start at the beginning. I had hidden all my pack stories from her, so she really didn't even know about T.J. and Candice. "He moved in after his parents died. He was family. I don't know what happened. Candice, his sister, is going to hate me. Gods, Sarah, I can't face her. I can't face any of them."

"Jade, they aren't blaming you."

"But will your parents?" The tears fell harder. "It's all been too much."

"Can we head back to the house?" Sarah grabbed my hand and started to pull. "Please?"

"I don't want to lose you, Sarah. I can't lose you. It will be one thing too many. Will your parents really do this?"

"I think so."

"Can we have a few more minutes?" Pulling my hand from hers, I wrapped my arm around her waist, needing more contact.

We ended up back in the house almost an hour later. We walked through the woods slowly, talking, holding each other, needing to touch. We'd always been close but being werepanthers had upped the need for contact. That may have been part of the rough week; I hadn't been giving in to the werepanther side at all, trying to ignore it for the human side. We talked about that among everything else.

When we got back, there was a tense silence in the house. I could smell all the people. Most had left, but the teens were in the basement and the parents were in the kitchen. Sarah led me towards the kitchen, knowing as well as I did that I needed calories. The last bit of the walk I had been dizzy enough that I'd almost fallen a few times.

As I approached, I could smell the meats of the deli

sandwiches as well as PB&Js. I took a deeper sniff and thought I could smell chili simmering. That was probably dinner.

In the kitchen I saw all the parents sitting around the table. My eyes were drawn to Cindy who was staring daggers at me. Tom didn't look as angry, but he also didn't look happy. Unable to handle the emotional judgment, I went in search of the food.

There was a pile of sandwiches on the island. Sitting on a stool, I couldn't stop myself from grabbing one and eating. Sarah joined me. My mom watched, looking sympathetic.

"I can't believe you can eat after what you did," Cindy said, a nasty edge to her voice.

The food was halfway to my mouth, my hand shook, and I didn't know what to do. My stomach cramped with hunger, but I couldn't eat in front of these people. Slowly, I put the sandwich down on a plate I found by the food. Eyes wide, I stared at them. Did I look as guilty I felt?

Sarah gave me a sympathetic pat on the hand before her head swiveled to her mom. "Mom, would you rather she let that werewolf kill her? She held the snout down so that she wouldn't get bitten. She couldn't control the others. It wasn't her fault."

Swallowing the bile that surged into the back of my throat, I glanced at my parents, who were letting the lie stand. They were going to let the decision be mine; Sarah was my friend.

I couldn't. "Sarah." Eyes down at my lap, my voice

wavered. "I hoped that the pack would do that."

She stared up at me in shock and I raised my eyes slowly to meet hers. "T.J. wouldn't attack me unless he meant to kill me. As soon as he attacked me, only one of us was going to get out of the back yard alive. I'm glad that the pack decided to help me, they didn't have to in what I'm guessing he saw as a dominance fight."

The shock and disgust rolled off Sarah, carpeting the room. Not wanting to leave this unfinished, I locked my gaze with hers, trying to get her to understand. "I've never fought before in animal form, and not being a werewolf, the rules aren't the same. I hoped that when I grabbed him the others would help me…choose me to live." *And him to die*, I thought. I couldn't quite say those words out loud.

My eyes dropped back down to my hands. "I knew that if they supported me, T.J. wouldn't survive. If they didn't, I probably wouldn't be here now. You have to understand the animal side of being a wereanimal—it's dangerous."

Sarah's face contorted in disgust. "Have you seen other deaths?"

"Yes." A tear escaped my control.

Sarah stood, starting to back away from me. "Is this why Annie left?"

"I don't know, maybe."

"Would you have chosen to become a werewolf if you hadn't become a werepanther, if you never changed naturally like Owen did?" she demanded, fire in her eyes. I could sense the volcano in her gut.

"Yes."

It felt like a door was slamming in my face with the whirlwind of emotions coming off Sarah. I could taste her horror that I would choose a life filled with such violent death.

"Why? How? How can you live with this kind of death and violence? I don't understand it, Jade." Sarah was looking at me as if I were a stranger.

Within the turmoil of her emotions, she was scared and confused. Her scent was all over the place. I didn't know if it was about me or T.J. I don't know if she knew either.

Her wide eyes never left me, she backed away until she stood by her parents. They had gotten up from the table when she had started yelling. I felt the line being drawn as I was losing the best friend I'd had for so long.

She and her parents would leave. They wouldn't tell our secrets, because they were their secrets, too, but we would lose them from the pack and from our lives.

The world was plunging me into an abyss. Sarah's emotions were a tumultuous twister of confusion, but Cindy's were a scalpel. She knew exactly what to feel. She was disgusted. She saw my family as disgusting animals and serial killers wrapped into one. Somehow, I was the center of her hate.

I didn't know how much more of this I could handle. Tears began to burn down my face.

"No!" Sarah yelled. "You don't get to cry!" She was

almost rabid. She was probably feeding off her mom's emotions as well. "You did this, Jade, you. You don't get to cry!" She turned and ran out of the house.

Momentarily shocked out of my misery, I stood there. A part of me wanted to go after her but knew I shouldn't.

Cindy glared at me and slowly followed her daughter out. Tom watched his family leave then turned to me. I suddenly realized he hadn't been emoting all the darkness and hate. His emotions had been tired and protective of his daughter. "I don't think you killed that person, Jade, but I don't know if pack life is for me or my family. I'm asking you to stay away from Sarah at school. I think it would be for the best." He looked sad as he turned and left.

I don't know when I stood, but after his words I would have fallen if my parents hadn't caught me. They helped me over to the table and brought the plate of sandwiches. Recoiling, I gaped at the food almost fearfully.

Mom's eyes were wet with tears, but she was insistent. "Jade, you have to eat. It will be dangerous for you not to."

Dad's voice was dangerously low. "Jade, you can't take it to heart what they said. You know our ways. You also know Sarah, like you, is a new wereanimal. She was picking up on, and reacting to, all the emotions around her. Give it time. I'm glad you're not dead. I know you are worried about your place here, and I'm worried, too. If we have to move to a new house, then we will. We don't need to live in the pack's den house to be alphas. It's helpful, but it isn't mandatory."

Confused, my gaze shot to Dad. "We? What? What are you talking about?"

Mom gave me a small smile. "Dad wouldn't let us leave without him, honey. I know he didn't react well on that first day, but Dad has a good heart, he just needed to get things figured out in his head."

With a bit more coercion, I finally took a bite. It was hard to swallow. Knowing my parents were right, I had to get my mind on other things besides Sarah's hate. "Did Sarah's parents call the police?"

Mom shook her head and huffed out a bitter laugh. "No, T.J. stayed in wolf form long enough for us to get them inside, so calling the police would have been… complicated. Ironically, they never asked if he would stay a wolf. He's probably back in human form by now. I'm just glad they didn't see it. Alejandro, Jackson, and Clare took care of the body."

"Does Candice hate me?" My voice was small, much to my chagrin.

Owen came into the kitchen before they could answer, followed by Bevin and José. Owen sat down next to me and engulfed me in a huge hug. He could be clueless sometimes, but I couldn't ask for a better brother. Then he got up and let Bevin and José in. They book-ended me and having friends, not just family, who supported me, made something inside click into place.

Dad watched us, still looking ready to fight. "Tanner took

Candice out. I'm going to meet them to discuss the situation later today. I want to see if she knows why her brother attacked you. Chris may come along as a calming influence."

Mom glanced at the boys and dismissed us with a wave. "Why don't you all go down to the basement?"

Not sure if I could stand or if I would be good company, I looked up at Mom helplessly.

Bevin grabbed my arm and pulled me up. "José, grab her other arm, Owen, get the food." Together, they dragged me and the food to the basement.

Bevin sat next to me on the couch with his arm around me. "You going to be okay?"

Curling into him, I shook my head. "How much did you guys hear?"

"All of it." Owen said. "You've had a messed-up couple of weeks, sis. Anything they missed, I filled in," he added helpfully.

José plopped down on my other side with some ice cream. "On the bright side, you have us. And, if all else fails, I'll adopt you to be my pet panther."

Laughing weakly, I straightened up and knocked my head against his shoulder then grabbed the ice cream.

Bevin's arm tightened around me in a squeeze. "I'm guessing, once the shock wears off, Sarah will come around. You two have been close friends for too long to let this end things. Also, she's a werepanther, like you. She'll need you in her life."

My head hit the back of the couch. "She really won't need me. If she wants to go off on her own, she can."

After a bit of research, I had learned that panthers were solitary animals and didn't live in packs as wolves did. My theory was my need for pack was because I had been brought up in a pack society. It was my human side, not my panther side, that craved people. As wereanimals we needed human contact, but I wasn't sure if Sarah would crave it as much as I did.

The four of us were too restless for sleep, so we stayed up late. It was nice having my friends to help with unpacking my thoughts about T.J.'s death, and the loss of Sarah. We pulled the mattresses off a few of the basement beds and piled them in the middle of the group space. It felt like a slumber party from when we were six, but much sadder.

Eventually we ran out of things to say, and we started a movie, a comedy. If my laughter was forced, no one said anything. And when one of the boys saw me crying, they brought more ice cream.

The next morning Dad informed Owen and me it was time to learn how to fight.

CHAPTER 29

Learning to fight wasn't as much fun as it sounded.

Dad's training was for both human and animal forms and included hand-to-hand combat, strength training, and cardio. Needless to say, the program sucked.

Dad paced back and forth in front of us holding folders. "Owen, Jade, I have devised a new schedule for you. It is based on a two-day rotation." Dad stopped and turned to Owen. "Owen, you've been doing this for a couple of months, but now that Jade is here, we can really push this into high gear."

High gear. Did that translate to torture? Looking at

Owen, he seemed thrilled. Stomach dropping, I wasn't.

Dad gave each of us the calendar detailing our training program.

After school we would mainly do independent training. We had the full gym in the barn, in which to get our "daily goals achieved." There was a whiteboard on the gym wall that kept our overall records. Today, much like Coach Nelson this past week, Dad wanted to get a baseline of our abilities. Unlike gym class, neither of us were allowed to hold back.

Although Owen had been doing this for a while, he didn't have any baseline numbers down on the whiteboard hanging on the wall. It looked new.

Today we had to run, lift weights, and spar against each other.

Basic hand-to-hand combat, such as karate, was taught to all the kiddos starting at about age six. Despite that, this was the most intense sparring event I had ever experienced, and somehow, I took Owen down. That was a first. I don't know which of the three of us was the most surprised.

Dad took notes on his clipboard. "So, we need to get you trained to fight in panther form. Your basic hand-to-hand isn't bad, though you are weak and a bit of a klutz."

Breathing hard, both Owen and I tried to laugh at that description. Dad ignored me.

"You should check out some videos online or from Allison that show how panthers fight, watch them, study them, become one with them. Then you need to practice the moves. I know how a wolf moves and fights, but nothing about panthers. I've set up times for you to work with Allison after school on Tuesdays, Wednesdays, and Thursdays."

My jaw fell open. "If yesterday is any indication," he added, "then you can't afford to wait to learn how to fight as a panther, Jade."

Despite knowing this was coming, my heart started to beat faster. Being a wereanimal was dangerous and, chances were, T.J. wasn't the only werewolf who didn't want me around. Dad's words confirmed the worst of my fears. Breathing deeply, I tried to calm myself down.

"Owen, I've given you a schedule as well, but I want you to go with Jade to train with Allison. The more people aware of the panther training, the better, that way when Allison is unavailable, you can work with Jade in both forms."

Owen's eyes sparkled with joy. "Awesome! Will there be multi-animal fighting drills?"

As excited as this made Owen, my body began to feel numb, and I groaned.

"Possibly. You'll probably be a better sparring partner for her in animal form. She needs to be able to protect herself against wolves and fight back when she's attacked."

"Do I have any say in this?" I asked.

Dad shot off a curt, "No," before continuing his directions. "I really need you both up to speed. Yesterday was more real than I liked. Now, begin with a forty-five-minute run. I expect at least five miles."

My mouth dropped further open, and my breathing became choppy.

"Yes, Jade, you need a good warm-up."

"Warm-up?" I demanded.

"Forty-five-minutes or five-miles?" Owen asked.

"Forty-five-minutes. But Owen, I know you can double that and then some; I want you to stay with Jade and push her. See what you can do."

Gaping at them, slack-jawed and frozen in place, I felt like a hatchling kicked from the nest before she's ready to fly. My run time in gym class had been just over nine minutes and I had been thrilled. What were these two thinking? Five miles? More than five miles? What the hell were they thinking?

Owen came over and nudged me. I didn't move. He nudged again, harder, and I backed up a bit.

Dad dumped water over my head. Crying out, I shook all over.

"Better?"

Blinking up at him through wet hair, my brain began to turn back on.

"Now go!" he yelled.

He was my alpha. What choice did I have?

Owen next to me, prodding me on, encouraging me, I ran.

Monday morning, Sarah wasn't by the lockers.

She hadn't met me for our walk, and I hadn't seen her anywhere along the way. Though it had been expected, I took it harder than I would admit to anyone. As I approached the lockers, I tried to be strong and hide my disappointment. Because I had been watching for her, I was the last of our group to arrive.

"Hi, guys, happy Monday." I didn't sound happy, but it was Monday. No one sounded happy on a Monday. It was probably illegal.

Bevin and José looked at me uncertainly.

"Hey, Jade." Bevin hugged me. "Sarah's already been through. She grabbed her books and ran. I tried to ask her about Sunday, but she wouldn't even look at me."

"It's okay." Not being a wereanimal, he couldn't smell the lie. Trudging to my locker, I got my backpack ready for my morning classes. Apparently, he could hear it fine.

"What did you do on Sunday, chica?"

"Dad set up a training program for me and Owen. Owen was probably already on one, but now we train together." What he'd been doing before hadn't been like this new routine.

"You don't know if he was on one?" Bevin asked skeptically.

I shut my locker hard. "He just became a werewolf before spring break. I'm not his keeper."

They both looked at me, their expressions half amused and half pitying.

Sensing my mood, José wrapped an arm around my waist. "How did the new training program go?"

"You know that fitness fun from last week? Yeah, well, Mr. Nelson has nothing on Dad. We had to get our baseline numbers. Sparring, running, weights, the works. He made Owen and me run for forty-five minutes to see how far Owen could push me. Apparently, on his own Owen can go over ten miles."

"And?" Bevin's eyes twinkled. He knew my hatred of running and my habit of falling.

I mumbled an answer.

Bevin leaned in. "What? I don't think you even said words."

Blushing, I mumbled again.

He and José narrowed their eyes in suspicion.

Owen chose that moment to join us.

"Jade telling you how she kicked my butt in one-on-one combat? Or is she telling you about running eleven miles in forty-five minutes? I almost couldn't keep up with her. Damn, she was fast."

My face turned so red it hurt. Quickly pulling out of José's arm, I opened my locker and started rummaging through it for good measure.

"What?!" Bevin yelled as I heard José laugh. Their voices rang down the hall causing a dead silence in its wake. Oh, no. I practically crawled into my locker trying to hide.

After our momentary drama, the hallway resumed its

normal level of noise and commotion. Relenting, I closed my locker to face the boys.

"You did what?" Bevin demanded, still too loudly.

I held up my hands in the universal sign of quiet and my eyes may have bugged out.

"Oh, did my little sister fail to tell you about her awesome Sunday?" Owen's smile was devious and evil. He knew I was embarrassed, and he clearly didn't care.

"Why are you over here, anyway?" Nearly losing it, I snapped at him. "Why aren't you with Brooke and the rest of your crew?" I may have sneered out Brooke's name.

"Just making sure my little sis is surviving." His expression was earnest as he grabbed my shoulders. "Seriously, Jade, are you okay? I know that Sarah not being here is hard. How are you? She's in your first class, right?"

After a slow blink and a deep breath, I answered. "Yeah, and I'm fine. Just, let me be. Okay?"

They kept asking questions that led to me thinking about Sarah. If I thought about her not being here, I would cry. All my will was working on my control, and it was a constant battle right then. Whatever shields I put up would fail and I wouldn't be able to handle the day. My hands started to shake as I thought about it.

Owen's hands slid down my arm, and he gave a bit of a squeeze. It helped. The shaking stopped, my breathing evened out.

"Thanks, that helps." Shifting my gaze up to him, I

shook my head in confusion. "Why does that help?"

"It's a pack thing. Whenever I'm about to lose it, Mom or Dad touches me, and I calm down. I think it is a wolf thing, but since you grew up in the pack, I was hoping it would help." He gave me a goofy half-grin, spun, and sauntered off to be with his friends.

Watching him leave, I shook my head, befuddled.

Bevin came up and swung his arm around my shoulders. "Just let us know when you need us, hon, you know we're here for you."

José came up and kissed my cheek. "You know it, chica."

Finally feeling centered, I checked the clock. It was almost time for class. "I have to get to English. See you in Bio," I said to Bevin, "and both of you at lunch."

They both nodded and we scattered in our different directions to our classes.

When I got to English class, Sarah sat across the room in a different seat. The class roster wasn't full, so she must have asked to be moved. I tried not to react as I sat down. Nothing to be done about it.

She believed I was a monster. Maybe I was. Who knew? My whole life had been lived in the pack. That was all I'd ever known. I had loved T.J. and it hurt to think about him no longer being around. Others had been killed during dominance fights, including T.J.'s parents. There would be other deaths in the future. It pained me to think of Owen, Bevin, and José possibly dying in fights.

Maybe Sarah was right, thinking I was horrible for always assuming my life, the pack life, was normal.

After English, I ran into Brooke. I tried to avoid her, but she was having none of that.

She stopped me by putting her hand on my chest, again, and pushing. "Freshman."

Sighing in exasperation, her glee at goading me oozed out of her. Sensing her hope that she could embarrass me, I tried to make my face blank. Being able to read her thoughts would've been nice, but she was almost transparent enough that it wasn't necessary.

Eyes neutral, I slowly raised one brow in the way Mom always did. "Are you stating your class level, or are you confused again? Say it with me, sophomore…or better yet, leave me alone."

Her face contorted into something ugly, her top lip half bunching up and her eyes slitting. She tried to push me, but I didn't move. At that, her face slackened for a second, but then I could taste her furry. "I hear you've lost your friend. I guess everyone knows what a loser you are now."

That hit below the belt and hurt. "Do you need something, Brooke?"

She knew she had struck the mark, and the pleasure was written all over her face. "Just letting you know that everyone here knows how much of a loser you really are. Pretty soon Owen will look at you with disgust like the rest of us, you know that, right?"

With that, she spun and sashayed down the hall.

Watching her, bile rising, I shivered in disgust before turning away to head to second period. There were people watching me, so I tried to keep an expressionless face before walking away.

To say the week was awful would only understate how bad it truly was. Sarah, my best friend and rock, now hated me. There was a torture, er, exercise program every day. And maybe worst of all, there was a cloud of ambiguity still over me that I just wanted solved. It left an air of tension with me and everyone else.

Thursday at lunch I sat with José and Bevin. We were still sitting outside. Sarah had joined her basketball friends inside. When I peeked in on her, she looked robotic. So many people in the lunchroom couldn't be easy.

Checking my texts, I pocketed my phone. "Dad wants to wait on the Aunt Allison practices until next week. I'm going to watch the videos and do some studying first."

José nodded. "That's not a bad idea. Catching up to the level you know about wolves will put you in a more comfortable place."

Bevin nodded. "He's not wrong. It's part of why you've been off."

I snorted. These two knew me too well.

"Owen's been watching the videos with me, you two should come and watch, too. Maybe Friday night?"

José rolled his eyes. "How romantic. Studying on a

Friday night."

Bevin raised an eyebrow. "Do you have other plans?"

José huffed out a negative and shook his head. "No, but it would be nice."

"You know, Owen has really gotten into the videos. His mind for strategy is actually fairly impressive. I think he's coming up with some training runs our Dad may implement."

Both boys looked at me in utter bewilderment.

I smiled and shrugged. "It's like sports, something he gets."

"What about you?" Bevin asked. "Any part of the training that you've really gotten into this last week?"

I thought about it. "Every morning Mom, Owen, and I get together for about forty-five minutes. We drink coffee and work on increasing our sensitivity to our senses."

José's looked at me questioningly. "Like sight, scent, and hearing?"

Nodding quickly, my body buzzed with excitement. "But it's more than that. There's touch, intuition, and this otherness." Circling my hands, I tried to figure out the words to use. "I can't explain it, but it helps when filtering out everything at school. Gods, I'd love to show what I'm learning to Sarah…if I could."

José wrapped an arm around me. "I know, chica, it'll happen."

Leaning into him, I sighed. "Anyway, mornings are turning out to be one of my favorite parts of the day."

The boys gave me offended looks. I smiled hugely. "Well, mornings and lunches, of course!"

Thursday night, I was home alone in my room studying the differences between panther and wolf healing when someone knocked on my door.

What? No one should be here. They had all gone out, giving me some alone time.

Feeling like an idiot, I remembered I was a werepanther. Lifting my nose, I used my newly honed senses and took a sniff. Candice.

What was she doing here?

Candice had lived here for long enough to feel that this was her house, too. She was still grieving her brother's death and probably wanted some familiar surroundings. She was probably searching for Mom.

"Yeah!" Setting aside the book I was reading on veterinary sciences, I rolled over and sat up.

Candice quietly opened the door and stepped inside. "Hi, Jade."

"Hi, Candice." Her eyes were a bit red, and she looked lost. I stood. We had always been close, but I wasn't sure why she was here. She was only twenty-five. She had turned furry at twenty, so she was a newer wolf and almost submissive, being near the bottom of the pack. She and T.J. were both low in the dominance hierarchy. Well, T.J. had been low, before I helped kill him.

Wrangling in my scattered thoughts, I needed to focus on Candice and why she was here.

"I just wanted to talk. I don't know why T.J. attacked you. I mean I can guess, but…he and I had discussed it, and we didn't think you should be part of the pack."

This hit me like a shot through the gut, and probably showed on my face. My eyes widened.

She started to pace around my room. "You're surprised? We're a werewolf pack. You're a panther, Jade, not a wolf. I don't think you belong in the pack. I don't even think you should be healer around here, but I know that I'll be outvoted."

Falling back down on my bed, hard, her words clawed at me. Her emotions washed through me as, dumfounded, I watched her pace. The pain each of her words caused was a knife to my gut, my heart, my soul. Breathing became difficult. Everything in my world was crumbling around me, and I couldn't seem to do anything about it.

She came over and grabbed my hand as she'd done so many times before. It felt warm, loving. "I just want you to know that I still love you like a niece." My mind reeled at this sudden change. Her emotions were oscillating from hate and disgust to love and caring. The roller-coaster ride wasn't one I could keep up with. Trying to imitate a statue, I even held my breath so as not to set her off.

She dropped my hand and moved over to my desk and sat down. The coldness returned before I could close my senses to more of her fluctuation. "But my wolf will never love you as a pack member. To me, they are very different relationships. My parents raised T.J. and me to think that way."

The different emotions I was getting from her and her wolf were shocking. It was almost like she and her wolf were at war with each other. It physically hurt. If she didn't figure it out, she would have a psychological break, I was sure of it. Two such different beliefs couldn't coexist peacefully. Was this the answer to why T.J. attacked?

She stood up and started looking at all the pack pictures on my mirror and wall. "My parents fought for pack, and they died for pack." Pride rolled off her as she stared at me. "Your parents and your grandparents ended up raising us after our own parents lost their dominance fight." Pride spiked into hate that I could block. "Speaking of which, you didn't win yours yesterday, did you? Your dad fought it for you."

This last was said with such venom, I felt poisoned. The whole situation was confusing and wrong. Her argument made no sense. Dominance was fought for placement in the pack. T.J. attacked me because I was a panther and he hated the idea of me joining the pack, not because I already had a place in the pack.

She stood again, pacing, fists clenched as tight as her jaw. "You just sat there, holding down my brother, while your alpha did the work for you." She was getting herself worked up as I wilted. Stung over and over with each word, each accusation, I sank deeper into my bed. "No, Jade, I don't think you should be part of the pack. I don't think you should run with us on full moon nights, and I don't think you should be our healer. You are *not* a werewolf."

She stopped her pacing to spin and face me, lips twisted in a sneer. "You could've been an amazing werewolf, and an amazing pack healer. But now you're a werepanther. You should go find your own way out in the world."

By the end she was spitting out the words with hatred. I could feel the venom piercing me like knives. All my blocks were gone, and every word hit its target. It was too much.

Sneering, she was through with me. She spun on her heel and left my room.

Stunned, I sat there, unable to think or move. Candice had done all this while I was the only one in the house, so no one else had witnessed her hatred, her loathing for me.

My heart pounded. The patterns on the carpet blurred as my eyes stung. Somewhere in the house there was a ticking of an old clock, and I continued to sit. Footsteps. Mom's footsteps. When did Candice leave? How long had it been?

My mom sat on the bed next to me. Slowly, I shifted my gaze from the floor to her knees. She hugged me. I leaned in. She could probably tell I was upset. My breathing was ragged. She tried to get me to speak but I didn't have the words. Anything I said could lead to another death, and I didn't want to get Candice killed. My parents wouldn't stand for their daughter to be treated in such a way.

Or maybe they would. So much had changed. Did I even know how things worked? Eventually, Mom tucked me in and left, telling me to get some sleep. Not thinking sleep was possible, I was surprised when the nightmares began.

Nightmares about school, Sarah, and Candice.

CHAPTER 30

Friday was mostly a haze. Dragging myself from bed, I had to separate nightmare from fact. My mind played tricks on me all day, making concentrating on school impossible.

"Jade. Jade?" Snapping in front of my nose finally got my attention and I looked up.

"Hi, Bevin, what's up?"

He shook his head and stepped over my legs that were thrust out into the hallway. "You okay? José and I have been talking to you," he used air quotes around the words 'to you', "for ten minutes."

Half in a trance, I gazed around the school hallway and back to the boys. "Yeah, I'm fine. Rough night, I guess. Just getting ready for English and no Sarah."

José dropped down next to me. "Don't you remember? There are those all-school events today in the auditorium." He waggled his eyebrows as he said, "School safety. No classes today."

Relief flowed through me at the thought of no classes, quickly replaced by anxiety. Shutting my eyes, I imagined all the student in one place. "Can we all hide in the back together? Wait…argh…we can't, can we? We have to sit by grade." My head fell back against the lockers. The clanging sound was oddly satisfying.

Sitting alone in the auditorium, Piper found me. We hadn't spent much time together this week. She didn't hang out with me at lunch because she was shy around my boisterous guy friends. During gym classes I had told her that I had to be home right away, and that my brother was driving me. She seemed disappointed but understanding.

I'll admit, I was the one falling short on communication.

"Hi," she said shyly. Digging deep, I gave her the best smile I could muster. She smiled back, which warmed my heart. "Can I join you?"

My smile became sincere. "Absolutely."

"You doing okay? I haven't seen you and Sarah together

all week." Her head swung back to where Sarah sat with the basketball team. Sarah had always had other friends. She simply joined another group. At lunch I could hear her laughing, even when I was sitting outside, and she was inside. Then, walking to class, Alyssa stopped me to gloat about some outing she and Sarah were planning.

A few times, when I had been at my lowest, I'd wavered between wondering if Sarah even cared about me and knowing I wasn't being fair. She'd always cared about me, but the violence of being a wereanimal was just too much for her. Recentering myself, I decided to be happy that she could move on. Or at least I tried…maybe I could be a better person next week.

I couldn't be sure, but I had the feeling Piper understood I was in a tailspin. Whatever the reason for her sitting by me now, I'd like to think that she sensed I needed someone at the moment.

Following her gaze, I tried to cover the low growl coming from my belly. "I'm surviving. We got into a…" How could I answer her question? I shook my head. "I don't know.… How are you doing?"

"I'm good, but still struggle in math. Do you know anything about Mr. Jorgans? I just don't understand a thing he says. You aren't in his class, are you?"

"I…um…no." The safety tips had started, so we were talking softly. "But maybe I can help you anyway."

"Oh, are you sure? Are you any good at math?"

"Yeah, she can," Parker, a boy sitting behind us said, interrupting us. He'd been in classes with me my whole life. He had obviously been listening in. "She takes classes with seniors."

Blushing, my focus turned to the assembly below. That was an exaggeration, but only slightly.

"Really?" Piper's eyes got wide, and her jaw dropped open a little.

"A few," I admitted.

"If you're willing to help, that would be great."

"Yeah. We have relatives visiting, so my place is out. Could we do it at your place?"

She agreed quickly and we set up a time to work together on Sunday.

The remainder of Friday was a blur of boring talks until they let us go home. I tried to keep myself numb but the memory of Candice's words kept seeping back to me, causing spikes in my emotional turmoil.

Saturday morning, I woke up with a powerful groan. This was one day I wanted to skip. According to Dad's program, I should run every other day. So far that had been Sunday, Tuesday, and Thursday. That meant that I was supposed to run today. Every other day, run.

Thursday. Thinking about Thursday and how badly that day ended with Candice, I crawled back under the covers for a while longer, putting off the inevitable.

If I could drag myself out of bed for my run and I

survived the day, my plan for studying with Piper on Sunday would be my reward. I had told Owen about it last night before bed, figuring if something went terribly wrong today at the pack meeting, someone should know my plans. He had just given me a weird look when I told him and walked away to find something to eat.

Today was the day of the big pack meeting. Again. The meeting, the one to decide my fate. Again. This time it was about the animals, which in some way seemed more important. I didn't know what would happen if they all agreed with Candice.

Maybe I could go live with my maternal grandparents. They didn't live far away. Their house was still in the same school district. I would just have to take the bus. If I did that, I wouldn't disrupt the pack.

Unfortunately, I wouldn't be the pack's healer anymore. I could still study medicine, but I would become a doctor or a vet. It wouldn't compensate for losing my place in the pack, my family, my role as healer, but at least I would be helping someone.

Despite being a cat, I couldn't sleep all day. I got up and changed into sweats and a T-shirt that read: "Relax: we're all insane, it isn't a competition." It fit my mood. I knew I had to run, and I wanted to do it before the meeting started. Making sure that I wore my fitness watch— Dad would probably make me run again if I forgot it—I headed to the barn.

Before leaving my room, I checked my phone. I had a text from Sarah from two a.m. My heart jumped but I really didn't want to face her right now and debated ignoring the text. Stuffing the phone in my pocket, I made it as far as the kitchen before pulling it back out to read the text.

`Jade, we need to talk.`

That was it.

It was too much for me to deal with…focus on the run, then maybe deal with other drama. Pulling on headphones, I strapped my phone to my arm, and headed over to the gym. After stretching out my tense muscles, I made my way to the track to start my hour-long run. I checked my watch when I got to the track; it was already ten. Four hours until the meeting.

About fifteen minutes into the run, Owen joined me, and then Dad, and finally Mom. This was unexpected. We didn't run together in a group, just all ran on the track, passing each other, everyone going their own pace. I ended up running until Owen was done.

"How far, how long?" Owen panted. Shaking my head, I grabbed my water bottle for a drink. He glared at me, and I shrugged, unimpressed. He narrowed his eyes further and moved closer, a wolf stalking his prey. Ignoring him I took another drink. My dad grabbed my arm, the one with my fitness watch. He looked at the tiny display screen and nodded with satisfaction.

He went to the white board with our stats and wrote:

seventy-five minutes, seventeen point five miles under my name. Then he checked Owen's watch and wrote *sixty minutes, thirteen point four miles* under his. The marker squeaked with each stark mark.

Always supportive, Owen hooted. Stunned, first I stared at the board, and then my watch in disbelief. The week had been so bad, I'd used my run as a balm to help soothe the pain and frustration I was feeling. I hadn't been paying attention to the time or distance.

"That can't be accurate. I've never—I can't—that can't—how could I?" Stammering, I was breathing hard, but not hard enough, given the distance I had run.

Mom finished her run and came up to us, half-laughing. "My goodness, put this on a calendar, call the presses, we have a first: the girl is speechless," she teased, hugging me from the side and giving me a quick kiss on the top of my head.

"But how?" I demanded, squirming out of her sweaty embrace.

Mom squared her shoulders and looked down at me. "You are a werepanther, dear. You have to let that fact sink in. You must embrace it. You have to stop fighting what it means."

Dad glanced up from taking notes. "Nice run. We should up the weekend runs for endurance."

Owen and I both grumbled at our future misfortunes. We all went off to shower and change for the day. After the shower, I stopped stalling and finally texted Sarah back.

Committee meeting today at two. I

don't plan on attending. I'll be in the back stretching or meditating.

Next on my list was breakfast and coffee. Dad and Owen were on the schedule for making lunch for pack members who showed up for the meeting. Though they could show up whenever, I hoped they didn't start arriving until one-thirty, I didn't want to see people any earlier.

At one, I heard the first car. Darn! The back door slid closed quietly behind me as I found a secluded area in the backyard. It was a few hours after my run, so I did some big moves to warm up my muscles before sitting down in the grass to stretch.

It occurred to me that I hadn't had a good stretch or meditation session since before the trip to Florida. Maybe this was part of my mind spiraling so much…I focused on each muscle group, really getting a good stretch. Centering on myself, I tried not to pay attention to the time, the house, or the people showing up. My goal was to re-center, become one with Jade, or some such nonsense.

Once I felt good and limber, it was time to meditate.

Shortly after beginning, I knew the meeting had started because the house got quiet. The goal was to not let the house interfere with my meditating, but with the quiet, came a release of tension and an overall calm.

Laughing, I recalled my shirt's advice: "Relax, we're all insane, it isn't a competition." A good life motto.

Yep. I was doing it, starting to relax. It felt like it had

been weeks. Why had I put off meditating? I took in all the smells and sounds of the background, the trees, the flowers, even some small animals out in the forest.

Then a new smell descended on me—Candice. What was she doing here? She should be in the meeting. Inhaling more deeply, I tried to figure out what my brain was interpreting. Was that fur? Was she in wolf form?

I was so deep into meditating that coming out of it took an effort. Before I could turn and open my eyes, a snarling lump of fur knocked me to the ground. My arm instinctively went up to protect my neck, and teeth sank into my forearm. Kicking out, I felt something soft and warm. Her gut. There was a crack. A rib?

My eyes finally flew open, and I saw her standing there, a small grey wolf with black and white markings. She was panting, her legs apart, her beady black eyes focused on me. She was ready to attack.

Lying on the ground, my feet pointing towards her, I began to pant. One of my arms was under me holding me up so I could see her, and the other was bleeding and mangled, still protecting my neck.

My mind reeled in disbelief. This was not happening. "Candice, what are you doing? Shouldn't you be in the meeting?"

I don't know why I thought talking would help, but I had to try to slow her down. Could I calm her down? Extended my calming influence, I tried to get her to stand down. Wait, I had to be calm to share calm, and currently

I wasn't calm.

Candice lunged at me, her claws digging into my thigh.

Pain shot through my leg like lightning. Trying to ignore it, my target was the grey wolf. This wasn't sparring, this wasn't a game, this was for real.

Swallowing a yowl of agony, I used my abs to shoot up and swung my back arm to punch her head. She held on and another wave of pain washed through my body.

She continued to claw at my legs and hip. Ignoring the pain, I snarled and punched her again. She finally let go, but immediately lunged again, this time sinking her teeth into my shoulder. Her jaws clamped down like a vise grip. Shuddering at a new sensation of pain and agony, my vision narrowed to only her.

Not believing what was going on I had been holding in my screams, but the bite was too much. The pain almost made me black out. Feeling and hearing the snap of a bone, I sucked in a shaky breath. Out of options, and seeing the blood dripping from the mangled shoulder, I slammed her head into the ground.

Candice's grip loosened and I worked my fingers into her mouth, to force a release. Everything was slick with blood. My blood. I drove a knee into her gut, and she flew off me. Crab-walking back as far as I could, my movements were stilted because of my shoulder and my arm.

Candice was back in a heartbeat. Her lunge was aimed at my throat, a kill-attack. Seeing the trajectory, I shakily blocked with the same torn up arm. Her fangs slashed into me again. Pain! I saw spots. So much blood. The backyard swayed back and forth.

As she gnawed on my arm, trying to get to my throat, the pain caused my mind to short circuit, there was no other reason for it. Random thoughts invaded. How many places had she bitten me? Three? I was quickly losing focus. The world was turning hazy. All I could see was a wolf and blackness. It was getting hard to think.

Should I shift to panther form? It would make me stronger and help me heal, but Candice would finish me off during the change.

A few more feeble punches and kicks drove home the fact that I couldn't defeat her as a human. She was a small wolf, weak compared to the dominant ones…I wasn't ready to fight a wolf. Why couldn't I defend myself?

Through the haze of my pain and loss of blood, I didn't see her go for my gut, but I sensed it. I rolled into a ball, and she bit into my sides and legs instead. She chewed, biting deep. This had to be the end.

There was a gasp. Through the pain it wasn't clear, but I didn't think it was me. Pushing past the ruination of my body, I tried to get a fix on who it was, but I was too far gone to reach out with any of my senses. Everything in me was being used to protect myself.

Candice had savaged too much of my body. She was eating into me. I lay on the ground quivering, trying to roll myself into a ball to protect my sensitive organs. Fading, I couldn't tell whether my eyes were open or closed. Everything was black. And cold.

There was no air, I was gasping.

Suddenly the weight of the werewolf was gone. There was a scream and a grunt. A meaty slam. There was more screaming. It sounded like despair. There were more sounds, I couldn't decipher them, was that my name?

All my energy was centered on keeping my body together. Oh, and on breathing.

Someone was talking to me, I felt it more than heard it, as if their voice were somehow inside me, talking to my panther. They were demanding my panther come out.

"Jade, shift or you'll die!"

That sounded like a good idea, but I couldn't. My insides gnawed on, my soul bleeding, pain flowing through me, all I could manage was…nothing. Thinking about it, I was pretty sure I was going to die.

"Jade, shift right now!"

Groaning in answer, I let the voice know I couldn't. Despite my protests, my panther heard the voice and she perked up. She started the shift. Gods, it hurt. There was so much pain. More pain. So much pain.

And then I felt nothing.

CHAPTER 31

So much pain…everything hurt.

"Will she survive?" A familiar female voice. She sounded anxious. Was it Mom, sad and worried? Aunt Allison? Sarah? It couldn't be Sarah. Was I hallucinating?

"She will, since you had the good sense to force her change. How did you know that would help?" That was a different voice. So fierce and strong…it also felt like Mom.

Who forced me to change? What was I right now? Was I human? Panther?

"When we went to Allison's office for tests and I changed forms, I had a sprained ankle before the change.

Afterwards, it was fine, healed."

"That could have been natural wereanimal healing."That one was definitely Mom. She was using her teacher voice.

Who was she talking to? It wasn't Owen. So, Sarah? If so, then this must be a dream. What a nice dream, it would be nice to have Sarah back in my life.

Things went hazy after that. Everything was hard to follow. Was that animal form?

"She looks better today."

Why couldn't I identify voices? *My mind must be playing tricks on me.* Everyone sounded like Sarah, or did they sound like Mom? Was I still asleep? Where was I? How could Sarah even be near me? She couldn't be here; she was gone from my life. I guessed anything was possible when hallucinating. Or was it sleep?

"Mom, I heard her heart rate go up. Is she waking up?" That was Owen's voice. That made more sense than Sarah being around.

Something cold and wet was placed on my forehead. It was rough. A towel? A washcloth? It felt good down to my soul.

"Honey, it's Mom. You were hurt. I don't know if you can hear me. You were hurt yesterday. You've been sleeping a long time and we need you to wake up."

The cloth moved across my head and everything inside relaxed. "Yesterday, while we were having our meeting, Candice slipped out and attacked you. We aren't sure why, though we can guess." This last was said with a growl.

She kept talking, but it was hard to follow her words. The cold felt so good. There was a gap in her story, maybe I fell asleep.

An edge that crept into her voice stirred me awake, and then the towel stopped moving. "What happened between River and T.J. was a father protecting his daughter. Dominance isn't an issue across different species. That was how we explained it to Candice."

Mom kept talking and I tried to focus, but I was so tired. Was she still talking about Dad? No, now she was talking about Thursday when Candice came over to talk to me. "Her scent was all over your room, love, I wish I knew what she said to you. I'm so sorry I didn't see this coming."

My heart ached with the tears in her voice. She hugged me. It was tight and it filled me with warmth. She rested her forehead against mine. "This is all my fault. Please don't leave us, love. I know you're in pain, but you can heal. Your body is almost completely healed, your heart can heal, too." She moved away after giving my hand a squeeze. "If you let it."

Huh, I had a hand. Human, not panther.

The apathy felt like a cozy blanket I could cuddle in, more alluring than waking up. As certain as my being was that it was time…I just didn't care. So much had happened that hurt deep down in the core of my soul. Lying in bed felt better than getting up to face it all.

"Hey, sis, don't know if you can hear me, but I texted

Piper from your phone that you were sick. Since you've been gone from school, your excuse should seem legit."

Gone from school? How could that be? I thought Mom said it was the day after the attack, the day after the pack meeting. Wouldn't this be Sunday?

"She's been texting you, but I've been ignoring it," he continued.

It felt later. Did I sleep? Was it minutes, hours, days? I really wasn't sure.

The bed sank down with a weight next to me. A warm hand took mine and then Owen spoke. "Jade, you need to wake up. We're all worried about you. Mom's losing sleep because she feels guilty you got hurt. And hey, think of all the homework I'm piling up on your desk." He snorted a laugh.

Leave it to Owen. I felt the spark of an inward smile warm the darkness inside of me.

Owen was gone. My hands were empty. My bed was empty of anyone but me. Floating in the abyss of nothingness…

"It's been three days; she should be up by now. I only work with animals, not humans. I really feel like you should get her to see a human doctor." Another female voice.

"But Allison, you've done great," I heard Mom answer. "Her wounds are almost all healed. I think she isn't waking up because she's depressed. So much has happened."

"Hazel, you are a great alpha, but you know nothing of medicine. You are making things up."

"Can I talk to her?" Sarah's voice again.

Another hallucination…these dreams were lovely. Obviously, I wasn't ready to face the world if I was hearing voices that couldn't possibly be here.

My heart hurt too much. The dream with Sarah continued.

"Jade?" The Sarah voice sounded so hesitant in this dream. Too bad we weren't floating on a cloud, that would be fun. "This being a werepanther is helpful sometimes. I can smell your fear and hear your heart rate jump. I know you can hear me. I'm confused right now, and I need you. I came over to talk to you last Saturday, to find some wolf trying to kill you, eat you."

There were footsteps and a sniffle. Was she crying? A cloud in the sky really would be better.

She growled at me. "I think if I hadn't walked into the backyard when I did you would have let her kill you. Were you letting her kill you on purpose? You are so strong. I can't imagine her beating you any other way."

If she only knew.

"Okay, maybe not. Now you smell annoyed."

I almost laughed aloud.

"Anyway," she continued, "I wanted to come over because this last week has been horrible. I've been doing a lot of thinking, and some talking with my parents, and I decided I wanted to learn more about the pack."

She sounded nervous. Her pacing sounded almost frantic, like she wanted to argue a point, but no one was there to argue with her. "They were totally against even discussing my joining. At least Mom was. They're scared. They didn't want anything to do with any of it."

She paused and took a deep breath. The edge of the bed dipped, and she grabbed my hand. "Then I came over here and saw my best friend being attacked by a wolf. Something primal took over. I grabbed the wolf, and I threw them against a tree. Then I went over and snapped the wolf's neck."

Sarah's voice sounded fierce and protective. "I couldn't keep myself from killing the beast which was trying to kill you. And before you ask, yes, I knew the wolf was really a person. I was pretty sure I could even smell who it was. That was when I started to understand what you meant by the violence involved in the world of wereanimals."

My mind stopped for a second. *What? Sarah had killed Candice.* Sarah had killed Candice to save me? Was that possible?

"Apparently I was loud," she continued, "because I turned around and most of the pack was at the door, even the kids. Your parents and Allison rushed over to you. Lots of stuff happened quickly. Once I calmed down enough to let people near me, Owen, Bevin, and José gathered around me. I guess they figured I might need comfort, too."

She moved her hand to my shoulder, rubbing in a soothing motion. "When my parents came over, they saw Candice as a human. They didn't know the dead wolf changed back into a person. Nice trick to not tell them about T.J., by the way. This time, when it was their daughter doing the…" Sarah's hand stopped moving for a moment and there was a hitch in her voice before she continued, "killing…they were less inclined to call the police."

She took a breath and her soothing motions continued. I could feel her turmoil as she aligned the killer within her with the person she had always been. After a few minutes she continued. "The discussion about the pack and what it means to be a wereanimal was much longer and more complicated. It was also a bit more complete than last time."

If felt like she was done talking. She was sitting on my bed rubbing my shoulder. Was Sarah really sitting next to me? Dream or real, it was comforting to have her there. This was a good dream.

But then she continued. "My parents are still deciding for themselves if they want to join the pack, but either way, I want to join…if the pack will have me. Nothing can undo this change in me, and I need to understand. Moreover, I need you."

"Don't you know you'll have me either way?" Did I say that out loud? My voice sounded rough with disuse.

"Jade?" Sarah sounded hopeful.

There was a sudden commotion. It sounded like a herd of elephants stampeding into the room.

I sat at the kitchen table. There was a bowl of soup and a mug of coffee in front of me. It felt like everyone from the pack was in the house. There were too many people. I could feel them, almost taste them. Their sheer numbers made my heart beat faster. Holding my hands in my lap to keep them from shaking, I wasn't sure if I could handle it.

My breathing was ragged. "Have they all been here since Saturday?" I whispered softly.

With so many people around, I wasn't sure who I was asking. Though the house was full of people, the kitchen wasn't. Mom was in the kitchen buzzing around, refilling coffee and soup bowls as needed. Owen and Sarah sat on either side of me. Sarah was close enough that her leg touched mine, a half-empty bowl of soup and a cup of coffee in front of her. Owen's soup bowl was empty, of course, so he nursed his coffee.

There were people on the couches in the living room who I could see. The people in the basement and other areas were discernible by scent and sound.

Owen nodded. "Most have been here since Saturday. Not everyone, not all the time, but everyone was scared. No one knew what would happen if you didn't wake up… if you died."

He threw his arm around me. It helped to center me and separate me from all those other emotions.

Mom came over to fill his bowl. "The pack needed to be together, dear. People have been leaving the house to go to work and school, though Owen took today off. He was stressed. Some of the pack have been staying in the pack guest rooms. If you didn't wake up, the pack was afraid for the future."

Confused, brows coming together, I looked up at her. "But why?"

Mom's body sagged a bit. She seemed to be taking on the enormity of the question. "Your dad and I have given our lives to the pack. If their thanks is taking away our daughter, then we will disband the pack. Tanner can reform a pack, but not here, not in southern Wisconsin."

She sat down across from me and took my hands. "After we found you, I made my feelings clear to the pack. I'm done playing around. The pack can still decide on if they are comfortable with you as a panther in a wolf pack. They can vote on full moon night runs. But attacking you is off the table. You are not a wolf."

My hands shook at what she just told me. I wasn't used to being important. I slowly took a sip of soup.

Mom got up to fill our coffees.

Sarah gently rubbed my arm to help me relax. She threw a teasing grin over my head to Owen. "When I got here, Owen was in your room holding your hand."

Owen scowled at her, face turning red.

"You're my sister and no matter what anyone says, you are *my* pack." He spoke with such strong emotion I felt warmth flow from my toes on up. My breathing evened out. Just as quickly, I deflated when I realized what Owen's declaration meant for the pack meeting the previous weekend.

He saw the emotions play across my face and backpedaled. "No vote was taken. We had only begun the discussion of what to do about you. The discussion was lively and there are definitely pack members on both sides of the vote. Sort of."

He paused to think about it, gazing off into space. "I think the direction the vote was going was why Candice broke down and did what she did. She knew she was on the losing side. It looks like she decided to take matters into her own hands. I think T.J.'s death was harder on her than even she knew."

Owen gave me a squeeze. "What did she say to you on Thursday, anyway?"

Dropping my head onto his shoulder, momentarily forgetting the three of us weren't alone, moreover, forgetting we were surrounded by people with extremely sharp hearing, I spoke slowly and softly, still feeling numb about everything concerning the attack. "Basically, she said that I shouldn't be here. I could never be pack. I shouldn't be pack. I shouldn't even be a pack healer and she didn't know why everyone didn't see and understand her point of view. She all but told me to pack up and leave town." I paused to take a sip of my soup. "It was awful."

If I had really thought about all the people in the house who could hear me, I probably wouldn't have answered the question, but I was still too tired and overwrought to think straight.

I felt the tension in the air before I heard anything. Tanner and Clare were suddenly standing by the table.

"Tell me she didn't say that to you," Tanner said. His tan face had turned pale.

"What?" Confused, I forced myself to look up at him.

"Tanner was one of the few who was starting to side with Candice," Owen mumbled, so low I could barely hear him. I doubt anyone else knew he had said anything. Thankfully, I was too tired to react.

"Please tell me Candice didn't try to run you out of town. A fifteen-year-old girl who is a new werepanther," Tanner said, sounding pained.

"Jade, hon, why didn't you at least tell your friends?" From the way Clare said this, I knew José was sharing some of my more painful moments with his mom. I didn't really mind; I knew he did it because he trusted his parents and, in the end, knew they would protect me.

Still numb, I nodded. "She did. She said Dad shouldn't have helped T.J. in a dominance fight, that I shouldn't run with you on full moon nights, and that I should find my own way in the world."

The memory caused my body to shake again. Sarah leaned closer to me and put her arms around my waist in a hug. I rested my head against her shoulder, comforted by her support. Somehow in all this awful, I had my best friend back.

"It wasn't a dominance fight," Tanner said with some heat. "As of last Saturday, no decision had been made on pack status, so no dominance placement could be fought over. Besides, if you are to become part of the pack, I don't think you will be part of the pack dominance. You aren't a werewolf. I don't think you, as a werepanther, could ever be part of a dominance fight."

Well, wasn't that an interesting take? No wonder Candice attacked me.

"That's why you were blank on Friday." I was shocked by Sarah's words. "Yes, I know I was avoiding you, but our connection is so deep. Friday you seemed to be trying to stay emotionless but kept having these eruptions of pain and sorrow. It was distracting and awful."

She took a sip of coffee. "It's why I reached out to you Friday night. I had to know what was wrong. I was so worried about you. It just became too much. If we're going to be connected on such a deep level, I can't just ignore your pain."

Everyone in the room just stared at her. My mind went blank with my confusion. If I worked at it, I could tell her emotions, but it took effort unless her feelings were very strong.

Mom came over to the table. "Sarah, what is Jade feeling right now?"

"Besides confused?" Sarah asked. "She's feeling guilty for starting this, guilty about T.J., guilty about Candice."

Sarah hit me upside the head.

"Ouch!" I rubbed my head.

"Also, she's starving." Sarah lifted a brow and pointed at my soup bowl until I picked it up. She continued, "She is intrigued by what Tanner said but nervous about him wanting to run her out of town, and a few other things. She's complicated. Why?"

My mom gave Sarah a quizzical look. "Because you're Jade's alpha."

My head snapped up at this proclamation.

Mom focused on Sarah. "Most people don't realize how much alphas take in about each pack member, but it helps us to know, among other things, when to comfort and lend that extra hand."

Mom shifted her gaze from Sarah to me and back again. "Your extra knowledge of her points towards you having the dominant alpha position as a werepanther. I bet this is why you could force her to change the other day. I can read all of this with her, as well, which is really interesting." She collected our coffee mugs, then hesitated. "She somehow has two alphas, which I've never heard of."

Having finished with her lecture she went to get us more coffee.

We both just watched her, stunned, as she filled our mugs. Dragging my gaze from Mom, I saw that Sarah's mouth was hanging open. Then, I realized mine was hanging open as well, and shut it.

Owen started to laugh, like really laugh, so much he

almost fell on the ground. "Two alphas? Leave it to you! And if you count Dad, and who wouldn't, you have three!" He slapped his knee in amusement.

There were so many people in the house, but aside from Tanner and Clare, no one had heard this last bit. However, others did hear Owen's laughter.

Several people ran into the kitchen wanting to know what was so funny, including Bevin and his dad Jeff.

My mom gave Tanner and Clare a look and then shifted her gaze to us. She sighed.

Before she could say anything, Owen looked over at Sarah, gave a final chuckle, and said, "This is freaking hilarious! You should definitely go with double trouble for an ice breaker idea. Damn near had coffee coming out my nose."

Mom looked at him as my face split with a grin. She wanted to keep the fact that Sarah was an alpha secret for now, and Owen had just created a cover story. People underestimated my brother.

I turned to Sarah whose face was clearing from confusion to understanding. She nodded and smiled. Her eyes met mine and then Owen's. "Okay, thanks. I wasn't sure."

Mom cleared her throat and then turned to Jeff and Bevin, who had just reached the kitchen. "Do you two know where River is? I need him in the meeting room with Sarah's parents."

Bevin stared at everyone in the kitchen and gave me a huge smile. He hadn't seen me since I woke up.

His dad spoke up first. "I'll find them." He turned and headed out.

My mom then turned to us. "Sarah, I'd like to talk with you and your parents. I think Owen can stay with Jade for now and be her protector. Bevin can help."

Mom took Sarah and her parents to the group room with Dad to have a long discussion about what it meant to be alpha. Sarah was my alpha…but she wasn't a typical alpha. I had to agree to listen to her. That would be more than interesting since we were both only fifteen years old.

This development made it even more important for Sarah to join the pack and put herself under Mom and Dad's alpha umbrella. Then I could be under her alpha umbrella, and by the transitive law of alpha umbrellas…

Bevin plopped down next to me and leaned over. "Ready for tomorrow's math test?"

CHAPTER 32

Going back to school on Wednesday felt weird. It felt like it should be Sunday or maybe Monday.

It started out well meeting up with Sarah at our usual spot. Even though it had only been a week, it felt like we were freshly back from spring break. It felt new again.

Bemoaning our fate, I complained to Sarah. "It's been two weeks. No resolution. The full moon is next week Friday. This weekend is our last chance."

"I have a good feeling about this." Sarah smiled wide and waved her arms. She bounced as we walked to school. She was hyped but was trying to restrain herself to match my pace. When she got ahead of me, she spun around and walked backwards to slow herself down.

We didn't have to move slowly, I was healed, but I was still feeling out of sorts. "Have you seen any of the panther videos?"

Her eyes almost glowed with excitement. "Yeah. After school Monday, while waiting for you to wake up, Owen showed them to me. I'm heading over to Allison's with you two tonight after school."

Heat expanding from my chest, I shot her a quick look. Despite my effort, I couldn't hide the grin spreading up my face. And now that I knew she was my alpha, I was sure she felt the emotions bubbling up inside me.

Her eyes narrowed. "Whaaaat?" She drew the word out.

"I guess I forgot to tell you. I'm studying with Piper tonight after class." My breathing shallow, my focus was on the trees and houses across the street, anything but her.

"A date!" she squealed as I cringed.

"No." Raising my hands in a gesture of silence, I didn't need everyone hearing her words. "Studying," I said with some finality. "We will be studying." The finality in my words was as much for her as for me. "Piper has exams coming up. She needs help."

Sarah started to dance around making happy sounds. It didn't matter how much I protested; she had decided it was a date.

The day slipped by without event, though I did take some teasing at lunch about my study date. This time I didn't mind the ribbing as much since I could tell how happy Bevin and José were at hearing the news.

Owen met Sarah after school to train at the house. Tanner had agreed to drive me and Piper. With the pack on high alert, they were also in protective mode. Over-protective mode if you asked me. I didn't know if I agreed with my parents' decision that Tanner was the best protector for me, but apparently, I didn't get a vote.

Piper hesitated as I directed her towards Tanner. "Who's he?" she asked.

Tanner's car was a black SUV, very official looking. So was he; a six-foot-four, dark-skinned, blue-eyed beast of a man wearing a Men in Black suit.

"He's my, ah—" Faltering, I debated how to describe him. He ran security for a local firm. He was a bounty hunter for fun on the side, and sometimes worked as a bodyguard, like now. Usually, it wasn't for pack business. So, yeah, he wasn't a horrible choice to protect me, but he had been leaning towards Candice's side.

"I'm her uncle," Tanner said smoothly. "You can call me Tanner. Jade has been sick, and there's still a chill in the air." It was fifty-one degrees outside, according to my watch, so that was as good a reason as any.

Piper was shy and still didn't quite seem to be buying our story, but she climbed in the back. I climbed in beside her.

"Where to?" After Piper gave the address, we were off.

Piper usually didn't speak up, but she boldly asked

Tanner, while watching her knees, "You aren't going to stay, are you, Mr. Tanner? My dad's home. I'm sure he can give Jade a ride home if you're really that worried about her health."

Tanner flashed a quick peek back through his mirrored sunglasses at the two of us. "Just Tanner. I'll come up and talk with your dad when we get there. Afterward, I'll decide. Chances are I'll leave and just have Jade text me when she's ready to come home."

"Are you really still so sick? Should you be coming over at all?" Piper sounded worried.

"I'm fine. I really am. Tanner is just being extra careful, that's all."

The drive didn't take long, and when we got there, I opened the door to get out. I was halfway out when I saw Tanner's scowling face.

"What? Did you want to get the door for me?"

"Yes." It was somewhere between a growl and a sigh.

Smiling at him, I was unsure if I should be shocked or amused. Piper had no problem with it. She laughed, her whole face lighting up like a sunrise.

I thought about closing the door to let Tanner reopen it. As if he had read my mind, Tanner gruffly said, "Just don't. Stay back while I check things out."

Piper gave me a quizzical look.

Squeezing her hand as I slipped out, I assured her, "He's in security. Hyper paranoid. Just let him do his thing, it's easier that way."

Piper lived in a one-story ranch style house with an attached garage. It was blue with a cute red door that Tanner was currently approaching. He made his way to the door and knocked. We had made it halfway to the door when Piper's dad opened it.

And then the situation turned upside-down.

All my senses went on high alert: werewolf. *What the hell?*

Piper's dad had begun to extend his arm to shake Tanner's hand but then he froze. His whole body began to vibrate before he growled low in his throat. And then he lunged at Tanner. His hands aimed for Tanner's throat.

Tanner tried to hold Mr. Schneider back as they started to grapple. Instinctively, I pulled Piper back towards the car to protect her. She seemed numb with shock.

In a controlled but annoyed voice, Tanner asked, "Jade, did you know?"

Damn, he was in the middle of a struggle, but in complete control. You would not know that he had just been attacked by another werewolf and was in a serious fight for his life.

"No."

Mr. Schneider's eyes popped out when he saw me, and he froze. When he stopped, Tanner stopped.

"What the hell are you?" He couldn't get much more out because Tanner's hold on him was so tight.

"Tanner, as much fun as this is, especially when the

police may be called, Piper and I really need to study math. She has a test tomorrow." Though my tone was conversational, my mind was reeling. A werewolf? I was trying to keep this part of my life separate and here it was smacking full force into Tanner. I tried to steady my breathing and pacify my face.

Mr. Schneider's head turned to me again. He swallowed audibly and tried to get a full breath. "Get away from my daughter," he hissed. "What are you?"

Closing my eyes, I had to find my center. Today had been better so I had less tension to release.

Approaching the two werewolves, I left Piper near the car. Tanner was holding Mr. Schneider in a half-nelson, and we needed to get off the street. "Mr. Schneider, you really need to *calm down*."

Piper's dad slumped a bit, blinking at me with surprise. Tanner seemed to rock back a bit, but he'd probably had mental walls up.

"Jade, you've got your mojo back." Tanner sounded impressed.

"Yeah." He wasn't the only one baffled. "I guess you have to be calm to give calm. But when did I get any calm back?" My confusion was real. "Mr. Schneider, could we possibly go inside before the police get called?"

He nodded, body shaking in uncertainty as he breathed slowly. Tanner let him go. He started to fall. Tanner grabbed his arm to steady him.

Piper, on the other hand, wasn't doing so well. Her face was drained of color. I could see the whites all around her ocean-blue eyes. She was completely hunched into herself as if she were trying to disappear. Her breathing was rough. She was freaking out.

Approaching her, I touched her arm. She flinched away from me. A light breeze sent chills down my spine as I closed my hands and stepped back. She slowly got herself under control. Looking over my shoulder, I saw her dad and Tanner watching me. Speaking slowly and patiently, I put my hands out in front of me in a placating manner. "Piper, let's go inside. Your dad will explain why he attacked my uncle, and everything will be peachy, all right?"

Everyone just stared at me blankly. Well, no one was fighting, I'd take that as a win. I spun on my heel and headed for the door. Once inside, we sat around the dining room table. I gazed at Piper. She was studying her hands. My heart hurt. "Is your mom around?" She shook her head, still not ready to talk.

Seeing no help there, I shifted my gaze to Mr. Schneider. "Does she know?" He shook his head, too. Like father, like daughter. To be honest, I wasn't sure he knew whether I was talking about Piper or Piper's mom, but apparently it didn't matter.

Finally, I turned to Tanner. "So, now what?"

"This is your show." He sat back and smiled. Darn it all, not again.

Everyone at the table watched me with varying degrees of amusement and confusion. Lowering my defenses a pinch, I felt for their emotions. Tanner was entertained, Mr. Schneider was terrified, and Piper, like a frightened mouse, wanted to run and hide. More than anything, I wanted to reassure her. Was there anything I could do to make her smile again?

Slumped back in my chair, I put my hands in my pockets and tried to relax. Here goes it. "Piper, Tanner, here, and your dad…" I paused to give him a very piercing stare and he nodded, appearing resigned. Oh well, good-bye secrets. "…are werewolves."

Piper snorted and guffawed as if to say, "Funny Jade." Obviously, she thought this was a joke and in bad taste. Her eyes got huge when she realized no one else was laughing.

Shifting, so that my hands were on the table, I tried to stay calm, but there was too much strain running through the room.

"Wait, Dad?" She glanced between us, looking worried.

Her dad just glared at me as if it was all my fault.

A slight thrill ran through me when I grabbed her hand, and she didn't pull away. Speaking softly, I tried to explain. "Piper, there are werewolves in the world. They are real. I don't know how many because, as you know, most people don't know about them. They like to keep it secret, for obvious reasons. Your dad, here, is what is known as a lone wolf. I imagine he was attacked and bitten, maybe even a long time ago."

Shifting my gaze to Mr. Schneider, I silently asked him, and he nodded. As I spoke, I could feel his anger turn to confusion and interest.

"Jade," Piper said softly, "I've seen the movies, I know getting bitten by a monster is the only way to become a monster."

We all flinched at the word "monster."

"Let's start by not saying, 'monster.' Most people responsible for the horrible crimes in the world are not werewolves. Wolves kill for food, not sport. Sport-killing is a human thing. I would put the humans at the top of the monster list."

Letting go of her hand and moving mine around, I sorted out my thoughts. Over the years I found that I spoke better when I could use my hands. "Most werewolves aren't monsters, or you would have heard about them before now. They've been around for a long time and know how to stay hidden. I know your dad was attacked, but lone wolves who attack others are usually taken out by stronger wolves who are trying to protect their pack."

At these last words, I shifted my eyes from Piper back to her dad.

Focusing on Mr. Schneider, I continued, "My family, my mom and dad, are the alphas of the local pack. Any lone wolf in the area should check in with them."

I shot my gaze back to Piper, then fully faced Mr.

Schneider. "Is this why she wears body scent and perfume? To cover any possible scent of werewolf?"

"Yes," Mr. Schneider confirmed. "We've run into other werewolves—lone wolves—and we've had to run. I'm tired of running. I thought if people couldn't find us, we could stay. I told Piper and her mom I really like the soap and perfume, pretty much guilted them into wearing it."

He looked down at his hands. "I guess we should start packing."

Tanner sat forward, brows furrowed in confusion. "Why? We have a strong pack here. You just need to check in with the alphas, like Jade said. They've let other lone wolves live in the region. All the others have either moved on or joined the pack. You can live here as a lone wolf, as long as you are known to the pack."

"You would let me join?" He almost stopped breathing. His brows shot up with hope and a little bafflement. This was all new to him.

"I can't answer for the pack, and neither can Jade. The first step is to bring your family over to meet the alphas and then we can introduce you to the pack. There's a pack meeting this weekend if you're available and interested."

My hand rubbed my forehead as a groan escaped me. It caught everyone's attention, but I shook my head. There was no need for Piper or her dad to know about my little problem. Not yet.

Tanner glanced at me and chuckled softly before

continuing. "I would suggest you come. In fact, I suggest that after this study session, you drive Jade home and meet the alphas. If everything goes well with them, then you could come to the pack meeting this weekend."

"Uncle," Piper said out of the blue. "Tanner is your uncle, as in, everyone in the pack is an aunt or uncle?"

Tanner laughed outright this time. "Of Jade? Absolutely. We are very protective of this one. Of her brother, Owen..." His silence spoke for him, though the answer really was as much "yes" for Owen, and for all the kiddos, as it was for me.

"As I was saying." This was the important part, something Mr. Schneider may not know. "Not all werewolves become wolves by being bitten."

Mr. Schneider cocked his head and leaned in towards me to focus more closely on my words. I spoke directly to him. "It's been studied within the werewolf community. If you're born to a werewolf, you might carry the werewolf gene. And then, in your late teens or early twenties you could become one naturally. About half the pack are natural werewolves."

"Is a natural born werewolf what you are?" Mr. Schneider asked. "Is that why you smell so weird?"

A snarl bubbled up, but I swallowed it. "No. I'm…I'm something different. We can get into that later. When did you become a werewolf, Mr. Schneider?"

"When I was twenty-three, just after college. I was attacked one night running on a dark foot path. I fought back hard enough that the wolf gave up. I made it home and was going to call the paramedics the next morning. I know, dumb, but twenty-three-year-old guys aren't always the smartest. However, when I woke up, my wounds didn't seem very bad." It dawned on him, and his eyes widened as he glanced at Piper.

Piper blanched.

"Am I a werewolf?" she asked softly.

Reaching over, I squeezed her hand as I answered. "No way to tell unless you sprout fur and fangs one day." She managed a wan smile, but still looked rattled. "This is the only reason I brought up werewolves in front of you. As a child of a werewolf, you needed to know, to learn, to understand." This last was said in rote and made Tanner crack a smile.

Tanner and I explained a few more facts of werewolf life before Piper jumped up and offered, a little breathlessly, to get everyone drinks. Tanner refused. I could tell my friend was overwhelmed. There was a lot of information flowing that she wasn't prepared for.

Searching the faces, I asked hopefully, "Can we get to math now?"

"Jade," Tanner replied in his rich voice, "you've only told part of the story. That isn't really fair, is it? Explain why you smell so weird, or Mr. Schneider will be distracted all night."

My lip curled up and I sighed. "Fine." Then I glared at Tanner for good measure. "I was on a trip a while ago and I was bitten, but not by a werewolf…a werepanther."

Piper had just returned with drinks and was sitting down. She missed the chair and hit the floor. With this news her eyes grew to the size of saucers.

Mr. Schneider nodded, brows raised, like something was making sense that had been baffling him mere moments before. "Cat," he mumbled.

"I haven't been this way long, and until this happened to me, no one in my pack even knew any other type of wereanimal existed. I guess werepanthers are from Africa. So that's why I smell different."

"No," said Mr. Schneider, "the cat is only part of it. It's weird, you also smell of wolf and," he glanced at Tanner, who started to chuckle, "is it possible that she smells of a stream through a pine forest? Chamomile tea? Calm? Is that a thing?"

Groaning, I rested my forehead against my arms crossed on the table.

This was getting out of control.

CHAPTER 33

Somehow, some studying did get done despite all the drama. Tanner returned home to report on the new lone wolf as soon as he answered Mr. Schneider's questions. We spoke long enough to be assured Piper could focus on school. My parents sent a few texts checking up on me to ask if I was safe. Once everyone was sure, they finally let me and Piper study.

Piper and I had only studied an hour or so before Mrs. Schneider returned from work. We were working in the dining room which was attached to the kitchen. My attention was split between Mrs. Schneider cooking and

Piper working through some of the harder math problems.

When requested, we moved our books over to the buffet and set up dishes for dinner. The smells of the baking cornbread while I gathered the flatware almost made me swoon.

Just before dinner was served, Mr. Schneider decided to broach the topic of werewolves with his wife. He'd asked me to be there for support during the big reveal.

"You're a what?" Mrs. Schneider low voice belied the turmoil rolling off her. Her eyes were wide, but her scent was telling a strange story. Overall, she was angry.

"A werewolf," confirmed Mr. Schneider. He looked so peaceful, but his emotions were a whirlwind of terror and depression. He obviously didn't want this conversation to happen, but it was time.

"Well, that explains a lot," her voice started to raise, and her anger came out in her voice. She saw me and frowned, prickling with hostility. "Why is Piper's new friend here? Shouldn't this conversation be more, I don't know, private? I would think a big secret like this would be told to me first, then Piper, and outsiders, say, maybe never." Outburst aside, I approved of her instinct for privacy.

That said, she sounded more upset that I was there than the fact her husband was a werewolf. She got up and started to gather the food. The sound of the dishes hitting the counter were loud enough to make even Piper jump. Piper and I watched the exchange go back and forth like a tennis match.

"Dear, this isn't what it seems." He stood up to grab plates from the kitchen and help set up. She gave him a death stare from the pass-through window. He froze, dropped his hands, and sat back down.

"It seems like you told this random teenage punk your secret before me."

"No, it isn't like you think." His voice deepened. "You have to understand…"

"Did you tell her before me?" she demanded.

"No, not really? Honey, listen…"

The fire in her eyes at what she thought was a lie was impressive. She was bringing dishes from the kitchen and suddenly something broke. *Oh, no!*

"Did. She know. Before. Me?"

Mr. Schneider swallowed audibly. His scent was turning spiky as his hesitation morphed to ire at not being listened to. "Dear, you have to understand."

She threw a towel at the counter and was about to storm out of the kitchen.

Mr. Schneider growled low in this throat, "Helen, listen!" His heart rate jumped and sweat broke out across his forehead. He was furious and terrified all at the same time.

Gods, if Mrs. Schneider ever became a wereanimal, she would be as dominant as they came.

Mr. Schneider was focused on his wife but kept giving me quick hopeful glances.

Taking pity on him, I finally jumped in. "I smelled it.

He didn't tell me." It came out quickly and quietly. I *really* didn't want to get into the middle of this fight.

She stopped and whirled towards me. A sudden urge swelled in me to duck under the table to hide. "What did you say?"

Gazing into her eyes, I *so* didn't want to repeat what I had said. She was staring daggers at me. If looks could kill…

"I said I smelled the werewolf on him. My parents are the alphas of the local pack," I explained. Leaving Tanner out for now seemed to be the better options. She fumed and it seemed to me, less was more.

She didn't seem like she was going to kill me now. She smelled like she was interested, maybe. Her scent shifted again. Holding back a sneeze, I hoped I wouldn't get a headache.

Mr. Schneider's eyes sparked with hope. His smell followed suit. He gave a small hand gesture for me to continue, so I did.

"Your husband is a lone wolf. I don't even think he knew about werewolf packs. When I arrived today, I smelled the wolf on him. I've invited him, and you, and Piper to come back to meet my parents. This way they can do all of this explaining." I waved my hand around vaguely. Taking a breath, I tried to slow down. "They explain it much better than I do."

Mrs. Schneider turned from the door and gave me a warm smile. "I don't know, dear, you didn't do too badly." She returned to the kitchen to clean up the broken glass.

Her change in mood was staggering.

Watching her in awe, I finally worked through all of the information she'd thrown off in her scents. "You knew."

"Of course I did, love," she said with a quirk of a smile. Once done cleaning up the glass, she came back to the dining room and sat back down with us.

Piper's eyes were huge. She smelled hurt. Mr. Schneider started to sputter. Through it all, Mrs. Schneider continued to talk to me. "My husband has always had weird hours. I followed him one night." She finally glanced at him for a second and then looked back at me. "Can you imagine my shock when he stripped naked in an empty park and turned into this creature?"

That word wasn't much better than monster. *Creature.* Flinching, I could smell the sadness in Mr. Schneider.

Mrs. Schneider noticed the flinch and nodded, her face growing gentler. "I watched as he ran into the woods. It happened just last full moon, and you know what? I didn't hear about any attacks. I didn't even hear about a wild creature being sighted."

She glanced over at her husband and gave him a loving smile. "I've been trying to get things figured out in my head. Part of me wondered if I was wrong. I mean, he's my husband, I know he's not a monster." She turned to Mr. Schneider and gave a small smile. "I wanted to confront you, or to have you tell me, but I get it. Sorry I blew up. I just wish I'd been the first person you'd told…first person you trusted."

"To be fair, you were. Until you, he hadn't actually told anyone," Piper said, speaking for the first time. "Jade has been doing all of the explaining."

Heat rose to my cheeks.

Shortly after our conversation, Mrs. Schneider served dinner. Chili with freshly baked cornbread. It was amazing. Our talk had given the chili enough time to bring all the spices together nicely. They even gave me a doggy bag for lunch the next day. Day-after chili was the best. If they stayed in town, Dad would be thrilled with this kind of cooking.

Afterwards, we were off to the pack house. The drive between our houses was quick, and my parents were ready and waiting when we got there. When we walked in, I started to perform introductions. Piper said hi, but not much more. Before I got far, I realized I didn't know everyone's full name.

Mom took over. "Hi, Mr. Schneider, Mrs. Schneider, I'm Hazel Stone, Jade's mother, and this is River, her father." She shook hands as she did the introductions.

Mrs. Schneider took their side. "Hi, thank you for this welcome. I'm Helen, and this is my husband, Greg."

There was a low growl. Piper's dad was snarling. I shifted my gaze between him and Mom. Oh, no.

"Oh, damn," Mom muttered softly.

Greg stepped forward, arms raised as if to attack. Mom grabbed his shoulders before he could get far. Mrs.

Schneider yelped. Piper squeaked.

On instinct, I grabbed Mrs. Schneider's arms so that she would focus on me. "Mrs. Schneider, look at me."

Mom led Mr. Schneider away. I was trying to radiate whatever calm I could. She was a norm, so I wasn't sure if it would work. "This is okay. Your husband is a wolf, and my mom is alpha. I don't know if he knows what's going on inside his own head. They are just going off to have a little discussion."

"Discussion!" she screeched. "Growling isn't a discussion! It was a threat. My husband doesn't do threats!"

"Well," I said, trying to remain calm, "they're wolves, they are communicating as wolves do."

Dad came over to help me. Putting a hand on Mrs. Schneider's shoulder, he said, "Jade, why don't you take Piper to your room? I'll take over here."

More than willing to leave this situation, I grabbed Piper's hand and ran. The sounds from the backyard were rough but I knew things would clear up soon.

Piper and I made our way to my room. There weren't many places to sit, so I took the bed and left the desk chair for Piper. She was staring at all the pictures of my friends on the wall.

She pointed at one of my family. "Where's your…brother?"

Snorting, I shrugged. "Owen? He's probably at Brooke's house." I couldn't say her name without a sneer. "Or maybe out with other friends. He's usually out late."

She continued to look through my pictures. "You really have been hanging out with your friends forever, haven't you? You and Sarah look so young in some of these."

Face flushing, I wasn't sure why I was embarrassed, but I was. "Yeah, I guess. Is there anyone you've known for a long time?"

She continued to investigate my life through images for a few minutes before answering. She reached out to touch a few of the pictures of me and Sarah or me and Bevin throughout the years. "No, just my family."

After a few minutes, her brow furrowed. "This is you, Sarah, and Bevin in middle school, right?"

Standing, I saw my life through her eyes. In the picture she pointed out, the three of us were eating ice cream cones outside the school at an all-school sports day. Sarah was wearing a jersey and had a ribbon pinned to her chest. We all had ice cream all over our faces. A smile split my face at the memory of the day. "Yeah. Sarah had just won the three-legged race. I'd gotten about two feet before landing on my face…I know, shockers. Bevin had done well, but he was in the eighth-grade races not seventh."

"Why isn't he in any of the younger pictures. You two are with this girl…but the girl looks like Bevin. Is it his sister?"

My breath hitched. It never occurred to me she didn't know. Everyone knew, but why would she know? "That's Bevin…from before. He's trans."

She froze for a moment, then slowly turned to me.

Eyes wide. "That's really cool that everyone seems so cool with it. *Is* everyone cool with it?"

Relaxing, I smiled enjoying her reaction. "Yeah, his parents are really supportive."

"Good."

A few minutes later my dad called us back out.

When we got to the living room, everyone was sitting on the couches. Piper's mom had a welcoming smile but smelled wild and nervous. Her dad smelled as relaxed as I'd ever smelled him. Interesting. Piper made a beeline to sit with them.

After surveying the room, I headed to the recliner and popped up the footrest.

Mom gave me a happy grin. She smelled proud for some reason. "Jade, Piper, we're glad you two joined us. The Schneiders have been learning about pack and have decided not to move, at least for the time being."

Piper let out a squeal of excitement and waved her hands in the air before realizing everyone was watching her. She froze, took a quick breath, dropped her arms, and sat still. Her smile, however, didn't leave her face.

A smile spread across Mr. Schneider's face, and he draped an arm over her shoulders. "I agree, hon. It's exciting to think about staying in one place for a while. Cheer all you want."

My Dad was watching them. "Just don't forget to come to the meeting Saturday to meet the pack." I couldn't hold back the groan.

On Thursday, Piper was convinced to join the gang at lunch. In her short time at our school, she had never established her own friend group. We sat outside despite the cooler weather. A few other groups thought about eating outside, but usually they ended up inside briskly enough.

The morning had been hectic, and I hadn't had time to warn anyone about why Piper was joining us, and I thought it would be best to let her tell her story. If this went well maybe she would join us in the mornings also. Anyway, showing up Saturday and finding everyone there would be a big shock, this was better.

Sarah plopped down with her lunch tray. "Is she really going to join us?" she asked, sounding sullen.

"Yes." There was a firmness to my voice, though it hurt that my friend felt this way.

"What the hell?" José asked. "The big meeting is in two days; shouldn't we discuss what's going to happen? Not to mention, you two are going to the first big panther fight training tonight with Allison. I want to talk. I get that you like this person, Jade, but did you have to invite her?"

His words cut into me, but I understood why he said them. Fighting the sudden tears by biting my inner cheek, I forced a smile.

Bevin sat down next to me. "José, that's kinda rough. I

mean, I get it, I want to hear about what you're doing with Allison, but Jade's had a hard month. This is a good thing." He smiled and gave me an encouraging hug. At least Bevin had my back.

"Tonight's going to be epic," Sarah said, her eyes sparkling. "I can't believe how much things have changed since Florida."

Piper was so quiet, no one had heard her approach, but Sarah and I smelled her. Sarah quickly changed what she was saying. "First our fight, then the end of our fight." Oh well, she ended lamely, but she'd tried.

Piper giggled. Her nervousness poured off her in waves.

Everyone looked up to see her approach. My heart started beating faster. This was it, either my friends liked her, or they didn't. The inquisitive glances from Sarah told me she was reading my emotions like a book. Trying to center myself, I had to relax.

Surveying my friends, I gave a quick, but hopefully joking warning. "Be nice everyone."

They all turned to me as I jumped up and took Piper's hand, guiding her to sit next to me. Giving her hand a squeeze, I said, "Piper, welcome to the group. I would like to introduce you to José, Bevin, and Sarah. Sarah has been my bestie since forever. Bevin and José, well, they have known me a long time, as well. I'll tell you after I explain to them why you're here. Sound good?"

She nodded. Her hand was as cold as marble. Her

emotions were spiking, which wasn't helping me to find my own calm. Closing my eyes, I took a deep breath. I felt Bevin's hand on my shoulder. It helped. One more breath.

I opened my eyes and looked into Piper's. I gave her an encouraging smile. She seemed to relax with me. Good. Finally, I faced my friends. Everyone waited for me to start talking.

Grumbling and craning my neck, I search the lunchroom windows. "Why is Owen taking so long?" Finally, I spotted him and managed to catch his eye. He gave me a look as if to say, "What do you want? Leave me alone, dork," all in one. I shrugged helplessly and turned back to my friends. There had been an attempt to include him. Really, there had! If he refused to come over, then he couldn't blame me when he missed out on important information.

"So." Bracing myself, I decided I had to pull the band aid off and just get this over with. "Last night when Tanner dropped me off at Piper's he walked me to the door. You can guess how surprised we were when we smelled that Piper's dad was a lone wolf."

As one, they all froze and gaped at me like fish drowning on dry land. And then they all rotated to look at Piper. Snorting, I tried to keep a straight face. Piper was astonished, too. I hadn't exactly warned her of my plan to be this forthcoming.

It wasn't like they wouldn't all find out on Saturday, anyway. The sooner this all came out, the sooner we could all move forward from this point of astonishment.

"Your shock wasn't even as big as Piper's. Before last night, she didn't know the truth about werewolves."

Everyone's shock turned to sympathy. "Oh, honey," Sarah said, giving her a big hug. "I feel your confusion. I have known about all this messed up imaginary-world-become-real stuff for just over three weeks. I really feel you."

Piper hugged her back. Her relief felt like a wave of warm water sweeping over me. Next, Piper looked questioningly at José and Bevin. "Are you two were... werewolves, too?" She stumbled over the word. No doubt it still felt weird to say it aloud.

"No, chica," José answered. "My parents were bitten... like your dad? I only ask because most lone wolves are bitten. Hereditary wolves tend to know there are packs out there." After a nod from Piper, José continued. "After they were bitten, my parents had me and my sister. I could become a werewolf in the next few years, just like you. Or if that doesn't happen, I could decide to be bitten and become a werewolf that way. Like Jade, and Bevin here, we've all grown up in the community. It's why we know each other so well. We were brought up like cousins."

Piper shifted her inquisitive gaze to Bevin.

Bevin nodded. "My mom, José's mom, and Jade's aunt were all college friends. They were attacked by a lone wolf, well a rogue wolf. Jade's mom took care of him, but not before it had bitten them, and, well, Jade's dad. They all followed her up here after college because she's their alpha."

Watching everyone, a warmth flowed through me, their acceptance filled me with hope and pride. Everyone was getting along. Not only that, Piper's heart rate was normal and she was steadily asking questions. She was talking with everyone. It was amazing.

Sarah looked over to me and gave me a big smile; she knew how important this was to me.

Taking Piper's hand again, I surveyed my friends. Bracing myself, there was more news I had to share. "On Saturday, Piper's parents will be at the meeting. They met my parents last night. They will be introduced to the pack at the," there may have been a bit of a growl, "meeting. Her dad will probably be invited to run with the pack during the full moon. As for joining the pack, that will be up to the family. So, Piper, you will be in the basement with José and Bevin and all of the non-wolf kids."

"I can't believe how calm you are right now," Sarah said, peering at Piper in wonder. "My parents and I are still in shock half the nights about all of this. You have only known since last night. How is your mom taking all of it?"

"I think it was easier for us. My mom knew something was weird. I mean, my dad has always been a consultant with the police and has worked weird hours. Disappearing on random nights has always been his modus operandi." Piper shrugged, smiling slightly. "I think my mom, being a nurse, knew there had to be more with him. We were at Jade's place late last night talking with her parents. Mom is mom. I'm just numb at this point. I'll freak out later, I'm sure."

She gave a little laugh. "I'm excited about being with everyone this weekend, though. Being with people and hanging out with friends should be fun. I've never had so many people to socialize with, it's weird. What about you? Will you be with all of us?" she asked me, a little nervously. She was probably shocked at the number of words she'd said to relative strangers.

"I don't know." I met Sarah's gaze. "I think I…I mean we, will be in the meeting."

Piper nodded.

"I'll be with you," Sarah said.

Piper's smile faltered and her scent shifted. Brows dropping a bit as confusion won out. She just shot a glance at Sarah before her focus settled on me.

"Jade didn't tell you?" Sarah asked.

Slouching, I said in a grumpy voice, "I told you, I don't tell other people's stories."

There were some head shakes and a few incredulous snorts from Bevin and José.

"I try not to tell as much as possible. Better?" I asked, a little indignant.

"Better," Sarah said, agreeing. "Jade and I were both in Florida over spring break when we were attacked by a werepanther. It wasn't a vicious attack; it was just a father protecting his daughter. His daughter wasn't in any danger, but he didn't know at the time. He tried to pull back, but it was too late. We've both been werepanthers for just over three weeks. This meeting on Saturday…. I still wonder. Can a werewolf pack include werepanthers?"

I was impressed. Sarah provided such a succinct summary of my hellish month.

"So," Piper said, pointing at each of us, starting with Sarah, "werepanther, not a were-anything, not a were-anything, me, werepanther." She ended on me.

"Werewolf," Owen said, joining the group. Piper jumped, startled. Glancing up at him standing behind me, his face was blank. He put his hands on my shoulders, squeezing them a bit painfully. His voice held a warning note. "Jade, why are we sharing pack secrets?"

Annoyed at his late arrival, I rolled my eyes. "Because I just can't help myself," I said, sounding vapid. Then to add to the act, I blinked my eyes innocently.

Piper stopped breathing. She shrank into herself. Owen eyed her like a tasty morsel. I elbowed him in the gut, not hard, trying to dislodge him. It didn't work. It felt like elbowing a stone wall.

Scowling at him, I growled. "You should have come out as soon as I signaled you, then you would have known." The bell rang. Automatically, we all started to get up to go to class.

"Not so fast, sis." He was livid, as if I would really be telling pack secrets to some random girl I liked. "Why. Are you. Spreading. Our stories?"

Wow. He was outraged, and he was squeezing my shoulders harder. Gently I laid my head against his stomach, as if giving in. Then, I jerked and elbowed him fast and hard enough to make him grunt. Owen loosened his grip enough for me to slip out from under his hands and stand up.

"See you after school, Sarah. We can head over to Allison's. We might have to walk," I said glaring at Owen.

Sarah simply laughed.

"See you there, Jade—and see you on Saturday at the meeting," Sarah said to Piper, giving a wicked smile to Owen.

His eyes popped out a bit. Seeing Owen's shock was very satisfying.

Following Sarah's lead, José and Bevin said the same as they all ran off to class. Funny part was, we'd all see each other tomorrow in school. This was just my friends having my back.

"Saturday?" Owen asked confused.

"I have to get to the locker room and change for gym class, Owen. I'll see you after school…or I won't."

Taking Piper's hand, we headed off to class.

CHAPTER 34

Saturday morning. Too early to think…coffee.

After coffee, I headed to the pack gym. Today was weightlifting. I jogged two laps to warm up and started in on weight training. My panther may have helped me with my running, allowing me to avoid falling on my face, but I was still pretty weak for a wereanimal.

Gradually, Owen, Mom, and Dad joined me.

This waking up early was a new development with the werepanther bit, and I didn't know if I liked it. If I started waking up at two a.m. to run up and down the halls, I was really going to call foul. Damn cat tendencies.

About an hour into our training, Sarah arrived. Watching her, I was confused.

"I asked if I could come early. I want to be here, with you, our own werepanther pack. We're a package deal. I think it's easier to see the connection if we're together." I couldn't disagree.

She jumped in and started training. I watched Dad adjust Sarah's machine and furrowed my brows. "Oh, yeah," Sarah said, "he set up a training program for me, too. Your dad is obsessed with training programs." Glanced at the whiteboard, which I usually tried to ignore, I saw, sure enough, Sarah had her own line.

Once we finished our routines and showered, we went up for a more substantial breakfast than coffee. Mom was on cook detail this morning. The smells coming from the kitchen made my stomach talk to me with anticipation.

Standing in the kitchen, watching Mom flit around making magic happen, I started to feel weird. Really weird. My breathing became…impossible. A numb sensation started flowing down my fingers and up my legs. Cold and sweating, my stomach felt like it wanted to turn itself inside out.

The room rotated…on several axes.

"Mom, Dad, I need…something…I think I need to…something."

Again, I tried to get air. What did I need? Why wouldn't the room settle down? The spinning made it too hard to think. My clothing suddenly felt tight and too warm. I yanked on my shirt.

Everyone looked at me, concerned. Mom's gentle voice soothed over me. "What do you need, love?"

"I need, Mom? I need…I think…backyard…please?"

Desperately, I stared at her. Panic rose as I realized I didn't know what was wrong. Breathing was hard. Surveying the room, nothing seemed right. The walls were…I needed to be outside. Things were distorted. I started to back up.

Everything turned topsy-turvy as hands grasped me. Oh! Dad picked me up with an arm around my waist and hauled me to the backyard. Once outside my body started to shake, my gut clenched.

"Mom…help me."

"What's wrong with her?" Dad.

Writhing on the ground, I couldn't focus on people. The world was spinning in a spiral of green.

"I think she is trying to shift, but her body is fighting the shift." Mom.

"Should I help?" Sarah.

"No dear, let's follow her lead." Mom.

Cramping, pain. I doubled over. "Jade, honey, take off your clothes." So much pain. Obeying automatically, not thinking about why, my body clenched in agony. Thoughts coalescing, I realized she was right. If this was a shift, that would make things easier. If it wasn't a shift, then who cared?

This was not a normal shift. It hurt too much. Three

weeks into shifting, I recognized the pain, and this wasn't it. Curling into a ball on the ground, I moaned. This was the wrong position if my panther wanted to come out to play, but the waves of sensation washing through my body were too much.

Closing my eyes on a particularly large wave, my breath hitched. If my animal was about to show herself, I had to uncurl my body. Slowly, I forced my body onto my hands and knees. Pain shot through me. Panting and crying fought for dominance.

Then, my face started to elongate. What? My hands dug into the dirt as my back arched. This was all wrong. Pain radiated down my spine. Hair, I felt hair growing. It felt rougher, coarser than my black panther pelt. My hands were shrinking. It hurt. Everything hurt. The pain, pain, pain.

Sniffing the cool air, trees, birds, alpha…but she was human. This was wrong and I growled low in my throat to let her know of my disapproval.

"Jade?" Words. Human words. My growl grew louder, vibrating up from my gut and I snapped. Words weren't need. Legs spread out, I could protect her in her weakened form. Her wrong from. A hand at my neck held me in place. A hand on my snout forced me to smell.

"Jade!" Someone called my name. A fog began to lift as questions swirled like a tornado. This wasn't right. I knew the voice, it was the human voice of my alpha. Her hand on my snout wasn't needed for me to know her, protect her. I snapped at the hand.

"Jade!" The hand hit my nose. Pain. I whined. Shaking again, as much as I could with my snout being held, the scent of alpha permeated my brain, alpha…alpha…Mom…

My body began to tremble, and I stared up at her, up into her eyes. No, that wasn't proper. She was the alpha. Whining, I tucked my tail and then hung my head. Everything was weird, everything seemed wrong. What was wrong? Gazing sidelong at my mom, I saw concern in her eyes.

"You okay now?"

Bracing myself, I forced myself to gaze up at her. Something was very wrong. What was wrong with me? What had gone wrong in my shift?

"Is she okay?" Sarah sounded scared. "How did this happen?"

"That was so cool!" Owen sounded reverent.

"How is that possible?" Did Dad sound nervous? He was never nervous.

"Jade, hon, go over to the glass doors and see if you can catch a reflection." I tried to walk, but my gait was weird… wrong. As I moved, I looked down at my paws and froze.

I didn't have big black panther paws; my paws were small, with short sharp claws. Whipping my head to my mom, I almost toppled over. *What?*

"Just go, hon."

Obeying my alpha, I slowly made my way to the doors, tail tucked. When I got there and looked up, I didn't see a panther staring back at me, I saw a huge black wolf with shiny, terrified, green eyes.

I whined.

Sarah came over to me, kneeling. Knowing she loved wolves, I stared up at her trying not to shake in fear. She too was my alpha and knew my emotions. "Jade, you're so beautiful." She petted me and gave me a doggie hug.

Her touch began to calm me. Over her shoulder I saw Owen, who had the biggest grin I'd ever seen. "Wow, sis, you're a werewolf *and* a werepanther. You have two wereforms. I knew it. You're the weirdest werecreature ever." Then he laughed. "But Mom, how?"

Gods above, I wanted to know too. *How was this possible?*

Mom turned, gazing at everyone in the backyard. "My only guess is that she was infected when Candice attacked her. I don't know if she would've developed a second animal otherwise."

Dad grabbed my snout. "Jade, you need to move, run. It's important for your first shift. Can you go out into the woods and find a rabbit, or some other lunch? Then come back. I want you to stay in this form for the meeting. I don't know if there will be any other way to explain this."

What about Sarah? I whined hoping my thoughts would translate.

He dropped my snout and stood. "I know you're worried about Sarah. But I don't think it will be an issue."

So, after head-butting Dad to say 'I love you,' I ran. It

felt good to move, but in this form, I couldn't climb a tree, or pounce. Per my Dad's command, my alpha's command, I caught a rabbit to eat, and then I found the river for a drink. This was my family's forest but exploring it as a wolf was new and different. I got lost in what I found. At one point I was sniffing deeply at a chipmunk burrow when I heard my dad calling me back.

"How dominant is she?" Owen asked. I ran up to him, tongue lolling out in a wolf laugh. He knelt and stared me in the eyes for a second and then backed off. "Damn, well, she outranks me. I'm not surprised, she has always been strong-willed."

"River," Mom said, "call in Tanner. If that doesn't work, we'll move on to Clare."

Dad got out his phone. It didn't take Tanner long to arrive. I was off in a shadowed corner of the yard exploring in my new form and I didn't think he saw me at first.

"What's up, guys? I was going to be here in an hour anyway for the meeting. What's with the rush?" He automatically took stock of the area around him. In seconds he had catalogued everyone and everything in the backyard. No danger on his watch.

He saw me and froze. "Who's the new wolf? That isn't Mr. Schneider is it?"

"Use your nose, Tanner." Mom became his alpha. To help him out, I trotted over and sat.

Between my scent and my eyes, he nearly landed on his

rump. "Jade? How the hell is that even possible?"

"We don't know," said Mom, "but we want to figure out her dominance before the meeting. She's a new wolf, but not a new wereanimal, so we're hoping dominance is possible early on."

"Right," said Tanner. He knelt in front of me, took my head in his hands, and stared into my eyes.

Look deep into my eyes, I thought, and my tongue lolled out in a laugh.

After a few minutes he looked away. "We're pretty even. I think she would be higher than me if it weren't for the panther. The wolf is in there strong as hades, then there's panther, all chill, and then her natural calm, a river with trees flows through. It's like the mood is somehow sitting back laughing at both sides. What is up with her?"

Mom just smiled at me lovingly. "Jade, you are just the weirdest being ever."

CHAPTER 35

Once again, I sat alone in the backyard.

Mom, Dad, Tanner, and Owen were at the meeting. Piper and her parents were with them, waiting to be introduced. They wanted to start the meeting with the lone wolf. Sarah and I would join them later.

Right now, Sarah was in the basement. She had left the door open a bit so I could hear when they were headed my way.

My hearing had improved, and I heard her talking to the boys. "José, Bevin, I need to show you something in the backyard."

José heaved a long-suffering sigh. "Sarah, I know you're new and don't know the rules yet, but we're working here."

"Fine, but don't whine to me when you're the last to learn about *everything*." Sarah's voice was as light as air, and I could imagine her flipping her hair as she turned her back on them. Her footsteps creaked on the basement stairs.

A bunch of rustling drowned out the murmurs that followed. I strained to hear, but they were talking too softly. Then, a feminine version of José's voice spoke. Estrella, his sister. "Of course I can handle it," she said.

Suddenly, what sounded like a herd of elephants came thundering up the stairs.

Quivering with excitement, I moved into the center of the yard and sat, facing slightly away, so they would have a great view of my profile, but not my eyes.

Bevin was the first one out the door. He stopped so abruptly José bounced off his back. Eyeing me suspiciously, his scent turned cautious. José eyed Sarah, confusion rolling off him.

Bevin stared at my markings and took another cautious step towards me. He stopped and pointed with his chin. No aggression, but still wary. "Who's that? I thought all the werewolves were at the meeting."

Sarah shot the boys a quick quirky smile and then strolled over to me. She plopped down to pet my ears. "This one? Come say hi."

José rushed to Sarah's other side and grabbed her

arm. "Sarah, you shouldn't approach unknown wolves. They're dangerous."

Amusement flowed through me as I gazed up at him.

He froze. Then his jaw dropped. "Jade?"

Bevin almost became a cartoon character. First his face and then his arms fell in complete disbelief. Then his eyes bugged out. Then he got a huge smile and bounded over with a whoop of excitement.

He checked out my eyes to confirm, but then his face split into a bigger grin and he tackled me in a hug. "It is her! How is this possible?"

Sarah spent the next few minutes explaining as much as my parents could figure out. Bevin just sat, all smiles, much like Owen. José was lost. He sat next to me, legs crossed, hands in his lap, following the story.

"But how? How is this possible?" he kept asking.

Sarah grabbed José's hand. "Don't know. No one does."

Still looking down at his hands, José asked, "Is Jade ok? Can she still go panther?"

They all turned to me. Staring back at them, I flopped on my side then closed my eyes. Thinking about it, I could still feel two animals in me. It was almost like there was a place in my mind they lived, in peace…but I didn't quite understand it. Opening my eyes, I jumped to my feet, and ran around them.

Sarah laughed. "I'm not sure, but I think that's a yes. I can still smell both animals, but she always smelled of both, so her myriad of scents isn't new."

Bevin tackled me again. "This is just amazing. Owen is probably green with envy. First a panther, and now this. Amazing."

We rolled across the yard, laughing.

Slowly, José came out of his shock and started to adapt to my new animal. We spent the next half hour talking and playing until Sarah and I were called into the meeting.

Mom had introduced Piper's family to the pack. So now they were happily amongst the pack members, waiting for Sarah and me. Finally, it was time to discuss panthers.

When I entered there was a bit of confusion. It filled the room, making me sneeze. Once I got to the stage, all I could hear were their exclamations. The cacophony of voices made me wish I had hands to press over my ears.

"Who is the new wolf?"

"What is going on?"

"I thought there was only one lone wolf?"

Their questions proved they didn't trust their noses or use them. Finally, I gazed at everyone, giving them all a chance to see my eyes. A hush settled over the room. Between my smell and eyes, just about everyone figured it out. Mouths dropped and arms got thrown in the air. Then an overall feeling of confusion took over the room.

There were whispers of, "Jade?" and "Can it really be her?" coming from every direction.

Coming into the meeting, I knew the pack would be

weirded out, but I also knew it would be about the theory, not me. There was one person in the room whose opinion I did worry about Steeling myself, I finally looked over to Piper and her parents. She had to have figured out who I was by now, and that I was an even bigger freak then I had been yesterday.

Piper's eyes were huge. She was looking back and forth between me and her parents. They were whispering. I tried to listen in. But even shutting my eyes to get a better focus on their words didn't help.

Dad came up to me and put his hand on my head. "Okay, we'll discuss my daughter in a minute. Well, the werewolf part, but we need to stick to the agenda. Let's start with the werepanther side."

Andy leapt to his feet. "She really has two animals?"

Clare chuckled. "Apparently."

Tanner shook his head. "Beware the black wolf, for she is dominant, yet weirdly calm."

Clare turned to him. "You checked out her dominance already?"

He nodded. "Yep, earlier this morning. It was trippy. You should give it a go." He saw Dad's glare, and added, "But later, after the meeting." Those words had the desired effect of quieting the room.

The discussion shifted to panthers. Ultimately, the vote was to allow the panthers to join the pack on full moon nights. The reason came down to the fact that Sarah and I were fifteen-year-olds and needed the guidance of adults and wereanimals who had experience. Running alone wouldn't be safe. Moreover, if we were seen or caught, the secret would be out for everyone.

The biggest voices against us joining had been T.J. and Candice. Without them in the room spreading their single-animal rhetoric, the rest of the pack followed Andy and Chris who were adamant about family first. Mom and Dad agreed but felt that the pack needed to have their say to maintain the family feel they had built in the pack.

In the end, we needed the pack and the pack agreed. After that, the pack members spent over an hour discussing what it could mean that I had two animal forms. Nothing was decided or figured out.

They did a dominance test on me, again, and everyone agreed I was even with Tanner, but I was chill. I had to shift back to human form even though they could smell it was me. Thankfully, Mom had brought in my clothing.

The following day, Sarah and I went to our practice sessions with Allison. Despite my attempts to become a wolf again, I shifted to panther form. If I were to be honest, I wasn't even sure how I had shifted to werewolf the first time. Maybe someday, I'd be able to find my wolf again and could control which animal I shifted into.

Sarah and I were improving our fighting skills, both individually and as a pair. Owen had fun during the training as a leader and a participant. We were even learning how to fight together as a trio.

Best of all, Piper started to come out of her shell and completely joined the group. Every morning she met up with Sarah and me on our walk to school. She joined conversations with the group at the locker. She even ate with us every day at lunch.

Piper's life was finally becoming more stable. Her parents had decided to stop running. They knew they were welcome to stay in the area. Though they still hadn't decided on whether to join the pack, for now Piper was taking advantage of having a group of friends.

At last, full moon night came. It was time to run. The shift to werepanther was still painful. In all reality this was my first full moon in complete control. Sarah arrived early and we went for a warm-up run together in the barn to discuss our fears. Then we made breakfast. Pancakes and sausage.

Throughout the day, pack members showed up. José and Bevin arrived early, both to set up so that they were ready for the night, and to hang out. Having first lost Owen and now me, they were going to have to do more and more work with the kiddos. They had Dillan, but he rarely did much. On the bright side, they did gain Piper.

Though she was joining us at school, the kiddos didn't know her. She also hadn't spent much time around kids, so this was a new experience all around.

After dinner, Sarah and I went out into the backyard. She looked at me. "You ready?"

"Yes. No. I don't know. You?" I shut my eyes and tipped my head back trying to breathe slowly. I wanted to be strong but was excited and nervous.

She laughed. "You've lived with this knowledge your whole life and aren't sure, and you're asking me if *I'm* ready? That's rich, hon."

I opened my eyes, felt a smile blossom across my face, and let my head drop back down. "I know." I shook out my hands, trying to release some of my tension. "I just didn't think my first time doing this would be as a panther, or with you. No offense, but you went from a norm to an alpha pretty quickly."

Her face went flat. "Yeah. Didn't notice."

My smile grew. Happily, it reflected on her face. "It'll be great. There is an energy. Once we start the run, we'll be one with the pack, it'll be amazing."

She looked at me, face blank. "How do you know?"

My face broke into a huge smile. "I don't."

"Just don't go werewolf on me and leave me alone."

"I don't know if I can control which animal I turn into, but I won't try for the werewolf. I don't think I could do wolf if I wanted to, truth be told." She heard the tension in my voice and gave me a quick hug. Taking a deep breath, I closed my eyes, and opened them again. "Ready?"

She nodded. We stripped and let go of our humanity for the night becoming werepanthers.

Gradually, the rest of the pack joined us. In ones and

twos, they came out and exchanged their clothing for fur.

Once everyone was ready, Mom led us on a run. Stretching our legs, we let the moon guide us as I yowled my first furry song to Mondara. The moon was making me want to run and sing. I was leaping over fallen trees with Sarah on one side of me and Owen on the other.

Eventually Mom found a scent to follow. We ran the trail and discovered an elk, wild and alone. The alphas, all three, got to eat before the rest of us mere pack members. Afterwards, we found a stream and lapped fresh, cold water.

After our hunger was sated, the pack howled at the moon, and we swam in the ice-cold water. In the end we made our way back to the backyard.

While the others settled down in a furry pile to rest, Sarah, Owen, and I gazed up at the stars. After sitting there in the safety of the pack, we nosed around the backyard, trying to find a place to sleep. I rubbed my head against Sarah's before leaping up into the treehouse. She followed.

Peace flowing through my body, I gazed down at the lawn full of werewolves, in piles and asleep. Shifting my gaze to the house, where my friends were safe with the kiddos in the basement, I realized, because the moon's light was so bright, I could see my reflection in a window's glass. Sarah bumped her shoulder against mine, gazing at her reflection beside mine.

We were pack...we were werepanthers.

ACKNOWLEDGEMENTS

I want to thank the people who have encouraged me when they read the first set of words that formed this story. It started with my oldest son and a friend who started as a math teacher but ended up as a librarian: Nina Seidler Wagner. After she showed support, my family read the story and began helping me clean it up: Gavin Rahr, Chris Meuzelaar, Emily Ochitill, Peggy Denker, Kathy Kane, Hal Offen. Then the work really began. I joined Tuesdays with Story, a local writing group who helped. Then Angela Grimes stepped in and things got rolling. Thank you also to Wes Imrisek, editor extraordinaire, and Katherine Danea Bowen, beta reader, mentor, and overall guide on my writing path. I had many beta readers who helped me along the way: Laura Winter-Owens, Promise Triplett, and Bill Keys, to name a few. The old adage "it takes a village to raise a child" could easily be adapted to "it takes a village to help an author"…especially this one, and I thank each and every one of you.

ABOUT THE AUTHOR

Huckleberry Rahr is a mathematics instructor at the University of Wisconsin-Whitewater. She spent many years teaching math around the Midwest and in Papua New Guinea with the Peace Corps. Her parents instilled a love of reading from a young age.

She grew up with lesbian moms who had a huge collection of women authors with heroines as the protagonist. Her favorite genre was fantasy and science fiction, that is, until she discovered urban fantasy. What her mom's library lacked were books with characters that looked like her family: diversity in background, gender identity, and sexuality. She decided if she couldn't find that series, then she would write it.